HATE STRUCK

NIKKI ASHTON

For Chloe Walsh who persuaded me that I was the little engine that could

PROLOGUE

The eyes of the blonde-haired girl in the bed, fluttered open and then closed again. Her Mum held her breath, a hand pressed against the ache in her chest as she waited for her daughter to wake up. When the girl's eyelids closed again, purple against pale skin, her Mum blew out a shaky breath.

"Please wake up, sweetheart," she whispered. Taking her daughter's small hand between both her own, she rubbed it gently. "Please."

The girl whimpered and stirred; her free hand clutched at the bed covers, but she still didn't wake. Her arms were thin and bare in the hospital gown, all except for the bandage at her wrist. Bound tightly it covered a failed attempt to escape her nightmare that had only resulted in a jagged scar.

The girl's mum thought back to the night before. She'd found her passed out on the bathroom floor, sticky with blood and a sharp kitchen knife next to her limp upturned hand. Her other arm had lain across her waist, as if she were hugging herself to hold in the pain. That hand had been wrapped around her middle constantly the last few months, a desperate bid to stop herself from falling apart, but her mum hadn't noticed. The girl had thought she was all alone.

Grief had swallowed them both whole and then spat them out as broken pieces of heartache, misery and pain; they'd become pieces of a jigsaw that could never be put back together.

As the girl became more withdrawn the more their lives became separated neither noticed the other was struggling and moreover the girl's mother didn't notice her daughter was frightened and hurt. She didn't notice the anger that had built inside the girl or the fact that she was withdrawing from everything and everyone. She no longer danced, and she started to hate going to school, but the girl's mother didn't see what was happening; she was barely surviving her own daily pain.

If she hadn't been doing the washing, she would never have found the torn and bloodied knickers in the back of her daughter's underwear drawer. When she did, an immediate cold shiver of dread clutched at her throat and realisation began to dawn.

The moods, the silence, the anger.

She'd thought it had been the grief of losing the man they both loved, but now she realised her daughter was filled with fear over something else.

She searched frantically through her daughter's things, desperate for anything to prove her right, but anxious to find something to prove her wrong. With drawers upturned, books on the floor and the cupboards emptied, she finally found the words that would shatter her already splintered heart.

Tuesday 9th March
Mr M asked for some help to clean the art room after school today, so I offered, and it was actually quite fun. We chatted about lots of

things, even Real Housewives! I talked about Mum too about how she's never home since Dad died – since he was murdered. I miss her but she doesn't seem to care and would rather work which was why it was good to talk to an adult. It was nice and I felt safe again.

Thursday 11th March

    The art room is still a mess, but we've nearly finished. One more night after school and I think it'll be done. I'll be sad in some ways I've enjoyed having something to do and someone to talk to. Mr M even got us pizza and Diet Coke delivered

Tuesday 16th March

    I feel sick to my stomach over what he's made me do. I didn't want to, I told him no, but he kept saying he'd be gentle with me and that he was the only person who cared. He wasn't gentle with me though. I couldn't do it, I kept fighting him and he got angry and tore my knickers off me, ripping them down one side. In the end he forced me, and it hurt, really bad. He kept saying it was because it was my first time and next time it would be better, next time I'd enjoy it more. I don't want there to be a next time. He tried to kiss me afterwards and told me that I was his special girl. He said I should keep it quiet because people wouldn't understand. People would think my mum was a bad Mum for letting us be together. He said they'd take me away from her and even though she doesn't care about me anymore, I care about her. She's all I have left since Dad was killed.

Thursday 18th March

    How could I have let it happen again? How could I let him do that to me? I feel so ashamed. I didn't go to art class, I hid in the library and waited for the end of school bell to ring, but when I was sneaking out he saw me and he told me that I needed to go with him to the Head, but he didn't take me there he took me back to the art room. This time he was angry and told me I was stupid and would definitely be taken away for skipping class as well as being in a relationship with him. We're not in a relationship - I hate him. He raped me in the storeroom with the smell of paint and turpentine clawing at my throat and nose and all the time whispered how special I was. I know I have to tell someone but what if he's right, what if they take me away from my mum? I'm so scared and I don't know what to do.

The girl's mother read more entries from the diary. Tears dripped from her chin and landed on the pages below with a splash. Each entry was the same until the last one, from only the day before.

Thursday 10th April

I finally gave in today. I didn't struggle and I didn't cry. I lay there and blanked him and the smell from my mind and sang a song in my head, one that Dad taught me when I was a little girl and somehow it gave me comfort. I still didn't let him kiss me, I moved my head away and that made him mad. He said I'd have to kiss him soon, everyone who was in love kissed each other. I don't know if I can take much more. I hate myself for being weak and needing my mum because if I didn't, I'd say no and I'd tell someone, but the truth is I have no one to tell.

The girl's mum fell to her knees and screamed, the pain she felt at not realising what had been happening to her baby was like a dagger being twisted in her guts – twisted and twisted before it was pulled out and then stabbed back in.

With rasping cries retching from her lungs, she called her daughter, but she didn't answer. She sent her a text, but it didn't even look as though it had been read. She even called her daughter's friends but none of them knew where she was and hadn't really seen much of her anyway.

She was still sobbing when she called the police and told them her daughter was missing and she knew why. Her face was sticky and wet when two officers arrived to talk to her and get any information that they could about her daughter to help find her. She remembered her heart thudding at the sight of the police car, because last time one of those had turned up at their home it had been with the news that would change their lives forever.

When her daughter arrived home, while she was still crying and talking to the police, she finally noticed how thin she was. She saw that the light had gone from her eyes, even more than the grief had robbed her of. She saw how her daughter flinched when the male officer touched her shoulder and she recognised hatred in her daughter's eyes when she looked at her.

It had taken almost an hour for her daughter to open up and to tell them she had been raped, more than once, starting on the day after her seventeenth birthday, and it took her another forty minutes to tell them who the man was who had taken something so precious from her without permission or care.

The police did everything they could but when it went to trial, he told everyone she'd lied, and the sex was consensual. He said they'd had sex twice and then he'd ended it, and this was her trying to get back at him. He was a good liar, convincing, whereas she got flustered and got her dates wrong and told them she liked talking to him.

In the end the jury didn't believe her, no one believed her, not even her schoolfriends; they believed him, and called her a whore.

He lost his job at her school for having sex with her, but he was allowed to go home exonerated of the rape he'd been accused of. She went home branded a liar and had already stopped going to school weeks before because of the gossip and the whispers. She had no one on her side, but it didn't matter she hated herself anyway and couldn't see a future for herself without the pain of memories. That was the night her mum found her on the bathroom floor with a pool of sticky blood next to her.

"Mum," she groaned as she finally opened her eyes.

"I'm here, sweetheart and it's going to be all right."

1

SARAH

You are my sunshine, my only sunshine
  You make me happy when skies are grey
  You'll never know dear; how much I love you
  Please don't take my sunshine away...

I sang the song over and over in my head to drown out my mum's voice as she told me all about the school and how great it would be.

"It has a very good languages department, sweetheart, you'll love it."

That made me sing louder.
I'll always love you and make you happy
If you will only say the same
But if you leave me and love another
You'll regret it all some day

"Sarah." Mum slammed her hand on the steering wheel and her

perfect mother mask slipped for just a second. I shuddered impulsively, and she raised the same hand to her mouth as tears crept toward her lashes. "I'm sorry sweetheart, I didn't mean to shout, I..."

"Mum, it's fine." My voice sounded so small I doubted if she'd even heard me. She grabbed for my hand but must have felt me tense, because she pulled it back like I'd sunk a fanged snake bite into her.

"Are you sure you don't want me to come in and help you fill the forms out? I can if you'd like."

I shook my head and reached to unbuckle my belt. "You have to go to work. You can't be late on your second day."

"I know, but Mr Henry would understand. You're my daughter and I need to be sure you're okay."

The words 'like you did for the last year?' were on the tip of my tongue, but I knew it would do me no good watching her drive away in tears, and she *would* end up in tears. I had the ability to do that — make Mum cry. All I had to do was sing the song currently going around in my head out loud; the song my dad taught me as a little girl.

"Honestly, Mum, I'll be fine. It's just a few registration forms. My buddy Alannah will be waiting for me anyway."

We were driving through Maddison Edge town centre, on the outskirts of Manchester, where we now lived. I looked out of the windscreen at the tired and neglected town as we drove down the high street, passing a few shops, a cinema and the Town Hall that lined the wide road. Above the street hung a banner that said '*Maddison Edge Britain in Bloom Winners*'. There were baskets hanging from lampposts and dozens of raised flower beds lining the street which, according to my mum, were all filled with Winter Jasmine and Crocus; but as we approached the huge, grey brick school building, which stood like a crown at the very top of the street, the displays got smaller until there it was, like a blot on the already murky landscape.

Maddison High School

It would be my place, my escape from home for the next six months. Miss Daniels the Head had arranged for me to have a buddy to settle in. Apparently, Alannah Fitzroy was a straight A student, talented artist and the head cheerleader of the newly formed football cheerleading squad. Miss Daniels had assured Mum she would be the ideal person to help me steer my way through the stormy waters of Maddison High School.

Yeah, she would be the perfect person to report back if I looked as though I was about to go crazy. There was a reason I was joining Maddison High School half-way through a school year.

And that reason was why I'd wanted to die.

2

ADAM

When Alannah Fitzroy walked past me with her nose in the air, I couldn't help but laugh to myself. She liked to make everyone think she was some innocent little virgin, but I knew different. I'd had her lips around my dick on more than one occasion and what she lacked in technique, she made up for in enthusiasm.

"Alannah," I crooned, holding a hand against my chest. "You wound me."

She flipped me the finger over her shoulder and the lads all fell about laughing.

"Shit, she's hot," Tyler said, spinning a football on his finger as he tilted his head to one side and watched her arse. "I need to fuck that sometime."

He looked at me and winked, a silent request for me to share. I nodded my agreement. Alannah may say no at first, but I'd soon persuade her otherwise. Only when the time was right though, because my current plaything was Mackenna White, and I had no fucking intention of sharing or being rid of *her* just yet. Now *she* gave amazing head. Her technique and enthusiasm were second to none, especially as she liked to touch herself while she did it.

"Fuck," Ellis groaned, looking down at his phone as it sounded out a message. "My dad has found the empty whisky bottle in my room." His eyes shot up to mine and his lip curled. "I told you to fucking take it with you."

I held my hands up in surrender. "It was you who fucking took it from your dad's cabinet, not me."

"Only because you wanted it."

"And you do everything I say, right?" I snapped.

Tyler and Kirk snorted out laughs. They knew as well as me that everyone did everything I fucking said. Everything I told them to do. I ruled the damn school and God help anyone who forgot. Maddison High School was not what you'd call a polite and genteel establishment. I'd learned from my first day here that if you wanted to have a half decent time, then you needed to be in charge. So, by my second day I was selling cheap cigs to the sixth formers, including Frankie Dawson who was my predecessor as 'top dog'. I hung around Frankie and his mates, running errands for them or nicking chocolate from the shop at the end of the road on their whim, fighting and generally making sure the other kids either hated me or were scared of me until Frankie left and it was my turn to rule the school.

Ellis cursed again and smashed his fist into a locker. "How long until we can leave this fucking shit hole, anyway?"

"Five months, two weeks and three days," Kirk answered. "Then we are out of here and I'll be at Leeds starting on my path to a fortune."

"I thought you already knew everything there was to know about computers, you fucking geek?" Ellis asked.

Kirk rolled his eyes. "I still need a degree, dickhead. Who the fuck would employ me just because I tell them I have mad hacking skills?"

"He's got a point," I said with one eye on Tyler as he did some tricks with the football that seemed permanently attached to him. "He'd more likely to end up in prison if he admitted to that."

"Whatever, we'll all be out of here soon," Ellis said. The three of them began talking about uni and I slapped my hand against my locker.

"Can we shut up about uni, seeing as my bloody mum wants me to get a job?"

"She can't make you," Tyler said. "Just apply for a course through clearance, if that's what you want."

"I would," Kirk muttered. "If it was a toss-up between parties, sex, parties, more sex and a little bit of studying, or getting a job, I'd tell her to fuck herself."

"Whatever, it doesn't matter anyway, as far as she's concerned it's a done-fucking-deal. I'm stuck in this shit, boring town until I'm useless or dead."

I took a deep breath and tried to let the rage seep out of me. When I felt a breeze from the direction of the main door, I turned my head towards it.

"Well look here," Ellis said, his concentration in the same direction as mine. "I do believe I smell fresh meat."

I watched as the blonde girl, wearing jeans and a baggy jumper, pushed her way through the door and hitched her backpack up higher. She looked frail beneath the red wool, but she held her head high as she walked toward us.

When she was level with me, I put my foot out and caught her ankle above her red converse, causing her to stumble a little.

"Hey, watch what you're doing." Her voice rasped with a hint of insecurity and when she wrapped an arm around her thin waist, I could practically smell the pain she was carrying with her.

"Sorry," I replied and turned to Kirk. "Looks like new girl is lost. You should take her where she needs to go."

"I'm perfectly fine," she said as she made a half-turn away from me.

I made to grab her elbow but before my fingers had a chance to brush the wool of her sleeve, she pulled away and shrank back against the opposite bank of lockers.

"Don't touch me."

My eyes widened and I made the same surrender gesture as I'd done with Ellis a few minutes before. "Only trying to help."

She glared back at me defiantly. "Well, I don't need your help. The office is this way, *right?*"

Part of me wanted to warn her who I was and that she shouldn't cross me, but the way her chest heaved and how she curled her delicate fingers into a tiny fist, excited me. No one had ever stood up to me like that and yet she'd barely done or said anything at all. She wasn't being threatening or trying to overthrow me as the power in the school; she was only being brave when she was actually scared.

When she let out a tiny breath, swallowed hard and then licked her lips, my dick twitched. Tiny and beautiful, her hair sat like a golden halo on top of her head. She was like sunshine. I already knew that I wanted her. I could practically taste how fucking sweet her pussy would be and I knew that when I made her come, she'd let out a little whimper, too afraid to let herself go. I knew that over time I'd persuade her that her body was mine to do with whatever I wanted.

I also knew that she could be the fucking undoing of me and that I would never let that happen.

"Go on then," I snapped at her and nodded my head in the direction she needed to go. "And if you don't want your time here to be the worst of your life, then maybe stay out of my fucking way." I grinned because I knew there was no way I'd let her do that. I'd most definitely be seeking her out at any opportunity.

Tyler hissed. "Burn," he laughed out and bounced the football to me. I caught it and threw it straight back so it landed with an oomph against his chest.

"Go on little girl," Ellis said and waved his fingers at her. "Go to the office."

The girl looked at us in turn and then finally brought her eyes back to me. I thought she would tell me to go to hell, but she didn't. She took a deep breath, hitched her bag up on her shoulder and practically ran down the corridor.

"She's going to be real fun to play with." Ellis laughed and nodded his head in appreciation of the challenge.

"Aww she's just a little girl," Tyler mocked as he fluttered his eyelashes.

"I need to shit," Kirk added. "Cover for me, I'm gonna be a while."

I shook my head and turned to my locker. Just before I opened the door, I couldn't help but look to where the girl stood. Halfway up the corridor, she had a hand against her stomach, her head back and eyes on the ceiling as she breathed deeply.

I knew she was trouble. I knew I was going to hate her, and I knew I was going to want her more than anything I'd ever wanted before.

3

SARAH

My heart thundered in my ears as I walked away from the group of boys. They'd make my life hell if I didn't stay out of their way like I'd been told. I knew I hadn't fooled them with my not easily scared act, especially not the one who seemed to be their leader. He'd watched me carefully and his eyes had focused on mine. The smirk on his full lips had told me everything I needed to know; he saw me as a victim.

I so didn't want to be. I wanted to be as brave and strong as I thought I appeared, but I guess my acting wasn't as good as I thought. Once I'd been dismissed by him, I stopped halfway down the corridor to gather myself together. It was one thing the school dickheads recognizing that I had issues, but I didn't need the school golden girl to know and feel sorry for me.

I put my hand on my stomach and dropped my head back to take in deep breaths like Eleanor my therapist had taught me; counting slowly to ten and then back down again. By the time I'd reached two, I could feel my breathing was almost back to normal and the only evidence that I'd nearly lost it, was the clamminess of my palms. I wiped them on my jeans and took another deep breath before I continued on to the office.

When I pushed through a set of double doors a girl my age stood outside an internal office door. I guessed she was Alannah. She wore black rimmed glasses and carried three huge books; a backpack similar to my own slung over her shoulder. The length of her skirt, which was short, and the tightness of her jumper, which was tight, didn't scream school nerd but it did scream bitch. Maybe I was stereotyping her, but in my experience, all the bitches at my old school had been those who slept around and wore the least amount of clothes possible, usually outfits similar to the one Alannah had on.

As I let the door swing shut, she looked up and smiled.

"Sarah?"

"Hi." I held out my hand, relieved when she took it and didn't look at me as though I'd just handed her a shit.

"Alannah, but I guess you know that already." She rolled her eyes and shifted the books in her arms. "Miss Daniels said you and your mum came in to see her over the weekend. She called me at home to tell me."

I chewed on the inside of my mouth and nodded, not sure what to say. The fact that the Head called Alannah at home must have meant that they were close in some way, or at the very least that she had trusted Alannah to do this sort of thing before.

"Maddison Edge is a pretty gossipy town," Alannah said. "Plus, my mum is on the PTA."

I widened my eyes and blew out a breath. "Woah, you kind of read my mind there."

Alannah gave me a bright smile and I noticed how pretty she was; her teeth were perfect and straight. "Everyone who's new here thinks the same thing."

"So, you buddy all the new kids?" I asked.

Her smile faltered a little but soon slipped back in place. "Depends," she replied with a shrug of her shoulders.

"On how fucked up they are?"

When Alannah's mouth dropped open my heart sank. This was supposed to be a new start. I wasn't supposed to alienate the only person I had in my corner on my first day.

"I'm sorry," I groaned. "I'm feeling a little defensive, you know being the new girl."

"Don't worry about it, I get it. I'm just surprised at your honesty. Most people who come here for a new start try to act all superior and forget about why they ended up here in the first place. Because, let's face it we're not the best of schools. All the council money goes to Sexton High School."

I shrugged. "We moved here from Kent, so I can't comment. When Mum did the application to change schools this was the only one with space."

"Sexton is the next town along," Alannah explained. "And is a cute little market town, whereas Maddison Edge is seen as the blot on the edge of North Manchester, so guess which school gets all the funding, and all the school applications?"

We both laughed quietly and although what she'd said hadn't been particularly funny, it felt pretty good to let out the stale air from my lungs for the first time in a while.

"So, not only are you the go-to buddy for the fucked up and deranged, but the whole school is."

Alannah scrunched up her tiny nose and thought about it for a few seconds before she finally nodded. "I guess so. Now, how about we get you registered and then I'll show you around? We got let off classes this morning, so I can give you all the juicy gossip about this place in detail."

I blew out my cheeks and nodded, totally relieved that Alannah seemed nice and genuine. I could so easily have been landed with a bitch who instantly hated my guts.

"Talking of gossip," I said and nodded toward the double doors which led to the corridor. "Some boy told me to steer clear of him and his friends."

Alannah's cheeks reddened, and she cleared her throat. "Adam Hudson is not to be messed with, Sarah and he's right. Stay away from him, otherwise he'll just suck you in and spit you out when he's had enough of playing his little games with you. Believe me that's not a nice place to be."

She averted her eyes and moved past me to knock on the office door, interrupting any conclusions I might make about her and the boy Adam. When a voice the other side called out to go in, Alannah pushed it open.

"Oh hi, Mrs Stubbs, I have Sarah Danes with me to register."

I moved up behind Alannah and saw Mrs Stubbs falter. Her hand went to her heart and her eyes sought mine.

"Hello, love," she said, her voice full of sympathy. "Come on in."

She obviously knew why I'd changed schools halfway through a year, it was written all over her face. She felt sorry for me and I hated that she did, but it was better than her just hating me, which was what most of the teachers and staff in my old school had done. I just hoped that my time here would be different.

Alannah and I were in the dining room after a morning of her showing me around the school. We'd spent some time in the art department even though I'd told Alannah it didn't interest me. As soon as I smelled the paints and saw the containers of paintbrushes lined along the windowsill, my heart had begun to speed up. The only way I could stop myself from running was to sing my song in my head, until I'd finally calmed down and been able to chat to the teacher, Miss Hughes.

You are my sunshine, my only sunshine
   You make me happy when skies are grey...

"You okay?" Alannah asked as I pushed my salad around my plate. "You've been quiet for a while now."

My lips twitched into a half smile. "Yeah, it's just a lot to take in, you know."

"I'm sure, but you don't have to suffer it for long, soon we'll be gone. I'm going to Swansea for Automotive Art & Design, what about you?" she asked.

"I'm taking a year out," I replied, avoiding eye contact with her. I had no desire to talk about the whys and wherefores of my decision, but no one ever ran with it when I informed them that I wasn't going to university... yet.

"Seriously?" Alannah's voice went up an octave.

"Yeah," I replied and looked at her spoon halfway between her bowl and her mouth. "I'm not sure what I want to do, so deciding to take a year out was the best option."

I expected her to argue, after all she was the A grade student, but she simply nodded. "Good idea if you're not sure on your plans for the future."

Surprised at her response, I smiled, and she went back to eating her soup, leaving me to look around the huge space we were in. It was much more modern and in better order than the neglected and scruffy rest of the school. The ceilings in the dining room were high with large round pendulum lights hanging from them. Aside from a few round tables scattered around, there were also long trestle type tables with round stools at them. One wall was all glass which looked out over the football pitch and along it from one end to the other was a high bench type table with bar stools at it. The floors were pale wood as were the walls and along the front of the counter and it all looked pretty new. Even the ovens and serving top were bright, shiny stainless steel.

"It all looks new in here," I said, my focus back on Alannah. "Has it been refurbished?"

"Let's just say," she said as she pushed her bowl away, "that there was an incident with burning books which pretty much decimated the place. The whole dining room had to be remodelled."

"Shit," I gasped. "What happened? I mean who set fire to the books?"

At that moment, the double doors opened and slammed back against the wall, allowing space for the boys who I'd had trouble with earlier in the corridor, to walk in, side by side. A lot of people continued to eat and chat, but the majority of the school stopped to watch. I had to admit they looked as if they ruled the damn world, never mind the school; they were cool and intimidating and I could see from the faces of all the girls, and some boys, watching them that they had reputations in other ways too.

I glanced at Alannah who focused her glassy eyes on them, her hands clutched on her serviette which was screwed it into a tight ball.

The one who I thought Alannah had said was Adam was slightly ahead of the other three, just one pace in front as he strode through the room. He had a red checked flannel shirt tied around his waist, his jeans were dark wash and ripped at the knees, and on his feet were a pair of white, Old Skool Vans. A white t-shirt covered his torso, clinging to his muscles, and when he lifted a hand to run it over his dirty blond hair the fabric stretched against his bicep.

I looked at the other three boys, scrutinising them as I hadn't dared in the hall earlier. There was another blond, but his hair was lighter, and his skin was pale. I remembered he had a smattering of freckles on his nose. The one who'd told me to go once Adam had warned me off, had rich caramel coloured skin and a tight cut afro. His features looked as though they were carved from marble, while the third, the one who had been told to take me to the office, had black hair and perfectly white, straight, teeth.

As individuals, they were all handsome, but as a unit, there was no getting away from the fact that they were beautiful; their reasons for attracting attention were obvious. They were a collection of perfect specimens who drew everyone's eye. Adam though, he was almost flawless with strong features, pouty lips and olive skin. He was the one everyone looked at first and for longest.

My gaze turned to Alannah who still watched them carefully, her eyes flickering between them behind her glasses, but lingering most on Adam. When they got closer to us, I kept my eyes firmly on my new friend and swallowed hard. I didn't need or want them to bring anything to my door. I'd heed Adam's warning because my life was crap enough as it was. I pushed my hands up the arm of my jumper and my fingertips found the raised skin on my wrist and rubbed it, up and down, up and down.

You are my sunshine, my only sunshine
You make me happy when skies are grey...

When I saw a flash of red checked fabric in my periphery, I dropped my gaze to the table and started to count the pieces of corn on my plate.

Eleven, twelve, thirteen.

"Alannah," a deep voice said. "You going to introduce us to the new girl? She ran off before we had chance this morning."

I didn't want to look up, I wanted to keep on counting the corn, but I knew if I showed any more signs of fear than I already had, not only would the four Adonis' make my life hell, but I would also be the easy target for the rest of the school. My dad had taught me that.

With my fingers still rubbing up and down my wrist, I lifted my head.

"Well," the boy with the dark skin said. "What's your name?"

"Sarah and what's yours?"

I flashed him a smile and moved my hands to between my legs and clapped my thighs together. I wouldn't show them my fear, they'd probably smell it on me, but I couldn't let it show it if I was to survive this place; that was another lesson I'd learned over the last year.

"I'm Ellis, and this is Adam, Tyler and Kirk."

The pale boy, Tyler, poked out his tongue and waggled it suggestively and I heard Alannah groan. All their eyes darted to her, and Adam took in a breath so deep that his nostrils flattened on both sides.

"Alannah," he drawled. "Have you told *Sarah,* how you like to suck my cock when your new little cheer squad and school are getting too fucking much and you're fucking stressed with everything?"

He turned his head slowly to me. I held my breath and heard Alannah whimper. I wanted to tell her it was fine, I didn't care what she did or didn't do and that Adam was just being a knob by telling me, but his Atlantic blue eyes mine held mine captive and no matter how hard I tried, I couldn't turn away from him.

"Oh yeah." Ellis sniggered. "She's not tried mine yet but fuck—"

He stopped abruptly as Adam gave him a side punch into his stomach.

"Thought you might like to know the company you're keeping, Sarah. We wouldn't want you to be corrupted by Little Miss Prissy now, would we?"

"She can do what the hell she wants," I replied as I swallowed to try and keep my voice steady. "I don't judge people no matter what their predilections."

Tyler whistled and Kirk raised his eyebrows.

"Big words for such a little girl." Adam dropped his hands to the table to lean closer to me. "Got to say, it makes me hard to think of you saying words like that while I..." He winked at me. "No, I don't think you're ready to know what I would do to you." He pushed himself upright.

"You'll be waiting a long time," I whispered as his bright blue eyes full of disdain and disbelief burned into my skin.

Adam leaned in again, closer this time, his breath whispering against my ear. "We'll see how long it takes before you're begging me to fuck you, because believe me, you will."

He sneered at me and without another word strode away with his posse of hangers on a couple of steps behind.

I took in a deep breath, gripped a hold of the table, and tried to ignore the way my veins buzzed with adrenalin as Adam's words continued to echo in my ear.

"I don't," Alannah said, forcing my gaze to her. "Well I do, but..."

Her eyes brimmed with tears and her complexion splotched with scarlet as she worried her bottom lip.

"Like I said, it's no business of mine." Feeling unsettled I gave her a wobbly smile and reached for her hand. "But if he's forcing you."

A cold shiver ran through me and I swallowed down the need to puke.

Alannah shook her head hard.

"He doesn't. I swear." Shame shrouded her features as she took a deep breath. "I can't say no to him, Sarah. I've tried but he's just so." She pulled off her glasses, threw them down, and then pushed the heels of her hands against her eyes and groaned.

"I get it, I do," I said and leaned across the table to her. "But be careful, I don't know any of you, but he seems dangerous and mean. I'm scared for you."

Mean.

Dangerous.

Magnetising.

Her head shot up and she looked me straight in the eye. "You don't get it at all, but you will."

I looked around the dining room and it suddenly struck me, no one had come to sit with us. No one was clamouring to talk to Alannah or find out who I was. Miss Daniels hadn't picked Alannah to be my buddy because she was good with the fucked up and the deranged; she *was* fucked up.

"Why will I get it, Alannah?" I asked, my voice soft and tentative.

She gave me a sad smile and then jutted out her chin in defiance. "Because you're on his radar now. He may have told you to stay out of his way, but I saw it in his eyes. He wants you and he won't stop until he has you and ruins you, just like he does with the rest of us."

She scanned the room and I swept my gaze with hers. Then I saw them, dotted around, and not easy to see unless you were looking for them; four or five girls, all sitting alone, and all with their eyes on me.

4

ADAM

I practically threw my lunch tray onto the table, *our* table, and sat down, dragging my stool across the wooden floor with a screech.

"What's got up your arse?" Ellis asked as he sat beside me.

Kirk and Tyler were messing around with a spoonful of mashed potato. It took all my effort not to stand up, lean across the table, and punch both of the fucking idiots between the eyes.

"Remind me again why we hang around with them," I snarled.

Ellis grinned and his brown eyes twinkled. "Kirk's brother provides us with weed and Tyler's mum is fucking hot, and when she answers the door in her dressing gown, I get to see her nipples."

I didn't feel in the mood for his crap jokes, but he managed to bring a smile to my face. Ellis and I had been friends since year five at junior school when we'd moved here after my mum's boyfriend left her with mountains of debt, and a kid in her belly. Back then Ellis always wore corn rows in his hair and big pieces of gold jewellery, because he was crazy for old school Snoop Dog at the time, and he'd greeted me like a long-lost friend. When you're nine-years-old and starting a new school in a strange town, someone just being nice to you makes them a friend for fucking life. Almost nine years later and we were still close; as close as I would ever be with anyone.

"Seriously though," Ellis said as he shovelled food into his mouth. "What's eating you, because it isn't just those pricks?"

I shoved my tray away and glanced over at the table where Alannah and the new girl sat.

Sarah.

I rolled her name around in my head, alongside a slide show of images of her on her knees as she sucked my dick.

Ellis reached for my untouched bread roll and ripped a chunk off with his teeth.

"Well?"

I let out a sigh and turned back to him. "Usual crap at home. Adam clean your room. Adam you know you're supposed to be home by ten on a school night. Adam suck my fucking dick."

Ellis burst out a laugh. "You know you can have him arrested for that," he said, spattering half-chewed crumbs of bread over the table.

"Mum doesn't say a word. She just stands behind him with her arms crossed, giving me this look that says; 'I'm not angry Adam, just disappointed'. Well guess what mother, I'm fucking disappointed too. I'm disappointed you married a man who thinks I'll like him if he just acts like a dad."

I dropped my head back on my shoulders and closed my eyes, letting out a strangulated groan at the damn unfairness of my life. A lot of fucking things disappointed me about my mother, and Roger was only one of them.

I lived with one parent who I had no respect for and a step-parent who I fucking hated. My mum had met Roger just over a year and a half ago and married him six months later. As soon as she married him, she pretty much checked out on parenting me and my sister and left it all to him. It was like she'd been playing a really tough game of football and had been working hard around the pitch, trying to score, but nothing she did was right. Then the manager subbed her for Roger and the fucking relief was written all over her face. She finally had chance to sit back and watch Roger do all the damn work.

When he came along Mum encouraged me to call him Dad, like she did with all her boyfriends. I knew it would make her happy if I did, but I resented her too fucking much, so usually I just grunted at him or called him Roge, which I knew he hated. The thing was, he *wasn't* my dad no matter how much he tried.

"I don't know why you don't divorce them or whatever it is," Ellis said, his concentration back on his food as he separated his peas from his corn. "You could get an afterschool and weekend job and then rent a flat."

"Yeah like there's plenty of jobs on offer around here."

Ellis shrugged and carried on eating, so I picked up my phone to text Mackenna. She should have been at lunch by now and I needed something to release the tension in my back, neck, and fucking bollocks.

As I started to type out the text, I caught movement in the corner of my eye. My head snapped up. I expected it to be Mackenna, but it wasn't, it was Alannah and Sarah, the new girl. Alannah had her head down and was moving slowly across the dining room, but Sarah held her head high and led the way.

It struck me as a pretty confident thing to do, considering it was her first day. I watched her take a deep breath with every stride and tuck errant strands of her blonde hair behind her ears; my dick twitch again.

There was something about her that excited me. I was going to love playing with her when I was ready. She wouldn't stand a fucking chance. All those attempts at being brave would come to nothing and by the time I'd finished with her, she'd wish she'd never even glanced at me. That was what I did. I played with people. Like a cat with a mouse, a dog with a rat. I played, I taunted and then I went in for the fucking kill.

"Shit," Tyler hissed. "You see where they're going?"

I watched in fascination as Sarah led Alannah to a table where Amber Smith was sitting, alone. Amber had been my plaything last term, but I'd had to humiliate her in front of the whole school when she'd decided she should be my girlfriend.

I didn't have girlfriends.

I played, I taunted, and I went in for the fucking kill.

"What you going to do?" Kirk asked stretching his neck to see around Tyler.

Sarah sat down next to Amber and held out her hand. Alannah was more tentative, and I didn't miss her glance my way, but then she pulled back her shoulders and sat the other side of Amber. Amber looked shocked as her gaze shifted between the two girls, but when Sarah moved closer and said something to her, Amber's face broke out into a grin.

"They can sit where they want to," I said.

I pretended indifference, but Sarah had thrown down a challenge whether she knew it or not.

"It's not like I told everyone to ignore her."

"Yeah but, Adam, you told the whole school she'd had a threesome with you and Ellis *and* you and another girl *and* that she'd wanted you to piss all over her." Tyler scoffed as he turned back to me. "Getting Kirk to flash that up on every computer in the school three times in one day, means no lad is going to want to go out with her in case she smells of piss and no girl is going to want be friends with her in case she wants to jump into bed with them *and* their boyfriend"

I shrugged, took a swig of my diet coke, and then grinned.

"The threesome part with me was right," Ellis offered.

"Although getting my cock sucked while looking at Adam's bare arse pumping away was kind of off putting."

We all laughed, but my attention was back on the table of three girls – actually strike that. It was on one girl as she took a band from her hair and let it cascade over her shoulders, before she gathered it back up on top of her head and wrapped the band back around it. She pulled at the bun and then combed her fingers through her fringe, all the time listening to whatever Amber and Alannah were saying.

"Hey, Kirk," I said.

"What?" He turned to me, his eyes were narrowing because he knew what was coming.

"Use those hacking skills of yours to find out what you can about her." I gave a chin lift in Sarah's direction. "What her secret is and why she's moved here with less than a year to go?"

"What makes you think she has a secret?" Tyler asked.

"Everyone has secrets," Ellis answered without taking his eyes from the spoonful of yoghurt which was halfway to his mouth.

"He's right," I said as I pushed up from the table. "Everyone does and I want to know what hers are."

5

SARAH

When I opened the door to our house after school, the last person I expected to see there was my mum. She'd only been at her job for two days and I knew she didn't finish until five, so I jumped when she walked out of the kitchen into the hall.

"Oh my God, Mum. What are you doing here?" I dropped my backpack to the floor and placed my palms against my stomach.

She smiled and threw the tea-towel she'd been holding over her shoulder. "Mr Henry knew it was your first day at the new school, so let me go early. Wasn't that kind of him?"

Her grey eyes shone with the tears that had seemed ever present for the last year, and she took in a shaky breath. Tentatively she took a step toward me and reached out her hand before pulling it back again. I knew I should have gone to her and comforted her, told her I'd had a great day at school, but the darkness inside of me told me to stay where I was, let her come to me, make her work for my love.

When I didn't move or even twitch a muscle, she finally took the step and pulled me into her arms.

"Was it okay?" she whispered against my hair.

My arms flopped to my sides and I nodded. "Yeah, it was good."

"And the teachers?"

I felt her body tense and the air around us stilled with anticipation as she waited for me to reply. Mum flinched as my hesitation became a long pause.

"They were nice," I finally said and pulled away from her strong hug.

She let out a long, breath and looked down at her shoes; navy leather stilettos that she'd worn for work.

"Good. That's good," she replied, flashing me a broken smile. "So, I made fried chicken for dinner." She laughed and pointed over her shoulder. "Well, I say made. I called in at KFC on the way home."

It was on the tip of my tongue to say I wasn't hungry, or that I had too much homework and would eat in my room, but she looked so expectant and anxious.

"That's great," I replied. "I'll put my stuff away."

I picked up my backpack and made my way to my room at the back of the bungalow which Mum had moved us into. My room overlooked the average sized garden and as well as a big window it had doors out onto a small patio. I was pretty sure it was the master bedroom as it had a full bathroom, whereas Mum's only had an en suite, but she was trying to make up for the last year, so I got the best room. I did feel kind of bad, Mum's room was a little smaller and looked out over the front driveway, but I didn't have it in me to offer to let her have it.

We'd painted it a deep cream with hints of violet and had done it together, which had been kind of weird. Mum and I had barely talked for ages and there we were spending a whole day together, painting my room, side by side. We'd still had little to say and at times the atmosphere strained as we avoided the two huge elephants in the room, but we got the job done and actually laughed when Mum stepped on the tray of paint and upturned it over her foot.

With a sigh I unpacked my back and stacked the books onto my desk, ready to do my homework later. I then pulled open my wardrobe and threw the bag inside; I wasn't a normal teenager who left things lying around, I hated mess and always had done. It was something I got from my dad, he had to be the tidiest person I knew... had known.

As images of him laughing swam around in my head. The pain in my chest that never really went away, gave me a punch in the ribs, simply to remind me that it was still there. This wasn't all a nightmare that I could wake up from and dad, a police officer, had been killed at the scene of a jewellery shop robbery. He really was gone. The pain never let me forget.

The memory still managed to blindside me and break my heart all over again. I took a hold of the wardrobe door, gripping it to steady myself, and blew out a long breath through pursed lips.

"Sarah, you ready sweetheart?" I heard Mum call. "It's on the table."

"One minute."

I took another fortifying breath and made my way over to my desk, opened the drawer and reached inside for the creased and dog-eared photograph of the three of us when we'd been happy. All of us smiling up at the camera, the sea behind us and the sun bright in the sky as Mum snapped away.

"I love you, Dad." I stroked a finger along the image of his handsome face with my low whisper.

It was the same thing I did every day, whether it was a bad, good or indifferent one. Every day I told my dad I loved him and stroked his face. I carefully placed it back in its place, under his precious and battered copy of Catch-22, and then closed the drawer and went to have dinner with my mum.

Dinner had been quiet, but not the uncomfortable silence that I'd grown used to over the last year or so since Dad died. At least Mum sat at the table with me and hadn't hidden herself working until all hours like she'd done when he first went. I understood why she'd needed to keep busy, but she'd forgotten she had a seventeen-year-old daughter who needed her. As a result, I'd been left alone most evenings with my grief, my nightmares and my pain.

"So, tell me about your first day," Mum said as she passed me the last dish to dry.

We had a dishwasher, but Dad had always insisted we did the dishes by hand. He said it was one of the best times to talk, to laugh and to be thankful for our little family, which was why after he died, I'd always run off to my room after dinner – our little family didn't exist any longer. Tonight though, Mum had insisted I stay and dry. I guess it was her way of attempting to make things seem as normal as possible, a year too late, but at least she was trying.

"It was okay." I shrugged. "Alannah is nice, the kids were okay, and the teachers were good."

I noticed the way her shoulders sagged and wasn't sure whether it was with relief or with sadness that we were having to talk about me having a new set of teachers.

"And Alannah took care of you okay?"

She turned her head to face me, and once again I saw sorrow where happiness used to shine. She and Dad weren't the perfect couple, but they loved each other and never went to bed on an argument; it was always their thing. We had been a happy little family until that day he'd answered a call on his Police radio about reports of gunshots at a high-end jewellery shop in the West End. The sad thing was, it had been his rostered day off, but he had gone in on overtime to help pay for one last holiday together before I went off to Uni.

"Yeah, Mum, she did." I nodded and gave her a small smile. "She's a really nice girl."

"Was there anyone else you got to know? Any other girls?"

She handed me a glass, slippy with soap suds, and I gripped it tightly to avoid dropping it.

"A girl called Amber," I replied as I thought back to the quiet, shy girl who Alannah had told me once used to be lively and popular before she'd hooked up with Adam. I had no details of what he'd done, but I guessed it was something bad because when he'd passed us on his way out of the dining room Amber's hand had started to shake and she'd dropped her gaze to the wooden table.

"Oh, that's so good, sweetheart," Mum said and flashed me a smile. "Really good."

We carried on with the dishes in silence, but once again it wasn't uncomfortable, and I started to feel my tension ease a little. Mum eventually let out the water and dried her hands.

"Have you got homework?"

I sighed. "Yeah, you'd think they'd be kind to me on my first day, wouldn't you?"

Mum laughed quietly and reached out a hand to me. I stood stock still as I tried desperately not to flinch from the touch that I'd missed for so long but now didn't welcome. Her warm fingers lightly touched my skin and her eyes softened.

"I hope that this is the start of something better for us," she whispered.

I swallowed and nodded, unable to say anything.

"Okay," she said as she pulled her shoulders back and gave a quick nod of her head. "You go and do your homework and I'll make us a cup of tea. That sound good?"

I nodded and started to make my way out of the kitchen when

Mum's phone started to ring. I looked down at where it laid on the table and saw a name I hadn't see for a while.

"Mum," I gasped. "It's Miriam."

Mum rushed to me and snatched up the phone, as if she didn't believe what I'd said. Her eyes were wide as she stared at the screen, and her breathing grew heavy as the call continued to ring out from one of the detectives of the Police station in our old hometown.

"You should answer it."

She looked at me, almost blankly, nodded and then punched at the screen.

"H-hi, Miriam, how are you?"

I tuned out the one-sided conversation and concentrated only on my mum's face, watching carefully and waiting. Finally, she pulled the phone from her ear and let her hand fall to her side. She'd gone pale and there was moisture in her eyes as she looked up at me.

"Mum, what is it?" I instinctively reached for the raised skin on my wrist. "Tell me."

She took a huge breath and pressed a hand against her chest.

"Joshua Mills has moved back into town."

I inhaled sharply, desperate to try and drag some air into my too tight lungs. My skin prickled like a thousand needles were being stabbed into me, even my scalp pulsated with the pain.

"When?" I whispered.

"Last week, it's the first time Miriam has had chance to call us. He moved back into his old house when the lady who was renting it moved out."

She stepped closer. This time without any hesitancy. She pulled me against her chest and held me tight as she made soothing noises and gently rocked us backward and forward. She knew how much any mention of *him* upset me.

"Miriam just thought we should know."

"I know and I'm glad he's there. At least he's nowhere near me."

The need to feel the skin of my wrist was desperate within me. I felt like I'd stop breathing if I didn't touch the raised scar; it was an addiction that I had to quell. My fingers twitched, but Mum had my arms trapped within hers. A pained groan escaped my lips as I fought against her until she finally set me free. Welcoming the space, I withdrew from her and backed up against the wall, sliding down it until my bum landed on the cool tiles. Mum immediately dropped to her knees and placed her hands against my cheeks.

"Sarah, sweetheart, look at me. He's hundreds of miles away and he'll never hurt you again. I won't let him, I swear."

"But you did, Mum," I whispered as the pain filled me with distaste and venom. "You weren't there. You left me alone and he hurt me."

Mum's face crumpled, and she drew in a shuddering breath, but her hands never left my face and her eyes never left mine as she shook her head.

"No, never again, sweetheart. I'd kill him first, I swear to you."

"I don't want to ever see him again, Mum." My voice cracked and I had to swallow hard to push back the vomit threatening to rise. "But I don't want anyone else to go through what I did either."

My gut twisted. Sweat started to roll down my spine, just like the cold trickle of fear had when I was trapped in that room; the room with the heavy, hot air that smelled of paint and brush cleaner.

I was there again and my chest began to heave with the effort of breathing. I was trapped with nowhere to go.

"Miriam said she'd keep an eye on him," Mum continued, gently caressing my hair with her shaking hand. "But she has to be careful because he's reported her for harassment once before. The point is though, she knows what he did and will do what she ca-."

"No." I shook my head and pushed my mum away from me. "She has to make sure, not do what she can. He can't do that to anyone else."

Mum's hands dropped to my shoulders and she gripped them tight. "Then I'll tell her that. We will make sure no one else suffers like you did."

There was a steel to her voice that I'd never heard before and a flicker of empathy for her filled my senses. She'd lost her husband, the man she'd loved since her second year at university, the man who was the father of her child and I'd made her feel guilty for grieving. It didn't change the facts though; she'd checked out on me and left me vulnerable to a monster.

Joshua Mills had been my art teacher and he'd seen the lost and grieving little girl who'd been neglected by her one remaining parent.

Joshua Mills had taken advantage of that.

Joshua Mills had raped me and now he was back in town living in his home when I'd had to leave mine.

Joshua Mills was the reason I had wanted to die.

6

ADAM

I pulled open the fridge door and snatched the plastic bottle of milk and lifted it to my mouth.

"Adam, really."

I turned to see my mum arching a haughty brow and holding out her hand. She fucking hated when I drank from the bottle.

"I promise no backwash." I replied and tilted my head back to drink a mouthful.

I expected her to snatch it from me and put it back. I kind of wanted her to. She just breezed past me, only pausing to give my back a rub of affection, a touch that irritated me.

"No one wants your germs, love," she said and then poked her head into the fridge and came back out holding a plate of raw pork chops. "How was your day?"

I put the milk down and reached for an apple and took a huge bite. As I chewed, I watched as she started to prepare dinner.

"Well?" she asked with her back to me.

"Just like any other day," I lied.

Except this day a new girl had started at Maddison High School,

41

a girl who fascinated me, a girl who I had decided I was going to ruin. The girl I had to ruin before she ruined me.

"I thought you had football training tonight," she said and looked at me over her shoulder.

"Mr Jameson changed it to tomorrow instead. His youngest kid has a school play or something." I shrugged and took another bite of my apple. "Where's Lori?"

"Gymnastics, Roger is picking her up on his way home from work."

My little sister, Lori, was a typical eight-year-old and was a member of any club that she could be. If it wasn't gymnastics, it was drama club or dance classes. We were pretty sure she'd end up on the West End someday, not because she was talented but because she was a real drama queen.

"Oh, and he called to say he picked up those football boots that you ordered last week." She flashed me a smile and I knew I was expected to smile back and say, 'wow that's really nice of him', but I just nodded and muttered an unappreciative, "Great."

"I have homework," I said, louder. "Call me when dinner is ready."

She dropped the potato she was peeling into the sink and placed the peeler on the drainer. "They'll be home soon, why don't you stay down here and do that jigsaw with Lori that she's struggling with before dinner?"

Why? Because I knew Roger, stepdad number four, was helping Lori too, and it would mean me sitting down at the dining table with him and acting like we were one big happy family. The thing was, he loved my mum, was a great stepdad to my sister, and would be to me too if I let him. But I hated the fact that he tried too fucking hard with me, like buying me a second-hand car for my seventeenth birthday. Yeah it was my pride and joy, but he was a dick for thinking it would bribe me into being nice to him. If that wasn't enough reason to hate him then him bollocking me for shit that really didn't matter was. All teenage boys had untidy rooms, or were late home, or drank underage, or were caught shagging a girl in their parents' bed. Yeah, maybe that one not so much, but they left me home alone for the weekend while they visited Roger's parents in the Lakes, so what did they expect? What I hated more though was that he was the fourth 'stepdad' I'd had in the last nine years since my dad left. He was wasting his time though, because I never let anyone get close to me, not Roger, not girls and especially not *Sarah fucking Danes*.

"I have two essays to do, Mum." I sighed, even though of them I could do with my eyes closed – I was a history buff and it was the one subject that I actually enjoyed.

She picked up the potato and the peeler again and nodded. "Okay, love, but please make sure you don't fall asleep over your books and actually come down for dinner."

I wanted to argue that I wouldn't, but it wouldn't be the first time I'd feigned being asleep over my homework to avoid having to sit with her and Roger for dinner.

"I promise."

She seemed happy at that because as I walked toward the stairs, I heard her singing.

Once I was in my room, I sat down at my desk and turned on my computer, intending to start my homework, but like I did most nights I just stared at the creased photo pinned to my wall next to it.

"Why didn't you call me, Dad?" I whispered as I stared at the man in jeans, a black t-shirt and wearing heavy biker boots.

It was the only picture I had of him. Apparently, we hadn't been into taking photographs as a family because Mum only had a handful of me when I was a baby and she had even less of her and Dad. Probably because she burned them when he moved out – or should I say she kicked him out. I only managed to rescue the one I had because she dropped it on her way out to the garden.

I stared at the picture and it struck me, as it did every day, that the only similarity between us was the colour of our hair, the rest of me was all my mum and that pissed me off. I wanted to look like him; Glen Hudson, my dad who I barely remembered; except for the fact he taught me how to kick a football with both feet and that he loved me.

He could have been dead, for all I knew, I had no clue. Mum told me he had often talked about going to live in Scotland, so maybe that was where he was, the only thing I knew was that my mum really had done a job on making sure we never had contact with each other ever again.

When I heard a car on the drive, I stood and went to my window and pulled down the slats of the blind to see Roger and Lori were home. Lori jumped out of the car first; she was wearing pale blue tracksuit bottoms and top and had her blond hair in a tight bun on top of her head. She bounced at the side of the car as she waited for Roger to get out. As soon as he did and had his door closed, she jumped into his arms and wrapped her own around his neck and gave him a kiss on the end of his nose. When Roger kissed her back, my chest constricted with a dull ache. I envied the love that they had for each other and the fact that it was pretty much immediate the minute Mum had introduced us to her new boyfriend. Lori had a big heart and was sweet, she had no problem in seeing the goodness in the man she now called Daddy. I hated it and loved it all at the same time because I hadn't had that sort of fatherly love for a fucking long time.

When their bodies disappeared around the side of the house, I let the blind slap back into place and threw myself onto my bed and toed off my trainers.

My hand went to my pocket and reached inside for my phone and pressed the code to open it up. I went to messages and scrolled until I found my last one from Mackenna just ten minutes after school had ended for the day.

Mackenna: Want me to come over after dinner? I'm feeling horny.

I was about to type out my response of yes, when my door swung open and a blonde pocket rocket rushed in and jumped onto my bed and bounced down onto her knees.

"Guess what," she cried, giving me the widest smile.

I did an ab roll and reached for her slim arms and gently pulled her next to me, so she had her head on my stomach and her knees tucked up close to my chest.

"I guess you found a pot of gold at lunch today," I said, draping my arm over her.

"Nope," she replied with a giggle. "Guess again."

"I guess you saw Daenerys riding her dragon?"

"The lady you like from that show?"

I nodded.

"No, but that would be really cool." She shifted and kneed me in the ribs, causing me to groan. "Oops sorry."

"You comfy now, Munchkin?" I asked and lifted a questioning brow.

She wiggled a little more and then sighed. "Yep. Okay want me to tell you?"

I pretended to think about it and then nodded slowly. "Yeah I think you're going to have to."

She grinned again, even wider than before. "I did a jump on the balance beam." Her eyes went wide and her tiny little fist did a pump.

"No way," I gasped. "I don't believe you."

"Truth," she replied, her tone serious. "Maddie my gymnastic coach gave me a clap."

Wow, a clap for a jump on a balance beam – Maddie was generous.

"That's fantastic. I'm so proud of you." I held my hand up for her to high five me.

"Are you really proud, Adam?" she asked, her palm hitting mine.

"Truth."

I pulled her body a little higher and kissed her forehead. When her arms gripped my neck like I'd seen her to do Roger, a chink of happiness broke through into my heart.

"Hey guys."

Roger was in my bedroom doorway and I couldn't help but stiffen at the glimpse I got of him over the top of my little sister's head.

Lori squirmed from my arms and turned to face him. "Daddy, I told Adam about my jump and he said he's proud of me."

Roger smiled broadly, but I noticed the wariness in his eyes. I couldn't blame him. Lori was his everything, her and my mum, and he knew what a fucking dickhead I could be at times — I was like that with him all the time, so I wasn't surprised that he would worry that I would be like that with his beloved step-daughter. I wouldn't though, could never be, because I loved the little Munchkin more than anything else in the world. She was pretty much the only light in my life.

"Yes, sweetie, you did great." He cleared his throat and held up a bag. "Your football boots."

I gave him a single nod and rubbed a flat palm over Lori's back as she scrambled to get up. Roger sighed, almost imperceptibly and placed the bag next to the door.

"Anyway," he said as Lori jumped off the bed. "Mum says dinner is ready."

"C'mon, Adam," Lori chirped. "It's pork chops and mashed potato, your favourite."

She flashed me a grin and then pushed past Roger who still had his eyes on me.

"I got you some new shin pads too." He paused but when I didn't say anything he turned to leave. "They were on special offer so..."

As he walked away, I could have easily thanked him. It wouldn't take much, but I didn't. I gave him time to get down the stairs into the kitchen and then went to join them all for dinner.

"Hey."

I answered my phone and reached into the shower cubicle to turn the water on.

"I can't find anything about the new girl," Kirk said, straight to the point but sounding a little distracted. "Her files just have her old school and home address in them, and some other shit."

"Like what?" I asked as I wedged my phone between my chin and shoulder and unzipped my jeans.

"Like she...*fuck*...she's allergic to banana, makes her throat itch and swell apparently." He groaned on the other end and then hissed. "If she eats it, she has some pen or something on her at all times, someone is supposed to stab her with it...*shit*."

"Please tell me you're not getting your dick sucked while you speak to me."

"Nope," he ground out. "I'm not getting my dick sucked while I speak to you."

"Shit, Kirk, you fucking are, aren't you?"

I laughed and dropped my jeans and boxers to the floor and stepped out of them as steam began to fill my small bathroom.

"Maybe. Point is, Adam, I have no shit to spill on her. She doesn't even have any social media accounts, not a... single one." He gave a quiet groan and I knew it was time I went. "My skills at hacking the school computer system are second to none, so if I can't find it, it's... woah fucking hell, Amy... not there."

The dirty fucking bastard.

"See you in the morning and don't get too pissed tonight, we have practice tomorrow."

"Okay cap-."

I didn't let him finish and cut him off. My need to shower was more immediate than my need to listen to him blowing his load into some girl's mouth.

I had considered texting Mackenna and getting her to come over, but for some reason, once I'd eaten dinner, I wasn't feeling it. The thought of fucking her was nice, but the idea of the banal shit I'd have to listen to her going on about after the act, not so much. Now the idea of a certain blonde's lips around my dick, and the way they pouted as she tried to act fearless around me, made my balls feel heavy and my dick spring to life. I could easily imagine myself holding that slight body of hers and slipping into her pussy. I knew it would be nirvana.

Under the hot water I sighed with relief. My neck and back muscles constantly ached, but today it wasn't from a hard practice session or a competitive game, today was from being tensed up like a fucking soldier on sentry duty all damn day. Truth was every day was pretty much the same. I woke up feeling angry and edgy and went to sleep feeling angry and edgy. The days I played football were the only ones where I felt some release from the blackness running through my veins.

I'd been that way since my dad left, since my mum kicked him out. She told me he was leaving; he kissed my head, said he loved me and would call me soon, and I never saw him again. He had had been everything to me and she'd made him leave over some stupid argument about him staying late at work too many times.

My head dropped back on my shoulders and as I let the water thunder down on me. I squeezed some shower gel into my hand and with thoughts of Sarah in my head, I reached down for my hard as steel dick. I wrapped my fingers around my length and gave it a long, slow tug. The pleasure was instant. It blazed around my body setting light to all my nerve endings like an out of control brush fire, easing my tension with every pulse. As I tugged harder, lathering my dick with the soap suds, a tingle started in my spine and crept around to the pit of my stomach. I closed my eyes against the beating water and opened my mouth on a groan as the waves of pleasure continued to build. The next pull I gave my dick was harder and as cum shot over my stomach a face appeared behind my eyelids.

That face was pretty, shrouded with blonde hair, and had the most fucking perfect cock sucking lips I had ever seen.

"Sarah."

7

SARAH

For a moment before I opened my eyes, I didn't feel the pain in my chest or see the pictures in my head. The relief however was short-lived. Images swam behind my closed eyelids of a man with a gun and my dad lying in his own blood. Then they mixed with those of a predatory man with cold, grey eyes. Vivid pictures that reminded me of the pain which was still deep inside of me; the pain that I didn't think would ever go away.

It constantly thudded against my chest like a battering ram, beating a rhythm that worked its way into my head and stomach. Anxiety was my companion every minute of every day and I could barely remember the last time I'd felt any peace. I didn't have a perfect relationship with my parents, what teenager did, but it was good. We were a little family who enjoyed spending time together, when I didn't have better things to do with my friends, or that was the way I looked at it then. Now I'd give anything to be able to go to the supermarket with Mum and Dad and then call at MacDonald's on the way home just because Dad found the whole food shopping thing stressful. I'd gladly go to the garden centre with them, just because it would mean he was still here, and Mum and I weren't heartbroken and drifting through each day because it was all we had the energy to do.

Mum watched me like a hawk through breakfast, just as she'd done the night before, checking on me every five minutes while I tried to do my homework; just as she did every night since she'd found out what happened to me. In the end I feigned tiredness and went to bed, pulling the duvet over my head to lay in the dark and try not to think about Joshua Mills and what he'd done. The only way I could do that was to think about the man who killed my dad with his brains blown out. Images of a man who'd eventually shot himself in the head were preferable to those of a man with a charming smile and a kind word, but they were what got me through some of my darkest moments in the last year.

Eventually I'd fallen asleep, but my night had been disturbed by nightmares and fear.

"Mum," I said, breathing out a sigh. "Stop watching me like I'm a fine piece of china about to break into a thousand pieces."

"So, talk to me then. Tell me what you're thinking about. You look anxious."

She looked as tired as I felt, with grey and puffy bags under her eyes, and a dullness to her normally bright, clear skin.

"I didn't sleep well." I shook my head. "I never sleep well."

Mum sat back in her chair and nodded. "I know. But you have to stop worrying about what he may or may not do to other people, it's not your responsibility."

"I wish I didn't, but I can't help it."

Mum's eyes studied me thoughtfully as she waited for me to continue.

"I need to try and get on with my life, Mum," I explained as the knife I'd been holding to butter my toast bit into the palm of my hand, pinching against my skin. I dropped it with a clatter to the plate as tears pooled at my lashes. "I mean it, Mum. I don't want to know. I don't want to be worrying and thinking about him every single day, but I can't stop." As my breathing sped up, I pushed my chair back from the table to try and get some space. Claustrophobia enveloped me in a tight grip. "I-I w-wish he was d-dead, but he isn't. He's still there in the town I should be living in. He's probably laughing and chatting with the people I used to call my friends. He might even be doing the same to one of them." My stuttered words mixed with sobs of destruction and I pulled at the neck of my t-shirt to try and get cool air onto my heated skin.

"Sarah, calm your breathing sweetheart, you're going to make yourself ill." Mum pushed out of her chair and crouched in front of me. Her pale grey eyes looked intently into mine as she cradled my face and breathed in and out slowly, silently begging me to copy her. "Please, Sarah, breathe, just like Eleanor taught you."

"Miriam has to keep an eye on him, Mum, she has to."

"Okay, okay. I'll tell her." She wiped the tears from my cheeks with her thumbs, her own eyes reflecting the fear in mine.

"Promise," I sobbed. "Promise."

"I promise, sweetheart. I'll call her today." She pulled me close and breathed in, her nose buried in my hair. We held one another for a few seconds before she pushed me to arm's length and met my gaze. "Okay, I want to see you breathing steady."

I stared at her and forced myself to mimic her breathing pattern until slowly my lungs calmed down and fell into their normal steady pace. Eventually the huge flock of birds stopped beating their wings against my rib cage. Mum smiled gently.

"Why don't you go back to bed and I'll call school for you?"

"No," I replied shaking my head. "I want to go; I have to go. I have my A-Levels in a couple of months, I can't afford to miss anymore school."

"I know, sweetheart, but you've not slept properly."

"I'll be fine." I got up from my chair, forcing Mum to stand, and picked up my plate with my half-eaten toast on it. "He's ruined my life enough. No more. I'm going to school."

Mum sighed and shook her head as she placed her hands on my shoulders. "Sarah."

"Don't try and stop me. I just want to be a normal teenager again."

Her lips parted and a quiet gasp escaped them because we both knew I'd never be a normal teenager ever again. Too much had happened, my heart was carrying too many scars and my soul was too blackened.

"At any point you can't handle it, you call me, and I'll come and get you." Mum's eyes were steely, and her hands gripped me tight. "Okay?"

I gave her a single nod and hoped that I was doing the right thing.

As I emptied my books into my locker, I knew someone was watching me. I felt it in the way my spine shivered, and my scalp pricked. I didn't turn around because I also knew it was going to be someone who I didn't want watching me. I felt that too.

I tried to regulate my breathing. *Never show any fear,* my dad had told me when I was around five or six and I'd been scared by dogs. He'd taken me to a rescue centre to try and help me overcome it. When we'd walked into the exercise yard and there were about ten or fifteen dogs all running around, I froze.

"You can do this sweetheart," he'd said as he gripped my hand. "Just don't ever show your fear, because as soon as you do, they'll see your weakness and try to dominate you."

I'd left the centre that day, not exactly in love with dogs but I wasn't scared any longer. Remembering Dad's life lesson, I straight-ened my spine, pushed my shoulders back and slammed the locker door closed. I was determined to get through the day.

I hadn't gone more than a couple of steps when I felt something hit my back. It wasn't hard and didn't hurt me, but it had definitely been aimed with precision. I decided to ignore it and continued down the corridor, but as soon as I did, I felt it again. I should have ignored it but instead I let my pissed-off mood get the better of me and whirled around.

"What?" I snapped before I even registered who I was facing.

Adman's handsome face smirked at me as he held up a piece of balled up paper and waved it in front of me.

"Morning," he said and tossed the paper at me.

I flapped around to try and catch it, as if it might explode if it hit the floor. I batted it into the air a couple of times before I caught it. Adam hissed out a laugh as I slapped it against his chest.

"You really aren't coordinated, are you?" he said with a smirk.

"And you couldn't say good morning like any normal person," I retorted as my chest tightened; my heart thudding to a fast beat.

Adam shrugged. "Maybe I'm not normal."

With a swift glance over his shoulder, I noticed his usual entourage were nowhere in sight, but while it was strange, I wasn't about to make it a conversation starter. I needed to get away from him. My palms had started to sweat, and I could feel a pulse tick beneath my eye.

He had to have seen how he affected me. It was so hard to hide my fear from him, because when he looked at me with his blue orbs, I felt as though he was looking right inside my head and was able to read all the thoughts that were swirling around in it.

"What do you want because I need to get to my French class?"

My gaze searched around, desperately hoping that Alannah would appear to save me, even though she was probably as much afraid of him as I was. I couldn't see her, so I had to face Adam alone as he stepped closer and his eyes considered me, slowly raking over me, as if memorising everything about me.

"Wanted to give you a..." He paused and then gave me a smile that barely upturned his lips. "A friendly warning."

With his head tilted to one side, he watched me carefully as a short gasp left my lips. "W-warning? What, you want to warn me again to keep away from you?"

"No, I want to warn you about the company that you keep. It can make or break your time here." He dropped the paper onto the floor and then folded his arms over his broad chest. His biceps, with the hint of a pale blue vein in each one, bulged against the sleeve of his white t-shirt.

"There's nothing wrong with Alannah," I said, trying to stand with my back straight. "She's sweet and nice, and—"

"Please don't let Alannah fool you into thinking she's sweet and innocent, Sarah. Because I promise you, she's not. And she's not the one I'm talking about."

He rubbed the pad of his finger around the outline of his open mouth and there was laughter in his eyes as the tip of his tongue followed the same path.

I frowned. "Who then?"

"Amber. The girl you had lunch with yesterday. Let's just say she has a reputation."

Amber hadn't told me anything about her and Adam, but I wasn't stupid. I'd seen how anxious he'd made her seem. My guess was they'd had some sort of relationship and after hearing what Alannah said about him, I was pretty sure it had been a sexual one. My other guess was that he was the one thing all the girls sitting alone in the dining room had in common.

"I'm not worried about anyone's reputation," I spat back, hoping that I sounded more confident than I felt – after all, hadn't I been the subject of the whispered comments in the corridors of my old school?

"Maybe not," Adam replied and leaned closer to my ear. "But this is me telling you to keep away from her."

His words were hissed with sharpness and I felt his breath ghosting over my heated skin.

"You can't—"

He put a finger against my lips. "Let me be clear, Sarah." He said my name like it was a curse and his eyes filled with disdain. "I'm *telling* you not to befriend Amber or anyone else who you think looks like they might need a friend. They're sad and lonely for a reason and that's usually because they deserve it."

I desperately wanted to run from this boy who had me tied up in knots, but I was so struck by fear, hatred and a sick sense of yearning that I was rooted to the spot. My hand went to the strap of my backpack and I clutched it tight, wincing when my nails dug into my palm around it.

"Alannah I'll let go," he continued, "seeing as Miss Daniels set that one up. Plus, I wouldn't want you to be totally alone in this big bad school now, would I?"

I drew in a breath and held it as I waited for him to continue, but he didn't say another word. He smiled and sauntered away. It was only when he reached a junction in the corridor that I noticed the other three boys of his gang leaning against the wall and waiting for him. Then I realised that most of my peers were stood still and watching our interaction. When my eyes met those of two girls and a boy huddled next to an empty water cooler, they quickly looked away to watch Adam as he high-fived each one of his boys in turn and then, without a backward glance, walked out of sight leaving me gasping for breath.

8

ADAM

My first class after lunch was History and I was glad of the peace because none of the lads had taken it as an A-Level. I needed a break from the constant talking shit and crap jokes, not to mention the size of their fucking egos. I guess that was my own fault though because as I'd earned my place in Frankie's inner circle, I'd introduced the three of them. Over time we'd got rid of a few people so that now it was just us four who everybody listened to. It helped that we were all pretty hard and didn't care who started a fight, just so long as we finished it.

I threw my bag down onto the floor and dragged my chair from under the desk, sinking down on it and relaxing back as though I was soaking up the sun on some fucking fancy beach in the Caribbean. My legs stretched out and I tapped my pen on the desk as everyone continued to file in.

Some of the girls cast glances my way, one or two even smiled as they probably considered whether to come and sit in the empty seat next to me. I soon made sure that didn't happen by the look I returned; my piercing, 'I don't want you near me' look. And it fucking worked because they all diverted away from me.

"Okay, okay," our teacher, Mr Raymond, shouted. "Settle down and grab your seats. It's nothing unusual I'm asking you to do, so less of a song and dance about it would be appreciated."

Chairs scraped across the floor and voices started to die down as one by one everyone settled.

"We are going to continue to discuss Napoleon today, so please turn to chapter six of your textbook and read today's assignment from the board."

Mr Raymond paused to allow the groans to echo around the room. I was sure I was the only one who didn't join in. I liked reading about the little French fella and his ambition from an early age.

"Complain all you like, people," Mr Raymond shouted over the top of the noise. "But his ideas underpin a lot of our modern world."

"Woah who'd have thought a geezer with an eye patch would be such a Billy Big Bollocks." Danny Roberts the class idiot laughed at his own joke and slapped a big hand on the back of his best friend, Cameron.

"That was Nelson, you brain dead idiot," I groaned.

The whole class, apart from Danny, laughed and Mr Raymond shushed everyone.

"You're quite correct, Adam. However, if you could refrain from the name calling, that would be much appreciated."

I saluted my teacher and turned to Danny. "No offence meant, but I've got to say it how I see it."

The class erupted into laughter again and just as Mr Raymond moved to his desk the door creaked open. The noise of laughter dropped, followed by hissed whispers. I looked over to see what had caused the sudden change in the room.

"Well fuck me," I muttered as Sarah edged through the door and looked warily around at my classmates.

"Can I help you?" Mr Raymond asked.

"I think this may be my class," she replied tentatively.

"And who might you be?" Mr Raymond asked as he looked down at the register on his desk.

"Sarah," she said. "Sarah Danes. I'm supposed to be in History."

"Well, Miss Danes, you're in the right place. Please take a seat."

She looked around and was about to head for a chair right in front of Mr Raymond's desk with no one either side of it, when I kicked out the chair next to me and grinned.

"I have a seat here, next to me, Mr Raymond."

Sarah's eyes went wide and she took a little breath, her head turned to our teacher who nodded towards me.

"Take a seat next to Adam, he'll tell you which chapter you need to go to. We're talking about the great Napoleon Bonaparte today."

"I can sit there," Sarah said and pointed to the empty desk.

Mr Raymond started to flick through some papers. "Go and sit with Adam, you'll need someone to help you catch up." He turned and flashed a smile at everyone. "Okay, Monsieur Bonaparte."

Sarah opened her mouth to protest, but Mr Raymond waved her along. Her eyes searched the room for another empty spot, but there was only the one next to me. With a swallow, she walked slowly towards me. I couldn't help but notice that today she was wearing a tight pair of jeans, instead of the baggy shapeless ones she'd worn the day before. I was surprised I hadn't noticed earlier in the day when I'd made her squirm. I did notice now though, thanks to the baggy hoody which hung off her shoulder and stopped above her jeans, that she had a tight arse and trim waist.

"Nice to see you again." I smirked as she finally reached the empty desk.

She didn't answer, but her lips moved, and I was sure I heard her singing. Before I could make out what it was, Mr Raymond addressed the class and whatever he said caused another bout of shouting and talking.

I kicked the back of the seat of the kid in front of me.

"Hey, Eddie, what did he say?"

Edward Stokes, the class nerd, sighed and turned around. "We have to get into pairs and write Napoleon's victory speech for the Battle of Austerlitz." He turned back around and shook his head when Shannon Harper dragged her chair up next to him.

"Really?" he said. "You have no clue about history. Why are you even in this class?"

"Because," she hissed, "I got thrown off geology and need three A-Levels to get into Liverpool, so you better make this speech a good one."

"Well she's a charm," Sarah muttered.

I laughed. "She's one of Maddison High's finest, that's for sure."

As Shannon flipped me the finger over her shoulder, Sarah snorted. I cocked a brow and tilted my head to one side to look at her. When her cheeks rushed with pink, I couldn't help but wonder how much of her body was covered by that blush.

"What?" she asked and flicked her tongue out at the side of her mouth.

I pressed my lips together and slowly shook my head, watching her eyes as she looked anywhere but at me. When I didn't answer, she leaned forward and poked Shannon in the shoulder blade.

"You want to swap partners?" she asked.

Shannon screwed up her brow, looked at me, looked at Sarah, and then without any response turned back to Edward.

"That'll be a no then," Sarah grumbled, and I couldn't help but smile.

"I think you're misjudging my ability," I said as I opened up my textbook at the chapter headed *The Battle of Austerlitz*. "Now, you going to help or not?"

With a sigh she looked at my book and then opened her own at the same place.

"So, how do you want to do this?" I asked. "I vote we write it as a victory speech he's making to Emperor Alexander and Emperor Francis."

"But they're who he defeated," Sarah said, glancing at what Mr Raymond had written on the board.

"You'll notice," I replied, and nudged her with my shoulder, "it says to be as inventive as possible. Everyone else is going to write a series of boring facts about how he won the battle. We can include what those two dicks did wrong."

"You know that do you? Because I can't say I've read any of that in this chapter."

"Well they were stupid for a start, believing his right flank was weakened. Exactly what he wanted them to think."

Sarah looked at me in astonishment, her mouth parted on a quiet oh.

"Close your mouth, Sarah, I know it's a shock, but I do actually have a brain."

The pink was back onto her cheeks and as she leaned down to get a pen from her bag, I caught a glimpse of colour on her collar bones where her t-shirt gaped.

"So, do we agree?" I asked and shifted in my seat, pulling it closer to my desk.

Sarah gave me the smallest nod of her head, smoothed down the pages of her textbook and cleared her throat. "I'll write. So, where do you think we should start?"

As we left the class, I threw mine and Sarah's paper on top of the others already there. Mr Raymond smiled at me and then looked to Sarah.

"Did Adam help you to catch up with where we are, Sarah?"

"Yes, thank you," she replied, barely looking him in the eyes.

"I think you'll find I did a good job with Sarah, Mr Raymond." I smirked at him and wiggled my brows.

Mr Raymond shook his head. "Go to your next class, Adam and we'll see how good a job you did when I mark your paper." He rolled his eyes and smiled. "Sarah, let me know if you need some old tests, or study notes to help you get to speed. Your records say you missed almost two months of school before you came here."

That pricked my ears up. When I turned around to listen to some more, I noticed how the colour had blanched from her face.

"I'll let you know," she muttered and pushed past me out into the hall.

So, she'd missed a couple months of school – well that was interesting.

"I can give Sarah any help she needs, Mr Raymond." I said in my most sincere voice. "Seeing as she missed so much school."

Mr Raymond eyed me over the top of his gold metal framed glasses.

"Go to class, Adam."

"But..."

"Adam." He scooped up the pile of papers. "If Sarah needs help, she'll ask. Now I believe you have maths with Mrs Baker, so go."

"Okay," I sighed. "But if I can help in any way."

"Goodbye, Mr Hudson," he growled.

I laughed and walked out into the hall, wondering how in the hell I could find out why Sarah Danes had missed two months of school.

64

9

SARAH

I had no idea how Alannah had talked me into it, but she'd persuaded me to go and watch her cheer practice before going with her for a burger at a cafe called TJ's, which was apparently styled liked a 1950's diner.

"You know you could actually help me," she said with a quick glance, her green eyes much brighter without her glasses.

"Me." I let out a laugh. "I don't think so. I love dancing, but cheer is really not my thing. No, that I've got any experience of it anyway." I didn't elaborate that the thought of hanging around with a group of girls all in one place brought me out in a rash.

"You don't have to join the squad, but this is all new to me, to all of us. We've only had a squad for two years and you should have seen the hoops I had to go through to get Miss Daniels, the PTA and Mr Jameson to agree to it." Alannah rolled her eyes and sighed. "Anyone would think I'd asked if we could give the team a lap dance every half-time. Anyway, the thing is, I know you do street dance and if you could show us some moves to add to the routine, something to go with the usual pikes and thigh stands..."

I pulled to a stop and slapped a hand against her stomach. "How did you know that I do street dance?"

If she knew that what else did she know?

Had she read the notes from my last school?

Did she know about what happened to me?

Alannah frowned like it was a really stupid question, and why wouldn't she know?

"Miss Daniels told me," she replied. "Why?"

My throat clenched as I searched her face for any sign that she might believe all the rumours that I'd led Mr Mills on or that we'd been having an affair.

"You didn't read my notes?"

I was being irrational, there was nothing on my notes, was there?

"No. There's no way Miss Daniels would allow that. She asked me if I knew any place that taught street dance around here so that maybe you could join."

Where I lived before, had only been an hour from London and I'd had a whole host of dance classes available to me, Street Dance had been the one that had pulled me in though, and had been the one to exhilarate me more than any of the others. I'd lived and breathed it for almost five years, even training to be a qualified teacher. Me and my squad had won the national championship two years in a row before I left, and I'd done the majority of the chore-ography.

"And is there?" I asked, an unexpected ache to dance again hitting me.

Alannah shrugged. "There's the Starline Dance School on the edge of the trading park, but I don't think they do street dance. It's mostly ballet, tap and some sports hall that they teach, but you should go over there and ask."

I nodded and carried on walking with Alannah rushing to catch me.

66

"So," she said. "Will you help?"

I had thought I was going to say no, but when I opened my mouth the word, "Yes," came out. Alannah squeaked excitedly and I felt a surge of joy at the thought of getting back to doing something I'd loved with passion up until a year ago.

"No way am I joining the squad," I stressed. "And anyway, I haven't practised in ages."

Alannah shook her head. "Nope, no way would I ever ask you. We have a full squad and three reserves anyway, so I promise."

Eager to get started, yet apprehensive, I followed Alannah to the sports hall with thoughts of Which-A-Way's and Scarecrows already forming in my mind.

When we walked in, my Converse squeaking on the polished floor, the cheer squad were already there, all stood together talking and giggling about God knew what. As Alannah approached them, I expected them to quiet down as their 'leader' had arrived, but they carried on, barely looking at her while she walked over to a huge speaker by the climbing ropes and dropped her bag next to it and turned it on. She pulled off her hoodie to reveal a purple bra top underneath which matched her leggings.

As she messed around with her phone, I moved over to a row of chairs around the edge of the room and surveyed the group of girls. I noticed Amber in amongst them, but she wasn't talking, just listening and smiling occasionally whenever one of the other girls said something. Her arms were wrapped tight around her waist and if I hadn't spent lunch with her earlier in the week, I'd have said she was shy and quiet. We'd only talked for thirty minutes, but she'd been funny and engaging and had plenty to say about the failings of the new shopping centre that had recently opened on the edge of town.

My gaze then moved to Alannah who with her phone in her hand, approached the group. She coughed to gain their attention, but when they continued to chatter, she pulled a whistle from around her neck and blew it.

All the girls looked at her and while most stopped and turned to Alannah, two or three others continued chatting but with their heads together. When Alannah blew the whistle again, they finally stopped; one of them did an eye roll.

"Okay," she called, as she shifted her feet around. "We're going to practice the choreography we did to High Hopes, but I want to add a Deadman in the middle after Chloe does her flyer. We'll warm up first."

After the way they'd failed to acknowledge her when she'd arrived, I kind of expected them to complain or suggest something different, but to their credit they each agreed and moved off to the middle of the hall where Alannah took them through some stretches and warmup exercises.

For a while, I had one eye on them and one on my French text-book. Once the music started to boom from the speaker though, I gave the squad my full attention. They were good, no doubt about it, especially the girl Chloe who was the flyer. Alannah was right though, it was kind of... boring, nothing I hadn't seen before on YouTube or Britain's Got Talent. As they repeated the choreography two or three times, I jotted down some moves that I thought would fit in and where to put them. I was sure the girls could pull them off and if Chloe could do a Funky Guitar mid-air, it would add some fun to the routine too.

Eventually after almost two hours, the girls, all sweaty and breathing heavy, were called into a line by Alannah.

"That was great; you're all doing really well with this new routine. Practice is off tomorrow because the football team have a match against Manchester Met."

"So, we need to be here then?" a tiny girl with a high ponytail asked.

Alannah shook her head. "No, Mr Jameson doesn't want us here. The match is a friendly so he can take a look at the team against an older side and see how they go. He doesn't want us distracting them." She huffed out a breath and flicked her ponytail over her shoulder. "As if we would do that."

A beautiful black girl with an amazing afro laughed loudly. "You know we would. Any chance I can get Tyler Jordan to look at me, I will. It's those damn freckles of his, I just want to find out where else he has them."

The girls all laughed, well everyone except Alannah and Amber who both looked at the floor. A wave of unease swept over me. What the hell had Adam and his hangers on done to them? I needed to find out, especially as Alannah seemed to think he was interested in me. If he had that much power to make these two girls appear almost invisible to everyone then I didn't want to be his next victim. I'd had enough shit in the last year. I wasn't sure I would manage to wade through the darkness again if anymore came my way.

"Okay," Alannah said and cleared her throat. "Practice same time on Thursday."

As the girls all started to walk towards the changing room, the double doors into the sports hall swung open and a bunch of boys wearing training gear all pushed through. They were sweaty and panting hard and right at the front of them was Adam. He wore a football top and shorts and his hair was all mussed at the front; but aside from the fact that I could see it was wet with sweat, he didn't look as though he'd exerted himself like the rest of the team.

"Alannah," the teacher who I assumed was Mr Jameson called. "I take it you've finished your practice."

Alannah stepped forward. "Yes, we're just leaving now."

"Good because this group of ladies need to put in some more practice seeing as most of them appear to have forgotten that training continues throughout the season and not just up to Christmas. Too much chocolate and turkey, is that right Walker?"

A really tall boy with black hair and, as far as I could see, not one extra ounce on him grunted and wiped his face with his t-shirt.

"Does that mean those of us who managed to complete the session without puking can go home, Mr Jameson?" Adam asked.

I looked over to see a conceited smirk on his face as he stretched his arms lazily in the air.

"Nope," Mr Jameson answered. "You're a team and if one fails then you all damn well fail. Now get into some dry kit, boots and shinnies and be on the pitch in five minutes. And you, Captain," he said to Adam as he passed him, "should know better than to ask such stupid damn questions. For that you've just earned yourself a little one on one with Walker once everyone else has finished."

I couldn't help the smile that burst through and when Mr Jameson pulled off his baseball cap and flicked the back of Adam's head with it, I snorted a laugh. Adam spun around and when his eyes met mine, they narrowed, and he pinned me with a stare that literally took the air from my lungs.

It was as if he'd poured every black part of his soul into it and a cold shiver ran over my skin despite the warmth of the sports hall.

"We should go," Alannah said, quickly turning to me. "You ready?"

I swallowed hard and nodded. "Yeah, I'll just grab my stuff."

You are my sunshine my only sunshine
You make me happy when skies are grey...

With the calming words of the song floating around my brain, I quickly packed my books into my backpack along with my notepad.

The whole time I felt Adam's eyes on me. I didn't dare look up because I knew there would be no doubt how much he scared me. My mum always said the eyes were the window to the soul and if that were true mine would most definitely show fear and anxiety.

"Hudson," I heard Mr Jameson shout. "Go get changed or that little one-on-one is going to get longer."

When I heard the squeak of trainers on the floor, I slowly lifted my head to see Adam disappearing into the locker room.

"Anyone else coming?" I asked Alannah with my eyes still on the swinging door.

"No, just us."

"What about Amber?"

Alannah didn't answer but almost skipped out of the sports hall and with a feeling of uneasiness swirling in my stomach, I followed her out to the car park and to a black Renault 500 with a daisy decal on the side.

"Nice car," I said and stood back to examine it.

It wasn't particularly new but was cared for and was shiny and clean.

"My Dad got it for me for my birthday, it was his way of apologising for his affair with his new PA. I mean how cliché is that?"

"Oh." My mouth stayed open as I tried to process what she'd said. I wasn't sure how to respond, we'd only been friends for the sum total of two days. I wasn't expecting to hear something so personal from her.

"It's not a secret, the whole town knew, well except for my mum who was away for six weeks caring for my grandma. It only lasted a couple of weeks and he was the one who broke it off and then confessed to Mum. Apparently, he felt neglected." Alannah rolled her eyes and did air quotes around the word neglected.

"Did your mum take him back?" I asked as Alannah's chin began to quiver.

She nodded. "They're madly in love, the PA was moved to a different office and he just happens to be a dick but I'm loving making him pay."

Her voice was laced with so much anger that I really wanted to slap her face.

"We all make mistakes, Alannah," I snapped. "And you should really cherish your dad while you have him. I don't have mine and I wish every damn day that I did."

As I felt the emotion start to prick the back of my throat, Alannah gasped and took a step back.

"Oh God, Sarah, I'm so sorry. I didn't know."

I knew it wasn't Alannah's fault. Mum had asked Miss Daniels not to tell anyone, that way I wouldn't have to experience their sympathy when they found out. Even so, it didn't make it any easier.

"You weren't supposed to know." I wrapped my arm around my waist and tried desperately not to double over with the pain. "I don't want everyone's sympathy, I just..."

I trailed off to take a deep breath so that I didn't sob out the words, '*I just want my dad back*'.

Alannah clasped a hand to her mouth, but the other she gently placed on my shoulder. The expression on her face was the exact one my mum had every day.

"I'm not going to crack up," I said. "I know that's what you're good at dealing with, the crazy ones, the ones with so much baggage they're buckling under the weight of it, but I'm fine Alannah. I just miss my dad that's all."

Before I knew what was happening, I was wrapped in Alannah's arms and being squeezed tight.

"I love my dad," she whispered in my ear. "I really do. He's so sorry about what he did, it almost broke him, but I just want to be mad for a little longer."

She sniffed and her arms tightened

"Okay." My response muffled into her squeeze. "But make sure he knows that even though you're mad at him, you love him too."

"I will." She let me go and held me at arm's length. "Do you want to come to my house for dinner instead of TJ's? My mum always makes far too much, she forgets my sister is at uni now."

"It's fine," I sniffed. "We can still go, but let's ask Amber too."

Alannah chewed on her lip and looked back towards the school and finally nodded.

"Okay," she said and passed me her phone. "I'll drive, you call her."

"Thanks, Alannah."

"For what?" she asked and gave me a huge smile.

"For not asking questions."

"You'll tell me when you're ready. Now come on, otherwise all the booths will be gone, and we'll have to sit on a table in the middle. That's the worst place you can sit."

"Why's that?" I asked as I pressed the screen of her phone to get to Amber's number.

"Because," she sighed. "That's where the football team sit."

As I put the phone to my ear Alannah's words sunk in. Dread and excitement swept over me in equal measure at the thought of seeing Adam Hudson again.

10

ADAM

Practice had been so bad that Mr Jameson had kept everyone back, not just me. We'd split into two groups and he'd made offensive players work against each other and defensive ones work against each other, encouraging us to try new passes and moves that our teammate would have no idea about. To be honest it was a fucking disaster, and Lenny Kowalski, Ellis' back up as keeper, fell awkwardly after trying to save a shot from Tyler who played left back. At first, Lenny seemed okay, but within minutes his wrist was twice the size it should have been, so Mr Jameson decided to drive him to casualty and practise finished earlier than expected.

"I need a double cheeseburger with chips right now." Kirk rubbed his stomach. "It's been almost three hours since I last ate."

We all ignored him and filed into TJ's through the old-style revolving door which Tony the owner had rescued from some fancy hotel just outside Manchester. As usual whoever was ahead of the line stopped walking so that the doors stopped revolving, and Tyler almost shit his pants. He got claustrophobic and we all thought it was fucking hilarious that he had a mild panic attack each time. Tyler hit whoever was in front of him around the back of the head and they passed it on until it got to the culprit, who tonight happened to be Dylan Fuller our centre back. The fact that Tyler was too stupid to realise if he only took the lead it wouldn't happen every single fucking time, only added to our enjoyment.

Once we were inside, a couple of year tens who were sat at one of our tables, looked up and saw us. One was a cocky little shit and waved, but the other knew what was good for him and snatched up his food and moved. As we approached, giving off some pissed off vibes, it wasn't long before the cocky kid did the same.

We all fell onto the red vinyl chairs and I lounged back in mine, looking around for a waitress, only for my eyes to fall on Alannah, Amber and fucking *Sarah*. What the hell was it about that girl that she wanted to be getting in my fucking face all the time. Hadn't I warned her that life would be so much better for her if she stayed out of my way? As I watched her, she studied some sort of notebook, occasionally scribbling in it, while Amber and Alannah chatted. They were still wearing their training gear from practice, but Sarah was in a tee shirt and those fucking tight jeans, with the hoodie she'd had on in class folded up on the seat next to her.

When she leaned forward her hair fell in a curtain and my blood prickled with the need to go over there and draw it back over her shoulder just so I could see the look of concentration on her face. My fingertips drummed on the table as I shifted in my seat and tried to deal with opposing needs that battled inside of me.

I needed to touch her.

I needed to break her.

"Are there no fucking waitresses here today?" I grouched and reached for the salt, spinning it around on the pale blue Formica table. Anything to stop my fingers from itching. "We've been here ten minutes already."

"No, we haven't." Ellis frowned and looked over his shoulder. "Becca is on her way anyway."

Becca, Tony's wife sashayed over to us in her too high shoes and too tight 50's style uniform. When she reached us, she leaned over the table and smacked a kiss on Kirk's cheek.

"Mum, please don't," he groaned as he wiped red lipstick away.

"I missed you this morning, seeing as I had to come in and receive the delivery with your dad." She laughed to herself and then sighed.

"Mum, me and my friends do not want to know what you and Dad got up to once the delivery arrived. Just please don't let it have been on this damn table."

When Becca grinned, we all shuddered.

"Okay boys, the usual?" She looked at us all in turn, waiting for us to nod. "Kirky, you want to double up?"

"Please, Mum, I'm starving."

Becca popped her pen behind her ear and then walked away. I looked around the table and grinned as each one of us, except for Kirk of course, watched her arse swing. She was most definitely a Hot Mum, not quite as hot as Tyler's, because *she* was pure fucking wanking material, but hot all the same.

Even thoughts of Tyler's Mum couldn't distract me for long, so while the rest of the lads pulled out their phones and started to scroll through whatever social media shit they were interested in, I shifted my chair a little so that I could see Sarah's booth without either her or the lads realising that I was watching. To anyone else I was keeping an eye on the counter to see when our food was ready, but I knew it was the petite blonde who had my attention.

Sarah was talking to Alannah and showing her something in her notebook. Whatever it was, Alannah grinned and clapped excitedly. Amber wasn't as interested, but when Alannah turned to her and pointed at something on the page, Amber pointed at herself and then jumped up and down in her seat with a gleaming smile. As the girls began to laugh, something darkened in my heart. I fucking hated the fact that Sarah had done that for them.

I'd broken them and she was putting them back together.

Sarah then got up to go to the ladies and pushed the notebook between Alannah and Amber, who continued to read it with their heads close together.

"Hey, lads," I said and pushed my chair back. "I vote we have some fun and go and sit with Amber and Alannah."

Each of them turned to look towards the booths and without another word, Kirk, Ellis and Tyler stood up. Dylan made to stand too but I pushed him back down with a firm hand on his shoulder and without a word passing between us, he stayed where he was. As we walked over to the booth, I wasn't sure what I planned to do, but I knew whatever it was I wanted to mess with Sarah's head. If that meant messing with Alannah and Amber too, well so-fucking-be-it.

When we reached the booth, I cleared my throat. "Excuse me girls, mind if we join you?"

Alannah groaned and Amber shrank back in the seat.

"What do you want, Adam?"

"Now now, Alannah, no need to be rude. Scootch up why don't you."

Kirk snorted out a laugh as I flapped a hand at Alannah, acting all girly. When she didn't move, I sighed and picked up Sarah's backpack and hoodie and dumped them in the next booth. I then sat down and used my thigh to push Alannah along.

Amber scrambled to move too, and as each of us got into the horseshoe shaped booth, she was pushed closer to Kirk's rock-solid body where he sat next to the end. Finally, we were all packed in with barely any room to move.

"We're going to have to fucking take it in turns to lift our burgers," Tyler moaned as Ellis elbowed him in the ribs accidently.

"If you let us get out," Alannah suggested. "You'd have more space."

"You're fine," I said close to her ear. "It's been a while since we spent time together."

She shifted uncomfortably and grasped her neck which had a blush creeping up it. "Leave me alone, Adam." Her voice was pleading, and a better man might have felt sorry for her; but I wasn't even a good man, never mind a better one.

"I'm not ready to do that, just yet." I wiggled my eyebrows and reached for a chip from her plate and slipped it into my mouth.

Alannah gave another desperate groan and dropped her head into her hands.

"What's going on?" Sarah was back.

She stood at the end of the table and looked at each of us but settled her gaze on Alannah.

"Alannah?"

"They just shoved their way in."

I sat back and surveyed the discomfort that slowly washed over Sarah at the sight of us all crammed in at their table.

"W-where's my stuff?" she stammered as she pulled her arm up to her chest and began rubbing the inside of her wrist.

"Oh sorry," I replied taking a sip of the Tango which had been in her spot. "I put it in the next booth. There really isn't space for all of us."

"But I was here first," she said as she glanced over to where I dumped her belongings. "*We* were here first, and that's my drink."

"Please, Adam," Alannah said and pressed her hands against my arm. "Let us out."

I didn't budge. "No. You and I are going to eat together."

"Excuse me, can I get out." Amber's voice was quiet and her stare remained fixed to the table.

When Kirk didn't respond, Sarah placed both hands on the table and leaned closer to me. "Let them out, *Adam*."

Her tone was harsh, but her voice quivered on my name.

"We're just having something to eat, Sarah, that's all. Now if you don't mind, our food is about to be served, so run along."

Everyone turned to see Becca approach us with a huge round tray full of food.

"Why the hell did you move?" she asked as she flicked out a stand and placed the tray on it. "You never sit in a booth. Oh, hi love," she said as she glanced at Sarah. "You looking for a table, because I'll be with you in a second."

Sarah shook her head. "No, we're just going, aren't we, Alannah?"

"Oh, okay," Becca said.

She started to hand out all the dishes as Sarah waited for Alannah to respond. I saw the determination on her face and there was no way I was going to let her win. This was my fucking Battle of Austerlitz. I slipped my hand under the table and dragged a finger up Alannah's thigh and whispered it over her crotch. Her leggings were so thin I could feel the lips of her pussy and I smiled when she tensed her thighs and pushed them together.

"Alannah," Sarah said insistently.

As I started to rub her, Alannah let out a little sigh. She pushed her hips forward and I knew then she wasn't going anywhere. I'd won.

The feeling that gave me should have been epic, I should have been beating my chest that I was the big man who'd made a girl act on his command just by touching her between her legs. The feeling of victory wasn't there though, instead was a huge ball of nothing. Emptiness and boredom sat at the pit of my stomach and began to fester as I continued to study Sarah.

"I'll come with you," Amber said to her and then looked at Becca as she said, "Excuse me, Kirk. I'd like to get out."

"Move, Kirky," Becca said and prodded Kirk. "The young lady needs to get out."

As Kirk moved, I glared at Amber knowing she'd used Becca being there to her advantage. Fucking sneaky little bitch.

"Alannah," Sarah said again.

Before she could answer, I moved my hand up to the waistband of her leggings and pushed it inside and into her knickers. I quickly entered her with two fingers and smirked at how wet she was before I'd barely even started.

"That's everything, boys," Becca announced. "Girls, you sure I can't get you anything else."

"No, thanks," Sarah replied and smiled at Becca before she turned to leave. *"Come on, Alannah."*

"Sarah, leave her," Amber said. "Just get your stuff and I'll give you a lift home."

Sarah looked at me and I shrugged. She shook her head and turned away, snatching up her stuff and following Amber out of the place.

Our table overlooked the car park and once I saw Amber and Sarah get into Amber's crappy old Fiesta, I quickly pulled my fingers out of Alannah's hot pussy.

She gasped and whipped her head around to face me. She'd been close to coming, I could feel it the way her muscles clenched my fingers, but Alannah's pleasure wasn't something I cared about.

I looked at the lads who weren't interested in anything but their food and then I turned to Alannah and put both my fingers in my mouth and sucked on them. Red crept up her neck and cheeks, but I knew she found it a turn on because her already heavy breathing grew ragged as she watched me. When her mouth parted I leaned in close.

"You can go now," I whispered. "I need to eat my burger."

"But—"

"Kirk," I snapped. "Let Alannah out would you, she needs to leave."

Kirk groaned and with his burger hanging out of his mouth, got up once more. Alannah shifted rapidly around until she could swing her legs over the edge of the bench and then stand up.

"You're a bastard," she hissed, tears welling in her eyes. "Why couldn't you just leave me alone."

I grinned and then ripped at my burger with my teeth and ignored Alannah's quiet sobs as she almost ran out.

"Pass me the ketchup, would you."

Ellis pushed it along the table towards me and as I moved around to get some more space, I noticed the notebook that Sarah had been writing in and showing to Amber and Alannah. It was a series of scribbles with words like scarecrow, floor sweeper and pop and lock. While I had no idea what it all meant, I didn't care because I had something that belonged to the girl who was starting to haunt me and I wondered if there was any way I could use it to bring her down.

11

SARAH

I was sure that Adam had wanted to see me break down and cry in the café. But he had no idea the shit I'd gone through, and him pulling off some pathetic mean boy routine was not going to leave me in a heap on the tiled floor.

I was mad, no doubt about it, but more at Alannah for falling for his stupid tricks. I wasn't sure how he'd got her to stay, but I guessed he must have had something hanging over her. He was putting pressure on her somehow, and even though I liked Alannah, we were new friends and it wasn't up to me to tell her what to do.

Amber had dropped me home, which was dark and empty because Mum had decided to work late because she thought I was going to be out. Once I'd done my homework I went to bed. I didn't want to be up when she got home and making small talk about how my night with my new friends had been. What would I say, oh it was great until this hot football player who hates the sight of me manipulated my new friend to dump me?

Alannah didn't turn up for school the next day, which worried me until I bumped into Miss Daniels in the corridor and she told me that Alannah's mum had called in to say she had a stomach bug so wouldn't be in for the rest of the week. She offered to find me another buddy for a few days, but I declined the offer. I really didn't want to spend another day having awkward conversation with someone who didn't want to be babysitting me.

School wasn't great. No one really made an effort to talk to me in class, but at least I had Amber at lunch. She started to come out of herself a little bit more each day and by Friday had told me all about her brother who was at Uni in Plymouth, and that she was going to Nottingham to study nursing.

Now it was the weekend and I was about to walk into the Starline Dance centre to enquire about street dance classes. Helping Alannah with her cheer choreography had made my chest ache with the need to dance again, and I didn't want to waste that feeling. For far too long I'd allowed Mr Mills' actions to impact on me. I'd hidden who I was and allowed myself to be swallowed up by guilt and shame of something that I'd had no control over. Now was time to take one of the first steps to being me again.

"Can I help you?"

The small woman, pulling her hair up into a bun and wearing tight yoga pants and an oversized cropped t-shirt which had 'Born to Dance' across the front, didn't look to be much older than me, but I guessed she must be Clarice Kitchener, owner of Starline Dance Centre.

"Hi, sorry to bother you, but are you, Miss Kitchener?"

She nodded. "Yeah and who are you?"

"Sarah Danes," I replied and held my hand out to her.

Clarice shook it and then went back to pushing loose strands of hair into the band on top of her head. "So, what can I do for you, Sarah Danes?"

"I was wondering if you do street dance lessons, because if you do, well I'd love to join."

She scrutinised me with her head to one side. "You do street dance?"

"Yes. I actually teach it as well, but I've haven't danced in a while so would love to just get some practice in."

"What level do you teach at?" Sarah's tone wasn't exactly confrontational, but it was straight and to the point as if she didn't actually believe me.

"I have a level three diploma in Dance Instruction. The Imperial Society of Teachers of Dancing ran a summer program, so my dad enrolled me as a birthday present." I wasn't sure why I'd told Clarice about my dad enrolling me, it didn't really figure in the conversation. Saying it made my stomach ache with longing for him. The need to speak to him hadn't lessened over the year, it had become more intense.

"You spent a whole summer learning to teach dance?" she asked, her tone now disbelieving. "Not lying in bed or watching Netflix."

"No. I spent it learning to teach dance."

I swallowed hard and forced back the tears, which threatened to spill over my lashes. It had been a big sacrifice from Dad and Mum. Not only had it cost them a huge amount of money, but they'd forgone their summer holiday that year.

That Dad's last summer was spent working or sitting in the house and dodging the British summer rain, was one of the pieces of guilt that I carried with me. Maybe that was part of why I'd stopped dancing, or maybe it was simply that I was dragged down so deep into despair that I just didn't find the joy in it any longer. But I was ready now, I wanted to dance again.

"It must have been hard work, attaining the diploma in a summer, it usually takes a year." Clarice crossed her long, sinewy arms across her slim chest and tilted her chin. "You have the paper-work with you?"

I opened up my bag and pulled out the folded diploma and

handed it to her. She read it carefully and then handed it back to me without a word.

"My dance squad won the national championship two years in a row," I added, my heart racing as I hoped the information might persuade her to let me join her class.

"I don't teach street," she finally said, turning away from me to pick up a box of hats and feather boas.

"Do you know anywhere that does?" I asked as I pushed my diploma back into my bag.

"Nope," she replied and began to drop the props around the mirrored room.

"Okay," I sighed, feeling my newfound enthusiasm begin to fade. "Thanks for your time."

I started to trudge back to the door when a feather boa landed on my shoulder.

"Hey, toots," Clarice called. "Where are you going?"

I whirled around, the feather boa fluttering to the floor and faced the woman who I found a little intimidating despite her small stature.

"I was just…" I half-turned and pointed to the exit door. "Going home."

Her lips turned down and she nodded sagely. "So, you don't want to teach street to my class then?"

A punching sensation hit my chest as my heart got excited at the possibility.

"Really?" I asked, breathlessly.

"Well," she said, tilting her head and assessing me. "Depends on whether that diploma is genuine or not."

"Oh, it's genuine." I stretched her the biggest smile my lips had felt in a year and took a step closer. "When do you want me to start?"

Clarice held her hands palms out. "Hold on, toots. Maybe you should show me what you can do and perhaps meet the classes first, and maybe you should get prepared with some music first."

I blew out a breath, causing my fringe to flutter in the light breeze. "Yeah sorry, I'm just so excited at the idea of dancing again."

"Well I'm not going to pry why, and you look pretty fit, but if it's been a while, I suggest you get some practice and conditioning time in before your first class. How about we say two weeks from today but in the meantime, you come and observe each of my classes? How does that sound?"

I nodded enthusiastically. "Yes, yes that sounds amazing."

Clarice finally gave me a warm smile and I felt myself physically sag with relief. Not just my muscles, but my bones, organs and soul too.

"I have a class at six on Tuesday and one at six on a Thursday and I have two classes today. One due now, they're between five and ten years old, and then after lunch we have the eleven-year old's and upwards. Each class is an hour and fifteen and I'll be honest there's only one boy. He's called Jasper, is thirteen and is an angry little shit, but has to attend as part of his therapy otherwise he gets shipped off to some sort of reform school." She shrugged. "Crap choice for the kid, but at least if he comes here, he gets to go home every night and be angry with his family who love him rather than with a load of people who probably don't have enough time or money to help him. You think you can handle him?"

Handle Jasper? God, I was probably the female equivalent of him.

"Yes," I said resoundingly. "I can handle him."

"Good, because to be honest he doesn't exist, that was just a little test, toots. Jasper is a great kid, a little bit gangly to dance if I'm honest, but he tries hard and he loves the feather boa, if you know what I mean."

God this woman was confusing. One minute she was dismissing

me and then offering me a job within seconds and then she was testing me with fictious angry kids. Maybe that was all a test too. I didn't have chance to question Clarice's actions any further because the door pushed open and a herd of young kids swooped in, all shouting and chattering.

"Okay, okay," Clarice yelled from the middle of the room. "Quit the noise or I'll make you clean the studio toilets again."

The noise immediately stopped, and each kid stood still and gazed at her with wide, horrified eyes.

"Excellent," Clarice said with a wicked smirk and placed her hand on a blonde plaited head. "Toots, it's your turn to pick the warmup music. What's your choice?"

Thinking it was going to get confusing if she called everyone toots, I quietly stepped back towards a row of chairs which lined the only wall without a mirror. I slunk down onto one of them as the pretty little blonde girl flicked through Clarice's phone, supposedly choosing her favourite warmup tune. I couldn't help but smile as she screwed her angelic face up in concentration and then finally flicked one of her braids over her shoulder and grinned at Clarice.

"You got something for me?"

"I do Clarice. It's '*Jump Around*' by House of Pain." She looked proud with her choice and pushed out her chest when Clarice gave her a resounding nod.

"Good choice, toots, good choice."

Clarice looked over to me and arched her brows questioningly and I nodded back, telling her yes, I was in. I was ready to dance again.

12

ADAM

As much as I loved my little sister, her constant chatter was getting on my damn nerves. With Mum's birthday coming up, Lori wanted to get her something nice as a gift, so I'd offered to take her to the shopping centre. So far, we'd been in at least ten shops and still not found the perfect gift.

Roger had offered first, but my mood was so fucking mean I decided to step in and offer to take her myself. I'd told him I wanted to get Mum something too, which was a lie. I hadn't bothered for years and usually I just about managed to get her a card. But I wasn't in the frame of mind where I was happy to see him take my little sister shopping like he'd done a thousand times before.

"And do you know that our new dance teacher has really pretty hair?" Lori twittered. "And she said she wanted to try plaits like mine."

"Yeah, you told me, about, ooh *ten times*," I replied as I looked at her with huge eyes.

Lori pulled up and crossed her arms over the chest. "Why are you so mean?"

I laughed and ruffled her hair. "I'm not mean, I'm playing with you, Munchkin."

"Hah, Munchkin, toots, I just wish people would call me by my real name."

"Who the hell calls you *toots*?"

"Clarice, my *real* dance teacher." Lori's face lit up and when she took a breath, I knew a fresh round of conversation about dance class was about to start.

Ten minutes later and she'd finally given up talking and was looking at a pink crystal swan with a red heart right in the middle of its chest. Personally, I thought it was fucking ugly, but my little sister kept sighing and telling me how beautiful it was.

"How much money have you got?" I asked as she pulled a tiny purse from the pocket of her jacket.

With her tongue poking between her teeth, Lori counted out her cash into my hand.

"And eighty and ten more makes ninety." She finally looked up at me and her bottom lip pouted. "I only have two pounds and ninety pence. I don't have enough."

I looked at the ugly swan that she'd put back on the display stand and thought my mum totally deserved it. I reached into the back pocket of my jeans and pulled out my wallet. I opened it up and took out twenty quid and handed it to Lori.

"Go and pay and ask them to wrap it carefully."

She flung her little arms around my legs and hugged me tight. "Thank you, Adam, you're the best." She pulled away and looked up at me with a frown. "It is just from me though, right? You're going to buy her something else?"

I glanced at the swan and nodded. "Oh yeah, my little Munchkin, that's all down to you."

With another grin, she turned and carefully picked up the swan to take it to the till. I stood by the door and watched the shop assistant wrap it up as she chatted to Lori. Finally, she came skipping back with a small bag clutched in her hand.

"Now your turn," she said slipping her spare hand into mine. "But I need to wee first."

"Okay, and then ice cream."

"Really, oh wow, thank you, but what are you going to get Mummy?" Lori asked as she looked up at me.

I shrugged because I had no idea, I think I'd been Lori's age last time I'd bought Mum anything.

"I don't know, chocolate maybe." I shrugged and led us towards the public toilets.

"Boring," Lori sighed. "I'll have a think for you while I wee."

I couldn't help but laugh as she thrust the bag with the ugly swan in it into my hand and then ran to the ladies.

"Don't speak to any strangers," I yelled.

"I know the rules," she called back without breaking stride.

I'd tried to take her into the men's toilets with me earlier, but she kicked up a fuss insisting that at eight she was old enough to go on her own. There was a bench seat opposite the toilets, so I sat myself down to wait for her. I watched two old ladies shuffle out and then a girl who I recognised from the year below me at school, but when a group of five giggling girls wandered out almost five minutes later, there was still no sign of Lori.

I gave her another minute, because if I knew Lori, she may well have decided to sing some Taylor Swift song all the way through before realising she'd actually finished peeing; it was something she did a lot at home.

"Where the fuck is she?" I muttered to myself and got up and went to the doorway. "Lori, you still in there?"

There was no sound apart from a toilet flushing and I sighed.

"Come on Lori, hurry up."

She didn't answer, but a lady in a blue uniform and a towel in her hand came into view.

"You looking for someone, love?" she asked as she wiped her hands.

"My little sister, she came in about five or six minutes ago."

"No one in here," she said and looked over her shoulder. "I just checked the cubicles and they're all empty."

I felt the colour drain from my face at the same time as my heart dropped. "You sure? She's only eight."

She nodded. "Sorry, love, but she isn't in here. Which door were you waiting at?"

It was then that I noticed another exit at the opposite end of the toilets.

"This one." I looked over at the bench I'd been sitting on, with some sort of hope that Lori would be sitting there laughing at herself for coming out of the wrong door, but the seat was empty.

"She probably went out the other one then," the attendant said. "Go to the information centre, they'll put an announcement out."

My eyes scanned the shopping centre and the dozens and dozens of people milling around as I desperately tried to spot my sister. I felt sick and my hands began to shake as my eyes went back to the attendant.

"Can you check again, please."

She nodded. "Sure, you go to information and if she's in here I'll bring her to you."

I hesitated not sure whether to do as she said or wait while she checked.

What if Lori was there and this woman was trying to keep her from coming out to me?

I pushed past her and ran into the toilets, pushing the door of each cubicle open with such force they banged loudly against the wall. They were all empty, so I then checked the woman's little

92

office area where there was just a chair, a radio and small table with a flask on it, but she wasn't there either.

"I did tell you," she said from behind me.

"What did you expect," I snapped. "She's my little sister. Where's the information centre?"

I was already halfway out of the door when she said, "This floor, turn right and it's near the lifts."

I didn't even thank her and ran off in the direction she'd told me to. I barged through groups of people and almost knocked a man over as adrenalin pumped through my veins. When I reached the circular glass office only one person was manning it and he already had a queue of four people wanting his attention. Not giving a shit, I pushed to the front and shoved a woman with some ugly little dog under her arm, out of the way.

"Excuse me," she cried. "I'm-."

"Listen," I said breathlessly, "my little sister is missing."

"Okay," the man behind the counter said. "Where did you last see her, what's her name and what's she wearing?"

"The ladies' toilets on this floor and her name is Lori, Lori Bla-, sorry Crawford," I replied, almost forgetting that Mum had changed Lori's last name to Roger's. "She's got blonde hair that's down with the front pieces tied back with a ribbon and she's wearing..." I closed my eyes and tried to remember what Lori had been wearing. "Fuck, why can't I remember."

"Take your time," the lady with the dog said and placed a hand on my arm.

"Yeah," the information man added. "Take a deep breath and think carefully."

I did as he said and then smacked my hand on the desk. "She's wearing jeans, a blue top with a rainbow on the front and a pink denim jacket. And, and." I pinched the bridge of my nose. "Blue converse, yeah blue converse."

The man nodded and when he started to speak into a walkie talkie, I turned around to watch the shopping centre just in case Lori walked past. Every time a little girl with blonde hair came into view, I held my breath, hoping that it was my sister, but none of them were.

"I've called security," a voice behind me said. "The centre will go into lockdown and control are checking the CCTV. Do you want to call your parents?" he asked.

I let my head drop back onto my shoulders and groaned. My mum and Roger would fucking lose their shit. I knew they had to know, but what if I could get Lori back first?

"I suppose so," I groaned and pulled out my phone. After about five rings my mum answered. "Mum, I'm so sorry."

It had been almost fifteen minutes since I'd last seen Lori. With every passing second my heartbeat was getting faster and I was feeling more and more like I was about to vom. Mum had pretty much lost it on the phone, but Roger was calm when he took it from her to speak to me. They were on their way and as we only lived a couple of miles from the shopping centre, I was expecting them soon. According to Mike, the man from information, security would bring them up when they arrived.

I wasn't looking forward to it, because while it wasn't my fault, I'd been responsible for her and I knew I should have insisted she go into the men's toilets with me. I'd said all that to Roger on the phone, in what was probably the longest conversation I'd ever had with him, but he told me I wasn't to blame, and that Lori was too independent for her own good.

The announcement had gone out asking for Lori to go to any shop assistant or member of security and it was becoming a hideous fucking waiting game as I hoped with every harsh breath I took that she would be okay and come walking in.

Mike had offered me some water, but I had refused. All I cared about was that my sister was okay. The lady with the dog had left, along with the other people who'd been in the queue, leaving just me and Mike waiting.

At twenty minutes and forty-eight seconds, I almost sank to the floor with relief when Lori came running into the information centre with a security guard and none other than Sarah fucking Danes.

"Adam," Lori screamed and ran at me, throwing herself at my legs. "I lost you."

I dropped to my knees and pulled her into my arms, wrapping them tight around her.

"Where did you go?" I asked against her hair. "I was so worried."

"I came out and you weren't there," she said, her little body shaking with each hiccupping sob.

"There were two doors, Munchkin," I sighed, breathing her in. "I was waiting on a bench for you and when you didn't come out, I got so scared."

"I'm so sorry." She sniffed and wound her arms tighter around my neck.

"You have nothing to be sorry about, nothing at all."

"Sarah found me looking for you and she was bringing me here when we heard my name on the big speaker."

I looked over her shoulder to see Sarah talking to a security guard and a police officer who was writing in a notebook.

"She told me you'd be worried and that we should come here because this was where you'd be," Lori continued, her sobs slowing. "She's so clever, Adam, you *were* here."

"Yeah," I replied. "She did a good job."

It was at that moment that my mum and Roger ran in and when Mum saw Lori in my arms, she let out a pained cry.

"It's okay," Roger soothed her and wrapped an arm around her shoulder. "She's fine."

Mum pulled herself away from him and ran over to us and ripped Lori from me.

"How could you, Adam?" she cried, over Lori's shoulder. "You were supposed to look after her."

"She was in the toilet," I protested. "She left through a different door."

"Elouise, love, it's not Adam's fault."

"Well whose is it, Roger?" Mum snapped, crushing Lori's little body against her. "He's the adult, or he claims to be. She's just a baby. Can you not do anything right?"

Her words hit me like a fist to the gut and the pain ricocheted around my body. For years she'd let me down, I'd never once told her how that had made me feel. I'd played up and disrespected her mostly, but I didn't want her to feel the ache in her heart that I did. I didn't want her to carry that burden of being a shit parent, but she was happy to lay it on me without a pause.

I got to my feet and took a step towards her. "I'm so sorry, Mum, I didn't know there were two doors and I—"

"No, Adam, I don't want to hear your excuses." She turned from me and towards Roger. "I want to go home, now."

Roger looked at me and where I'd expected disappointment, there was only sympathy in his eyes. I couldn't stand to see it, so turned my gaze to Sarah who was hovering around the doorway. She was chewing on her lip with her eyes on my mum and Lori and when Mum started to walk out of the door, Sarah stepped in front of her, causing Lori to lift her head.

"Sarah found me, Mummy," Lori said and gave Sarah a teary smile.

"Thank you," Mum replied. "I appreciate you taking care of her."

"It really wasn't Adam's fault," Sarah offered with a quick glance in my direction. "There are two exits from the toilets on this floor, I got lost myself only last week when I was here with my mum."

Mum took a deep breath. "I appreciate what you're saying, but she's eight years of age. Adam should have taken more care."

"Elouise," Roger said in a warning tone.

Mum glared at him and then lowered her head to kiss Lori's cheek before storming out of the information centre, past Mike, the security guard and the police officer who were talking quietly.

Roger turned to me and sighed. "Do you need a lift, Adam?"

His sympathy caused a fire to start within me and I couldn't bring myself to be thankful that he'd been on my side. It was all part of his plan to bring me around, to get me to fucking like him, so I wouldn't see the pain coming that he was bound to bring upon me once he had my trust.

"I have my car, how the hell else did you think we got here."

Roger's shoulder's fell in defeat as he let out a long breath. "You know, Adam," he said in a low tone. "I'm not your damn enemy and one day you'll realise that hating me and everyone else wastes far too much energy and creates so much negativity in your life you'll drown in it one day."

"Whatever you say, Roge," I replied and curled my lip.

"We'll see you at home later then." He turned to leave and stopped in front of Sarah. "Thanks again for taking care of her and realising this was where Adam would be. You both handled it well." He glanced at me one last time and without waiting for a response from Sarah left to follow my mum who I could see was waiting by the lifts with Lori still in her arms.

"Are you okay?" Sarah asked as I watched my sister reach out to Roger.

I whipped my head around to face her and the first thing I noticed was that her hands were shaking at her sides. She must have realised that I'd seen them because she thrust them into the pockets of the huge cardigan she wore over the top of a long blouse with llamas printed on it.

"I'm just fucking fine," I snarled. "I almost lost my little sister. My mum thinks I'm a waste of space and my stepdad wants for us to be best mates and go camping and sing kumby-fuking-a around a fire. What do you think, *Sarah?*"

My nostrils flared as I stared at her and flexed my itching fingers in and out of a fist. Her just being there, and being the one to find Lori, made my blood boil with anger and fury, yet I yearned to fucking touch her. Put my hands on her. Kiss her.

She didn't move but kept her eyes on me and I felt sure she was waiting for me to erupt like an unstable volcano. She was waiting but was too scared to move, I could see the fear in every part of her body.

"Was there something?" I asked, pulling out my phone and stabbing at the screen.

Sarah shook her head, but still didn't move, even when I took a step closer to her with my phone at my ear. When I was almost toe to toe with her, she took a sharp breath and held it. I could practically feel her muscles tense.

"Mackenna," I said when my call was answered. "I'm horny. Meet me at the old BMX park in twenty minutes."

Sarah's eyes went wide and her body reared back as I grinned at Mackenna's argument that she was home alone, and we could have sex in her bed.

"I said meet me at the park," I replied and licked my lips as my dick went hard.

Sarah momentarily closed her eyes and then with a defiant lift of her chin turned and left. As I watched her go, and ended my call, I felt my skin heat at the realisation that it wasn't that I *knew* that I would be fucking Mackenna that made me hard, but the *idea* of fucking Sarah Danes until she cried out that she was all mine.

As I reached the lifts, I felt a hand on my shoulder. It was the toilet attendant and she was holding up the bag with the swan in it.

"You left this on the seat," she said thrusting it at me.

I looked at it and shook my head. "Keep it," I replied. "I don't want it."

The woman looked in the bag and as she did, I stepped onto the lift and left.

13

SARAH

I lay on my bed and looked up at the bare ceiling. Tears began to creep from the corners of my eyes and down the side of my face. In my old room, at our old house, Dad had stuck luminous stars up there when I was six years old and they'd still been there when we left. I remembered Mum laughing because they kept falling off, but Dad was determined until they finally stayed put. I thought he was so clever to get them to stick, but then Mum found an empty tube of super glue and it was obvious how he'd managed it. Looking up now, I really missed those stars; stars that some other little girl would be looking at every night. I could have really done with them to tell my secrets and fears to. To whisper how a certain boy had begun to make me feel as though I were losing my mind.

I couldn't deny that my run in with Adam at the shopping centre had unsettled me. I couldn't believe it when I'd spotted cute little Lori from Clarice's dance class wandering around sobbing and looking scared. I'd immediately rushed over to her and as soon as she saw me, someone she recognised, her face had crumpled with relief. When she told me she'd lost her brother, Adam, not for one minute had I thought it would be him, so when we walked in and I saw Adam Hudson, I'd been floored. He'd looked so worried and scared, unlike the mean, vitriolic boy I'd met in my first week at my new school. Then when his Mum blamed him, well that was when I saw something else. I saw him broken and pained, like her words were a knife slicing into his skin and everything in me wanted to hug him and tell him it was okay, I had his back.

I'd wanted to make him see it wasn't his fault. It was something that could have happened to anyone, but he hadn't cared what I had to say. All Adam could do, all he ever did as far as I could see, was fight back. Actually, no he didn't fight back, he always struck the first blow. He was constantly on the defensive, desperate to strike before he could be hurt, and I'd laid myself wide open for his attack.

Seeing him like that though, had made me realise he wasn't black inside like he wanted everyone to believe. He'd been soft and gentle with Lori, nothing like the hardened bully that he was at school. At least it showed he did have a heart – somewhere.

He had to have something redeeming about him, otherwise why would he have filled my every thought since I'd seen his face crumple with pain at his Mum's words. It made me think he wasn't as bad as he wanted everyone to believe.

As soon as I'd got home, Mum had wanted to see the clothes I'd bought. I didn't tell her that finding Lori had distracted me because then she'd ask too many questions, so I lied and said I hadn't found anything I liked. I gave her back the cash she'd given to me and then disappeared to my room to try not to think about Adam hooking up with Mackenna. As soon as I'd heard them on the phone, a conversation he'd wanted me to overhear, I'd felt an uneasy sickness in my stomach. It unsettled me and had done ever since.

To avoid any more thoughts of Adam, I thought about what to do for the rest of the day, and whether I should maybe start my conditioning regime in readiness for my dance classes. When my phone vibrated on the bed next to me, I picked it up and saw Alannah's name across the screen. I hadn't seen her since the incident in the cafe, and I still wasn't sure how I felt about her and how she'd let Adam manipulate her.

On one hand I wanted to tell her she was being stupid and needed to be stronger, but on the other, I was beginning to see why girls were so fascinated by him; wasn't I falling under his hypnotic spell too? I'd begun to walk the same rocky path others had.

"Hey, Alannah." I sighed.

"Sarah, I'm so sorry," she blurted out. "I should have stood up to him and come with you, but I..."

I waited for her to end the pause, but there was dead air on the line, so I answered her.

"It's fine. Let's forget about it." I screwed up my eyes with the guilt I felt at my lie, it really wasn't *fine*. Adam had controlled her, which was wrong on every level, but I didn't know how to tell her it was wrong because I totally understood how she might let it happen. His was a light I could feel myself wanting to bask in, even though I knew that light was dangerous.

"You have to understand, Adam is—"

"Alannah, I really want to talk about him." I cut her off. "Just tell me how you've been?" I asked changing the subject. "Are you feeling better?"

She hesitated slightly and I guessed I'd been right in that she hadn't actually been sick.

"Much better thanks, it was a stomach bug."

"Yeah, so Miss Daniels said." I stared up at my starless ceiling and chewed on my thumbnail, searching for something to say. "So, do you want some help to catch up, ready for tomorrow?"

"N-no, Miss Daniels dropped some work off with my mum, thank you, but I do need your help on something else though."

I shuffled up my bed and rested my back against the silver padded headboard. "Okay, what is it?"

"I tried to remember the moves that you suggested but couldn't. I'd like to put them into the choreography at practice tomorrow, so I was wondering, would you come over this afternoon and go through them with me? I know it's asking a lot, but we have practice tomorrow and it's the last chance to get it right before Tuesday."

"Why what happens on Tuesday?"

"I'm not sure you'll want to know," Alannah sighed.

"Why not?" I asked, unsure of why she'd think that.

"Well, because we have to show the team on Tuesday," she said hesitantly. "It's kind of a rule that they watch any new choreography and have to agree on it before we can perform it at a game."

"Oh my God," I cried and sat up straighter. "And who thought up that archaic and misogynistic tradition?"

"I think it was the PTA and Mr Jameson," Alannah replied with a quiet laugh. "To be sure we don't surprise them with any stripper numbers at half time. Like the team would say no to that."

"So, you're telling me, Adam fucking shithead Hudson, and his fucking dickhead teammates, get the final say on what your squad are allowed to dance. Shit, Alannah that's crap. You're the one who persuaded the school to let you have a cheer squad." I knew I was shouting, but I was so mad that they had so much control on something that really wasn't any of their business.

"Well, yeah."

"They should just concentrate on what they do on the bloody pitch, not what happens on the side lines." As my voice rose even higher, my mum's head popped around my door.

"Everything okay, love?"

"No Mum, it isn't." I held the phone away from my ear. "We've moved to a town that supports the prehistoric idea that men need to make all the decisions in life and I, for one, am appalled."

"Okay then," she said and grimaced. "I'll, well I'll leave you to it." She disappeared as quickly as she'd appeared, evidently deciding this was one battle I could fight for myself.

"Alannah," I growled. "I'll be at practice *and* at the meeting on Tuesday."

"Sarah, I don't know," she groaned. "I really don't want any trouble. You know Adam is the captain, right?"

"Of course, he is. That's why he acts entitled in everything he does." I rolled my eyes even though Alannah couldn't see me. "And you're okay with the fact that he gets to say how you dance?" I let out a long, agitated sigh.

Alannah cleared her throat and I could sense she was irritated by me, the new girl, questioning the idea of some stupid rule that she didn't have an issue with.

"Sarah, it wasn't his idea, you know," she sighed. "That's not to say he doesn't think it is a good one, but I don't want you at practice if you're going to cause friction. Quite honestly, I really don't need any more trouble from Adam Hudson and his little gang of idiots." She finally took a breath. "Is that okay?"

I couldn't help but smile at her sass. It was quite a relief if I was honest, because I was beginning to think she was a pushover, especially where Adam was concerned.

"Yes," I replied quietly. "I won't cause you any trouble, but I'd still like to come if that's okay."

She was quiet for a short time. "Okay but promise me."

"I promise." I didn't want to, but she was right, it wasn't her fault and I was new to the school, so it really was none of my business

"Good," Alannah replied sounding relieved. "But are you still able to come over?"

I moved over to where my backpack was sitting on my desk chair and opened it up. "Yes sure. Is 3 p.m. okay?"

"Perfect. Oh, Mum said you can stay for dinner if you'd like?"

I considered saying yes, but Mum was home and had been making a real effort for us to eat dinner together every night. She'd learned from her past mistake of losing herself in her work as an accountant, and now made sure she stuck to normal office hours and was here for me. I'd feel bad about leaving her alone when she'd told me she was making roast chicken for dinner.

"I can't, I'm sorry. Maybe another night, if that's okay?"

I wanted to be friends with Alannah. She'd made an effort with me and it didn't matter what I thought about her relationship or whatever she had going on with Adam. She and Amber were the closest thing I had to friends here. The thought of which reminded me of those I'd left behind at my old school; Grace, Lily and Harley They'd all believed I was a whore.

"No problem," Alannah replied, causing me to push the sadness and bitterness from my mind. "See you at three."

I said goodbye and feeling excited at the prospect of dancing later, I searched through my backpack for my notebook. It wasn't in the inside pocket where I usually kept it, so I pulled everything else out to check, but it wasn't amongst it all.

"Shit," I muttered and dragged my fingers through my hair. "Where the hell is it?"

I thought back to when I'd last had it and the realisation it was at the cafe made my stomach roll. I must have left it there, or what if someone had picked it up? Or worse still what if Adam or one of the other boys had picked it up? There wasn't anything incriminating in it, except for my poetry and would they really understand what I was trying to say with it?

Most people probably wouldn't, but someone with a black soul might recognise themselves in the hostile words and phrases and figure out that I had pain dragging me down.

Someone like Adam Hudson.

14

SARAH

As the girls got ready to show the new routine to the team, I could see how nervous Alannah was. I wasn't sure whether it was about the new moves she'd introduced with my help, or the thought that I might have an epic tantrum over the team having the final say so on it.

I really hoped they said yes, because at practice the night before, the girls had been amazing and had embraced everything that Alannah had added from what I'd shown her. By the end of the night they had it nailed, and it looked fantastic; it was fresh and new.

As the team filed in and took up their places around the room, I looked over at Alannah who had her eyes firmly on her squad. I was glad she didn't look at Adam, because the smug smirk he had on his face as he walked in with an arm around the neck of his friend Tyler, may well have put her off her game.

I quietly moved to the side of the hall and sat on the floor near to a pile of gym mats. I could see everything from there, but no one would see me, particularly not Adam. I'd managed to avoid him since the incident at the shopping centre. On Monday he'd been on a Geography field trip and today he'd missed History due to some interview he'd had to do for the Maddison Edge Guardian about the Maddison High Eagles chances of winning the next round of the Under 18's Schools Trophy. Here in the sports hall was the first time I'd seen him, and I couldn't help but think how hot he looked. His hair was sexy and messy, and he was wearing his usual attire of jeans ripped at the knee and a long-sleeved t-shirt. The shirt was a corn-flower blue and the colour matched his eyes and highlighted his olive skin.

It had been a long time since I'd been attracted to anyone, Jason Jones had asked me to the end of year disco, the year before my dad had been killed. We'd gone out for about three months, but when I wouldn't have sex with him, he dumped me for a girl the year above us. After that I decided I was done with boys for a while until someone could prove to me that I actually meant something to them – then Mr Mills happened, and everything changed.

Yet here I was, finding myself staring at Adam and trying to quell the weird feeling in my stomach whenever he smiled. His laughter was loud, and I found it hard to believe that this was the same boy at shopping centre; the boy who'd looked like the bottom had fallen out of his world. When his mum had said those hurtful words, his eyes had filled with pain. Now though, he was back to being king of the hill, sitting in the middle of all the team, wearing a cocky grin as he talked and joked with them all.

After a few minutes of speaking quietly to the squad, Alannah moved to stand in front of the boys and cleared her throat, surpris-ingly they all went quiet.

"If you're ready," she addressed them. "We'll show you the new routine."

"Off you go, Alannah," Mr Jameson replied and gave her a quick chin lift.

Alannah turned quickly, causing her short cheer skirt to flick up and show the maroon coloured shorts that all the girls wore under their gold and maroon uniforms. A couple of the boys jeered until Adam threw them a glare.

From my spot, I saw Alannah take a deep breath and then start off the booming voice of Eminem singing that he was not afraid. As the girls started their moves, my breath caught, and my heart pounded at how good they looked. The choreography had so much power now Alannah had changed to the song I'd suggested.

As they did a mix of gymnastics and some classic street dance hip hop moves, the team and Mr Jameson watched in rapt silence, their heads bobbing to the music or moving to look up as Chloe flew through the air. When the girls did a synchronised twerk in the middle, where Alannah and I had cut in forty seconds of Bring it Back by Travis Porter, a few mouths dropped open and almost all of them fell around groaning and clutching their crotches, muttering about how hot it was. Almost all, except for Adam; he remained calm and turned his head in my direction. I was afraid that he might have seen me but had no idea how he could have. I was hidden by the high tower of mats with my back against the wall.

His gaze stayed in my direction and I knew without doubt that it was me he was looking for, that he'd sensed I was there. That thought made me fizz with excitement even though my short time at Maddison High School had already taught me that I should have been afraid. He was a boy who could slice at my skin with his vicious words.

I knew that being attracted to Adam Hudson was wrong and it would only end with me being hurt and betrayed in some way. I should have wanted to stay away from him, but I was a moth to a light bulb; I knew it was going to burn like hell, but I couldn't stop myself from wanting it, because the pain and suffering were deserved.

I held a burden of guilt at putting myself in a vulnerable position with Mr Mills. I'd been the one to suggest I help him clean the art room after school. I was the one who didn't report him the first time he forced himself upon me. I would take whatever agony the boy with the dirty blond hair and full lips would force onto me if I stayed within his sights.

It would be my relief.

It would be my release.

I would relish the scars he inflicted on me much more than those I had inflicted on myself because the thrill was more empowering than the fear.

Adam's gaze moved back to the girls dancing in front of him and I let out a long breath. My heart kick started itself and thumped wildly as the music came to a stop and the girls held their final poses.

The boys watching all clapped and some whistled, and I was relieved to see all Alannah's hard work had paid off. Then my eyes went to Adam, who was lounging back with his hands behind his head.

Something about the smile on his face and the tilt of his head told me he was going to say no, and when his eyes flashed in my direction again, I knew I was right. Lori must have told him I was the new dance teacher at Starline, and that alongside the street dance moves the squad had performed, he must have realised that I'd helped Alannah.

Saying no was going to be his first action of damnation towards me.

"Lads," Mr Jameson said. "What do you think?"

Alannah didn't look worried she knew she and the girls had done a great job, so she stood poker straight with an air of confidence. I held my breath waiting for her to be disappointed and for the affliction of blame to land on my shoulders.

"I like it," Adam said and sat up straight. "Something different and entertaining; a change from the usual boring stuff you bring us."

My stomach turned at the harshness of his words and how they would no doubt hurt Alannah. It was his way of trying to cause shit between us. He wanted Alannah to feel resentful of me, but she surprised me and probably him too.

"That's because I've had some help," she replied and looked directly at Adam. "I haven't been doing this for long and only know so much, so thought it best to bring someone in who can turn us from a good cheer squad to a great one."

"Well job well done," Mr Jameson said. "It's takes a big person to know when they need help, so that was a good call."

Adam's eyes narrowed on Alannah, who quickly looked over her shoulder to where I sat in the shadows, giving me a quick thumbs up.

"Well, if you want my opinion," a tall rangy boy with a shock of red hair said. "I think it makes you look cheap."

"Davies," Adam roared. "Shut your fucking mouth."

Adam was halfway up from his seat, when Ellis dragged him back down.

"Yeah, Davies. Shut up, you dick," said a boy I didn't recognise, as he threw a plastic bottle at Davies.

"Thank you, that's enough." Mr Jameson sighed and pointed at Adam. "Watch your language otherwise I'm going to send you out."

"Me?" Adam protested. "He's the one being shitty about the girls."

"The girls," Davies said with a laugh. "Since when did any of us care about, *the girls*?"

"Oi, Davies," a boy wearing huge goalkeeper's gloves shouted across the room. "Just because you've been dropped the last few games, doesn't mean you can act like a dick."

Davies stood up and pointed at the goalkeeper. "Ah thinking about your sister were you, Walker. Thinking about how she dances around dirty old fucking men for money, were you?"

In an instant, before Walker was even out of his seat, Adam had launched himself to land on top of Davies. He threw a punch to his kidneys and then to his side all before his teammate could retaliate.

"Hudson," Mr Jameson barked. "Get off him now."

Mr Jameson ran to them while Adam kept on going, like a terrier dog on the attack. Red mist seemed to have fallen, and he appeared to hear nothing as he ignored Mr Jameson's angry cries and continued to rain punches on the leaner Davies. As he pulled his arm back to punch him again, Mr Jameson pushed through about four other boys who had surrounded Adam and Davies and put an arm around Adam's neck to pull him away.

"That's damn well enough," he bellowed and pulled the two boys apart.

"Apologise you fucking twat," Adam cried as he literally spat the words out, trying to tear free from Mr Jameson.

Davies reared back and I was sure he was going to try and head butt Adam, but before he had a chance Ellis appeared and got him into a headlock. As he did, Adam got free and landed a punch right in Davies' eye.

"You fucking bastard," he sneered and then staggered back against Mr Jameson, breathless and red faced.

Anger poured out of him. The way his rib cage heaved, and he clenched his hands in and out of fists, created a swarm of excited butterflies in my belly. His power and determination to get to Davies was intoxicating and I couldn't take my eyes off him.

"Get out of here now," Mr Jameson roared and pushed two hands in Adam's back, forcing him away from Davies. "I don't give a shit what he said, you do not damn well set about your teammate and you certainly don't ambush them. Byron, you get out too."

Ellis let Davies go and threw his hands in the air. "What did I do? All I was doing was trying to stop him head butting Adam."

"Yeah just so Hudson could punch me." Davies groaned and held a hand over his eye. "That's a fucking dirty coward's trick."

"Call me a coward again, Davies," Ellis hissed. "And I will finish off what he started."

"Both of you, out. Davies you too."

"Sir, I'm not going with them," he yelled. "They'll kill me."

As I continued to watch the confrontation from my spot against the wall, Alannah appeared at my side and dropped down to sit next to me.

"You okay?" she asked, her eyes still on the argument going on.

"Yeah and you did great by the way," I replied, my breathing a little ragged from the excitement of the fight.

Alannah smiled tentatively and then looked back to the girls. "Do *you* think we look cheap?"

I gasped. "No way would I give you choreography that makes you look like that. Davies is a dickhead."

She nodded and as we looked back over to the argument, we saw Adam striding across the hall and straightening his shirt.

"Shit," Alannah said. "He looks about ready to maim someone."

She was right, he looked homicidal as he strode across the sports hall towards the doors and pushed them open.

"Alannah get back over here," Mr Jameson cried as he shot Davies a hard look. "We're going to vote, everyone except for Davies and Hudson. Davies apologise to Walker, *now*."

"I'd better go," Alannah whispered. "We might be a while, the last time it took them almost an hour to agree. Will you be okay to get home?"

Alannah had decided as I'd helped her with the routine that a favour deserved a favour, so she was going to be my lift to and from school. It suited me as I had no car and lived just over three miles from school, but I really didn't fancy hanging around while a bunch of self-entitled footballers argued over whether my moves made the girls look cheap or not.

"I'll be fine, but listen, if anyone doesn't like it, I won't be offended if you drop some or all of the moves."

Alannah shook her head and pursed her lips. "Not a chance, we love your moves. They're staying."

I smiled and leaned in for a quick hug, which surprised me. I hadn't instigated a physical embrace with anyone but my mum for a long time.

"I'll pick you up in the morning," she said as she pulled away from me, ignoring the shocked look on my face. "And thank you so much for your help."

I gathered up my stuff, leaving her to head back to Mr Jameson, and shoved it into my backpack before I sneaked out of the door to corridor which led to the changing room and the main exit.

I closed the door behind me and turned, almost screaming as I came face to face with Adam leaning against the wall with his arms folded over his broad chest.

"Oh my God," I gasped. "You almost gave me a heart attack."

"So, you *were* in there."

"Well good for you." I made to move past him. "Aren't you the clever one."

"Were those new moves yours?" he asked and pushed off the wall, falling into step beside me.

I shrugged. "So?"

"They're good, like I said it made it entertaining. Better than the usual boring routine she puts together."

His cheek was a little red and I guessed Davies must have got a punch in.

"He caught you," I said, pointing at Adam's face and ignoring his shitty remark about Alannah's cheer routines.

"Lucky fucking punch." He sighed and reached for the door. "You need a lift?"

"What?" I asked and my breathing faltered.

"I'm guessing Alannah usually gives you a lift, and if I know anything that vote in there is going to go on for at least an hour."

"But you said yes, you're the captain, the king of the school. They'll say yes, right?"

Adam rolled his eyes. "Of course they will, but doesn't mean they won't try and act like a bunch of pricks and make the girls sweat. I promise you it'll be a while." He opened the door and waved for me to go through, but I hesitated. "Look, Sarah, I'm not about to let you walk home alone in a town you barely know, on a route you have no idea of, so come on."

"I'm not stupid. I can find my way home."

"Maybe you can, but I'm not letting you, so let's just get the fuck out of here."

He sighed impatiently and pointed towards the corridor. Every brain cell I had told me to say no. If I went with him, he would find some way to hold it against me, to hurt me, because that was what he did. If I was sensible, I would call my mum to come get me on her way home from work. I knew I should say no, and I would have done had I not seen the love and tenderness he'd given to his sister or hurt and shame he'd felt at his mum's words.

If I hadn't seen a different Adam Hudson, I wouldn't have allowed my brain to let my body know that it was attracted to him; but I had, and it did.

I nodded and walked past him through the door and into the corridor, hating myself because I loved it that his eyes were on me with every step.

I swallowed deeply as I realised I was going to be just like Alannah and Amber. I was probably going to become one of those girls who sat alone in the school dining room but at that moment I didn't care.

15

ADAM

As I watched Sarah walk down the corridor in front of me, I couldn't think of a single reason why I'd decided to be nice and offer her a ride. Well I could and it was her damn pussy. I'd done nothing but think about getting inside it since she'd walked away from me at the shopping centre on Saturday.

I'd met up with Mackenna and I'm not going to say I couldn't get it up, or didn't blow my load, because I did, I'm a seventeen-year-old lad, but I did wonder how it would feel being inside Sarah instead. Mackenna was a good shag for now, but when I'd had enough of her, I'd make sure she never bothered me again. If I was honest, it was getting to that point. Whenever she spoke or touched me, it felt like thousands of tiny needles were piercing my skin and her voice was fingernails down a chalk board. Her time had nearly passed.

"Get in," I snapped at Sarah as we reached my blood red Volkswagen Golf and she hesitated by the passenger door. "Because if you think I'm the sort of person that opens the door for you then you're fucking mistaken."

"I don't. I'm just not sure I should be getting in with you." She reached inside the sleeve of her thick jumper and started to rub. "I think I've lost my bloody mind."

"It's up to you." I shrugged and opened my door. "But it's dark, so if you want to walk the three miles back to your house then go for it."

"How do you know how far my house is?" Her brows arched and she took a step back from the car.

Fuck, I'd let my guard down. I either had to admit to Kirk hacking the school computer system or think quick about how I knew that she lived on Cedar Avenue with only her mum.

"I'm guessing you live on the new estate a couple of miles from where I live. I saw you going that way with Alannah. Most people who move from out of town move there."

It wasn't exactly a lie. I had seen her and Alannah go past my house in that direction, in Alannah's car with the stupid flower on the side, plus it was true that most people who moved from out of town moved to the new estate; unless they rented one of the many terraced houses around Maddison Edge. We'd been lucky that an old friend of my mum's, from years back, knew someone who knew someone who had gone to work in China, so had let us have his detached house at a pretty cheap rent. Then, a year and a half ago he'd dropped the bomb that he was finally selling up because he wasn't coming back and needed the cash. Mum had tried to find us something else to rent, but whatever was available was either too small, too shitty or too expensive. And then, as luck would have it, Roger came along and before we knew it, we were moving in with him. It wasn't that my mum didn't love him, because I knew she did, but was he the great love of her life? I doubted it. Was it a love that came from anything but gratitude? I sincerely doubted that too.

"Well, okay, thank you." Sarah's hand reached for the door a little tentatively, but once she had it open she quickly jumped inside and buckled up before I'd even got comfy.

I started up the car and glanced at her. She'd moved right up to the door and had her back pressed against it; her knuckles were white as her tiny hands clutched the strap of her backpack.

"What do you actually think I'm going to do to you?" I asked, unable to keep the anger from my tone.

Did she think I was some sort of fucking deviant who would force myself on her? Manipulate maybe, but never that.

"N-no," she stammered, her damn hand disappearing up the arm of her jumper again. "I just wonder why you're doing this. You actually seem to hate me."

I laughed out loud and shook my head. "I hate every fucker. Please don't think I'm giving you any special attention."

"You don't hate your *boys*."

Her words were heavy with sarcasm, but she was still rubbing her fucking wrist with one hand, while the other hung on tight to the backpack. Yet again, she was desperate to appear brave, like me even breathing in her direction didn't scare the shit out of her, and it made my chest feel tight. It made me want to protect her and aside from Lori that wasn't something I ever felt about anyone. I protected myself and fuck everyone else, but this tiny girl with the golden hair made me feel things that I wasn't comfortable with. She made me feel like I was being worked and controlled to do things that I wouldn't normally. Like my life had suddenly become the fucking Truman Show.

As we drove through Maddison Edge, the streetlights were starting to come on and the traffic had started to get heavy with people traveling home after work. When I pulled up at a red traffic light, in my peripheral vision I noticed Sarah's body had relaxed a little.

"My sister thinks you're amazing by the way," I said as I drummed my fingers on the steering wheel. "She said you showed them some of your dance moves when you were introduced to them."

Sarah shifted in her seat and when I looked at her, she was smiling, and fuck, it lit up her face. Even in the half-light of the car, I could see how it sent her from pretty to beautiful.

"Yeah," she sighed. "Only a couple of little things, but they all seemed keen to learn more in a couple of weeks."

"A couple of weeks?"

The light turned to green and I put my foot down, burning off some old bloke in a Focus next to me.

"I'm excited to get started but Clarice wants me to get my fitness levels back and prepare properly first."

I frowned and manoeuvred the car to turn right towards the area where we both lived.

"Why the hell do you need to get fit?" I took a tighter grip of the steering wheel.

I had watched her arse and seen her tiny waist when she occasionally uncovered from those big, baggy clothes. I had no idea what Lori's dance teacher was talking about.

"I-I haven't danced in a while," she replied and moved to flatten herself against the door again.

"How come?" I glanced at her and felt anger rise that she'd gone back to feeling threatened because I couldn't help but open my big mouth. "Sarah, you really don't need to sit practically outside the car, I'm not going to fucking do anything."

Hesitantly she moved a little to the middle of the seat, not much, but enough for me to let out a breath and feel the tension ebb a little.

"So?"

"So what?" she asked.

"So why haven't you danced for a while? Why does the dance teacher think you need to get fit?"

As we turned into the estate where she lived, the lamplight lit up her features and she was biting on her bottom lip as she stared straight ahead through the windscreen.

"Things got in the way," she said quietly. "I just didn't have time."

She swallowed and placed a hand against her slim neck. My fingers twitched on the wheel, wanting to stroke along her pale skin. The need to touch her was getting stronger every time I saw her.

"And now you do?"

She smiled and let out a long sigh. "Something like that."

She wasn't telling me everything, I could see it in the way she eyed me warily. The fact that she was lying, hiding something from me, caused the blackness in my soul to make an appearance. It was like her lie had broken the dam I'd made to keep it away and inch by inch the hate slowly began to seep back in, soaking up any positivity. I wanted to know why she'd stopped dancing. It was something huge, something big enough to make her not want to do the one thing that brought that beautiful smile to her face.

"So, what made you so busy you couldn't dance?" I asked.

Sarah shrugged. "I don't know, just stuff. Why are you so interested anyway?"

"Just trying to be friendly."

She huffed and shifted her backpack closer to her chest. "You're never friendly. Not to me, not to any girl at school."

"Someone is salty today. After I gave you a lift home too."

"Yeah well, I'm still undecided why you felt the need to offer," she replied.

I chanced a glance at her and was met with narrowed, speculative eyes. Her arms were wrapped tightly around her bag as if it was a life jacket and it would save her life, while one hand was hidden up the arm of her jumper.

"What's wrong with your wrist?" I asked. "Why's your hand always up your sleeve?"

I heard her gasp and from the corner of my eye saw her pull her legs up closer to the seat. As the traffic slowed, I turned to look at her and saw her whole body was stiff and rigid. Her shoulders were hunched almost up to her ears and she was staring out of the window looking up at a white Range Rover Evoque next to us. The driver must have sensed her looking and turned to face us. He was about our age and obviously liked what he saw in Sarah because he waved from what was probably 'mummy's car' and gave a smile that as a lad I knew meant only one thing.

"Arsehole," I said and revved my engine.

"You see." Sarah sighed. "You hate everyone. He was only being friendly."

"Yeah because he wants to get into your knickers, *Sarah*." I spat out her name and then flipped the finger to the dick in the Evoque when the traffic started to move.

"Why do you say my name like that?" Her voice was quiet and tentative. The leather of her seat squeaked as she moved around in it.

"Like what?"

"Like it's a curse word, or you get a nasty taste in your mouth whenever you say it."

I turned and grinned at her. "Not sure what you're talking about."

She let out a long breath but didn't respond. I sneaked a glance at her and when I saw her tits heave up and down my dick twitched in my jeans.

What the fuck was it about this girl that had my head in such a mess. One minute I wanted to fucking crush her, break her and stop that brave act she tried putting on. The next minute I wanted to pull her against me and kiss her until she moaned out my name and begged me to fuck her.

At this moment, in the confines of my car, I wanted to do the latter. I couldn't think of anything other than stripping her of her clothes and worshipping every inch of her pale, naked skin.

"The thing is, Sarah," I said, repeating her name softly and sweetly. "You interest me a great deal."

"No," she replied with a little quake in her voice. "There's nothing remotely interesting about me. You should just keep your focus on the other girls at school."

"Maybe, I don't want to," I muttered, not sure if I wanted her to hear me or not.

She heard me. "Well, I certainly don't want your attention, so just leave me alone." She was being petulant and sounded a lot like Lori when Roger wouldn't let her eat sweets before dinner.

"Where would be the fun in that?" I asked, loving that she was most definitely feeling uncomfortable with the way the conversation was headed. "It's so much more entertaining making you squirm."

Her leg bobbed up and down and she grew fidgety. If it wasn't because I was getting to her it would be irritating and fucking piss me off, but her actions just made realise she might want me just as much as I wanted her.

I didn't want her like I wanted Mackenna or Alannah, or any one of the other girls I'd had. They were quick and mostly unsatisfying one night, one-time only hook ups. Her though, the tiny girl who wanted everyone to think she was brave, the one who constantly shook like a leaf in the January wind, she made me feel like I was drunk. When I was around her, my head swam and my body lurched through each moment of the day desperate to see her; desperate to play with her.

Desperate to see her; desperate to save her.

"Drop me here." Her words were harsh and they pierced the stifling air within the car.

I peered through the windscreen to see we were still on the edge of the estate where she lived.

"Nope," I growled. "I told you it's dark and I'm taking you home."

"I don't want you to. Now pull over."

Sarah's voice cracked as she slapped a flat palm against the dash and then drew in a breath that sounded like it was tattered and torn at the edges with fear.

I slammed on the brakes, having no desire to deal with Sarah having a breakdown in my car. As soon as I pulled on the handbrake, her door flew open. She moved to jump out but was still buckled in.

"Shit," she muttered and snatched at the belt.

When she finally managed to unbuckle it, she let it shoot back with force so that it smashed against the door.

"Hey," I cried. "Watch my fucking car."

Sarah didn't answer but practically threw herself onto the pavement. She stumbled and had to put her hand down onto the concrete to stop herself from falling. As she lurched forward, her feet caught up in her bag and despite all her efforts, she face-planted the floor.

"Fuck." I unbuckled my own belt, got out of the car, and ran around the front to reach her.

"Leave me alone," she spat out.

I knelt next to her and placed my hand on her arm. "I only want to fucking help you." I didn't wait for her to answer but put my other hand at her waist and hauled her up with me as I stood.

When she was upright, she winced and turned her hand over to study it.

"Are you bleeding?" I asked as I peered down. In the darkness I couldn't see any blood but could make out a graze along the surface of her palm.

My hand was still at her waist and I could feel how tiny she was. In fact, all of her was small. Her height, her waist and her arms, but she wasn't thin like I'd expected her to be. I could feel muscle in her bicep and my hand at her waist rested against the curve of a hip.

"Ouch." She poked at the pad of her hand, hissing with her touch.

"You need some antiseptic and a plaster."

Sarah looked up at me through long, sweeping lashes that curled at the ends, and my whole fucking body wanted to sigh with appreciation.

"I'm fine." She turned to pick up her backpack. "I'll walk from here."

As she took a step away from me, I felt a swell of anger build in my chest like a tidal wave. She was fucking stubborn and her need to challenge me suddenly wasn't so enticing. I had told her that I was taking her home and she needed to respect that. I growled out her name and she stopped, pulling her shoulders back.

"Leave me alone."

I hesitated for a moment and wondered whether to demand she get back into the car, but something about Sarah Danes and her fucking attitude told me that I would have my day with her, but it probably wasn't today.

"Fine, fucking walk, if you have any clue where you're going."

"I'll-I'll call my mum if I need help."

She breathed out the words as though she was trying them for size; saying them tentatively in case they hurt her. When I didn't respond but simply continued to watch her, Sarah carried on walking away.

I was almost at my car door when I did a stupid thing and looked back to see she was hobbling a little and cradling her hand close to her chest.

"For fuck's sake." I started to jog towards her. "Sarah wait!"

She looked over her shoulder and shook her head before taking one more slow, unsteady step.

"You're so fucking stubborn," I grunted.

"Leave me alone, Adam. I'm fine."

"You're hobbling and your hand is hurt. Just get your arse back in my car."

She ignored me and continued to move further away from me, but as I watched her go, with her shoulders slumped and a slight limp to her step, a hand reached into my chest and punched me from the inside out. Its power urged me forward; towards her.

What the hell was she doing to me?

All the hatred I used to push me through each day, the blackness that helped to focus my brain, faded away when she was around. It came like waves; high and dangerous until they hit the shore and then ebbed away slowly. Sarah Danes was my shoreline.

"Sarah." I reached out a hand. "Just stop."

She swung around and when I looked at her face, I saw fat tears at those damn lashes of hers. I didn't know how she did it but one look from her and all my need to hurt her disappeared. She was already in pain and I had the strangest feeling in my gut. I looked at her and my fingers itched and twitched, and warmth like that from the sun heated my skin.

I felt tortured and messed up. My feelings for this girl changed every minute, every second, and I had no fucking clue what I was supposed to do, or who I was supposed to be around her.

A tear crept from Sarah's eye and slid down the apple of her cheek. "I can't do this," she whispered. "I can't be the next person that you crucify, Adam. I've had enough."

Enough?

I hadn't even started, she'd had nowhere near *enough*, but that wasn't what I wanted, not at that moment.

"I just want to go home. Let me go home."

I shook my head, no.

"I'll stay out of your way, please just leave me alone."

I shook my head again and Sarah stomped her foot in frustration, but I didn't answer. I was too busy listening to her breathing and watching her lips as they parted slightly with each inhalation.

My fingers itched and twitched.

The need was too great, I couldn't stop myself any longer. I pulled her to me, lacing my fingers in her hair and wrapping an arm around her waist. Without any thought other than I had to taste her, my mouth smashed against hers. My breath mingled with her breath. My body moulded against her body. My heart thumped in time with hers.

I kissed her and when Sarah Danes opened her mouth to allow my tongue in, when she kissed me back, like grains of sand in a timer, some of my pain slipped away and I hated her just that that little bit more for it.

16

SARAH

I felt more alive than I had done in over a year. As Adam's tongue touched mine, he pulled me closer to his body and all the parts of me that had been long dead woke up and tingled with a slow sense of excitement and pleasure.

Desperate for more, I pushed onto my tiptoes and gasped against his mouth. His hand trailed from my waist to my bum, urging me to remove any inch of space between us. I felt his hardness in his jeans and all I could think about was that it was for me; *I* had made him feel like that.

He kissed me like it was going to be his last action on earth and I felt bold and empowered. I didn't feel scared or want to hide my face so his mouth wouldn't find mine. Every emotion that a kiss had evoked in the past disappeared with each stroke of Adam's tongue.

Wanting Adam like I'd never wanted anything in my life before, my fingertips clutched at his suede Trucker jacket, gripping it tight and pulling him towards me despite the fact that almost every part of both our bodies were already pressed together like two halves of a vice.

There was no fear passing through my veins, only euphoria.

I didn't taste bitterness on my lips, only sweetness.

I didn't want to die at his touch, I wanted to live for more.

"Fuck, Sarah," Adam groaned and picked me up with my legs wrapped around his waist.

I had a sense of us moving but was too immersed in Adam to know for sure until a brick wall pressed against my back. He pinned me tight and a slight burn flared as he thrust his hard, jean covered dick upwards and hit me right where I needed it.

I moaned and my knickers grew damp as my pleasure amped up. Adam thrust again and groaned as one of his hands left my bum and moved between us. His fingers fumbled for the button of my jeans and for a split second I froze.

"What?" Adam asked against my mouth. "You don't want this?"

I could let my past rule my life. I could allow it to put me on a path that would only see me seeped in misery for the rest of my time on earth, or I could push it behind me, chase away the fear and let myself feel.

"Yes, I want this."

There were no thoughts of how he would treat me afterwards, no worry that I would become one of those girls like Alannah and Amber. Greed and hunger made me unconcerned with the consequences. I'd dealt with worse and I could deal with whatever punishment Adam Hudson chose to give me for allowing him to have me.

"You drive me fucking mad," he said as he deftly undid my button and pulled down my zip. "So, fucking mad."

I smiled against his mouth, gasping for air as his hand snaked down into my knickers and a long finger slowly stroked me.

"I know for a fact," I panted. "That's not a good mad. It's a bad mad, a mad that makes you want to make me suffer."

"Absolutely," he said with a smirk, pushing a finger in, "right."

Adam then pushed a second finger inside of me and began to pump them in and out in time with the rhythm his hips had started.

I gripped his shoulders for purchase and rode his hand as he went back to kissing me. With his mouth on mine and his fingers inside of me, all my inhibitions flew away on the cusp of my bliss and I moved my hands from his hair to the crotch of his jeans and rubbed him.

"Shit."

Adam pulled his mouth from mine and let his head drop back. His mouth parted on a gasp, his eyes were closed, and his chest heaved rapidly as I undid his jeans and slipped my hand inside his boxer briefs. He was like steel; as hard and as smooth as it. His dick was warm to the touch and when I trailed my thumb over the end, I could already feel his pre cum. I spread it over the head and then gently pulled down before pushing back up, repeating it slowly. Every stroke up, I matched it with a stroke of my tongue against his and every stroke down I sucked on his bottom lip.

It was hard to concentrate on my own orgasm while I was trying to please Adam and I knew he sensed it because he moved his mouth away from mine.

"You get yours first," he growled and started to pump his fingers harder, adding his thumb to rub against my clit.

It wasn't long before the rush of warmth washed over my entire body and the pulsing which had started between my legs, fanned out until even my skin felt like it had its own fast and thudding heartbeat.

"Oh my God," I cried, only for Adam to muffle it with another searing kiss that prolonged the sensation taking over my body.

Adam's mouth moved to my neck and sucked it hard, while his hand grabbed my wrist and pushed it against his hard on. He needed his own release now I'd had mine, so I began to pump his dick while still riding out the gentle decline of my orgasm on his hand.

"Slow down," he gasped, resting his forehead against mine.

I watched him carefully and did as he requested, changing the pace of my movement. Up and down I went, breathing heavily and looking into his eyes, daring him to punish me for what we'd done. My eyes telling him that I didn't care what he chose to do because in that moment anything would be worth the way he'd made me feel.

As Adam's breathing sped up, I couldn't help but increase the speed of my strokes, but when he flexed his body and I felt his perfect, high, tight bum tense beneath my calves wrapped around him, I knew he was about to come too.

Two more stokes and with a kiss that was soft and gentle, he came, blowing his load over his stomach and my hand with a cry that almost sounded anguished. Instantly, his hand in my hair loosened and fell to my waist as he slowly pulled the other from my jeans and blew out a breath. His eyes were hooded, so I had no clue what was written in them. I didn't know whether there was regret, hatred or satisfaction showing in them. Adam Hudson gave nothing away and I would have to wait to find out my fate.

"You okay?" he finally asked as he slowly dropped my legs.

They felt like jelly and as my feet hit the concrete and I wobbled a little. His hand came out to my elbow to steady me and I breathed out a sigh, mostly of relief but also a little contentment too.

I'd been intimate with someone and it hadn't been painful or petrifying. I'd done something I hadn't thought I'd ever be capable of; I'd allowed a boy, a man, to touch me. I didn't feel dirty or ashamed even though this boy, this man, had the ability to make me feel regretful with a simple look or action.

"I have wet wipes in my backpack," I said as I looked down at his stomach.

The cum was drying on his skin in the cool night air, and I guessed he'd want to clean up. He didn't say anything but looked down and then over his shoulder. My gaze followed his and I saw my backpack was on the pavement, lying on its side where I must have dropped it as soon as he'd put his lips onto me.

"Hang on."

Adam moved away and left me leaning back against the wall, giving me an opportunity to take in our surroundings. We were in an alleyway between two buildings, and if I was right it was the new Tesco Express and a hair salon that were part of a group of shops that had been built specifically for the estate that I lived on.

There was one light at the far end of the alleyway which led to a service road at the back of the two businesses. It was fairly dark, and Adam had carried me far enough down that I was sure we wouldn't have been seen from the pavement. Thankfully, his car was parked in such a way that the view into the alley was blocked from the road, so no drivers would have seen us, yet for some reason I didn't give a shit.

I watched as Adam snatched up my backpack and then jogged back to me. He passed it to me, and I noticed his jeans were still undone as were mine. I reached into the side pocket for the small pack of wipes and pulled one out, before handing them to Adam.

"Thanks," he said and took one with a small smile before pushing the packet back into my bag.

We both cleaned ourselves as best we could and then fastened up without another word being spoken.

"I'd better get you home." Adam finally broke the silence and took the used wipe from me and pushed it into the pocket of his jacket with his own. "Will your mum be wondering where you are?"

I pulled my phone from my pocket and checked the time and was relieved to see I had no missed calls or text messages.

"No, she knew I was going to the cheer and team meeting. I wasn't sure how long it would go on, so told her to eat alone if I wasn't back by seven."

Adam nodded and it struck me that he hadn't asked me about my dad.

"How did you know it was just me and my mum?" I asked.

"Just a guess," he replied with a shrug. "You said you'd call your mum for help when most girls would call their dad if he was around."

The truth in his words made my chest crack open and allow a little grief to permeate into my system.

"When did he leave?" he asked with the confidence of a boy who'd evidently been disappointed by his own father at some point. I knew the man who'd come to the shopping centre was his stepdad so assumed his real dad must have been the one to leave him.

"He didn't." I shook my head, mainly to shake away the images that immediately played there. "He was killed just over a year ago. A jewellery shop robbery in London."

I gasped as I realised something; I hadn't even told Alannah that piece of information.

Adam pulled back and stared at me with his brow furrowed, like he didn't know whether to believe me or not.

"My dad was a policeman in the Met and when he was on duty one day, someone reported that they'd heard gun shots and he was first on the scene. It was a jewellery shop robbery and when Dad got there the man was about to get into a car that had been waiting for him. My dad tried to stop him but..." I paused to take a deep breath. "The man turned around, shot him at point blank range and then... and then they ran over his body."

"Fuck," Adam groaned. "That's...shit, Sarah, I'm so sorry."

He reached up to brush my hair over my shoulder and I shivered at the tenderness of his action. Was this the real Adam Hudson I was seeing in front of me? What happened to the angry, manipulative boy I saw wandering the halls of Maddison High School every day?

"The owner was shot too, but he survived," I replied.

"And the man who committed the robbery?"

"The police eventually tracked him down to some isolated farmhouse in Surrey. They surrounded the house and tried to get him to come out, but after three hours and him realising he had nowhere to go, like the coward that he was, he shot himself." I swallowed back the sob pushing at my throat.

Adam gasped. "What about the one driving the car?"

I shrugged. "The police never found him and Carl Jenkins, the man who shot Dad, was dead, so he wasn't going to tell them."

"And you get no fucking closure," Adam said, running a hand through his hair.

"No, we don't. No closure and no justice." I shuddered as I remembered clearly how it had felt seeing Dad's Chief Inspector on our doorstep and then having to hear him say the words that would change our lives forever. While my heart felt like it had been squeezed in a vice and then ripped apart, Mum and I had both screamed and clung to one another, my whole world tilting beneath me.

"Fuck," Adam groaned. "I'm so sorry. I wouldn't have..."

"It's fine," I said on a deep swallow. "You weren't to know."

Sensing that I probably didn't want to talk about it any longer, Adam turned and looked up the alleyway towards his car.

"Come on, let's go."

"I can walk."

"No." He sighed and shook his head in frustration. "We've talked about this and look how that ended."

He then smirked and my stomach lurched wondering whether this was when he turned back into the cocky shit who ruled the school. I inhaled sharply and wrapped my arms around my waist only to be surprised when Adam gently unfolded them and took my hand in his.

"Please, Sarah," he said, voice low. "Get in the car."

I nodded and followed Adam back to his car. This time he opened the door for me and waited until I got in. While he walked slowly around the front to his own door, it dawned on me that my life at Maddison High School would now change one way or another. How it changed would depend on the boy who had just given me the biggest shot of bliss I'd ever had.

17

ADAM

The drive to Sarah's house was done in silence, and I had a sense that neither of us knew what to say. I had no fucking words because I had no fucking clue how I felt about what we'd done; how she'd come apart under my fingers, how I'd come apart with her hand. I didn't regret it, but I also didn't know if I'd done the right thing. I'd finger banged her, let her wank me off, and had loved every damn minute of it. I wanted to do it again, more than I'd ever wanted a repeat performance with any girl. The real shitter though, was that I had no red mist clouding the thoughts in my head.

"Here you go," I said as I pulled up in front of her driveway.

Sarah had given me address, although I'd already known it, and I was surprised to see it was pretty compact, the smallest in the street I would guess. I wondered if they'd had to downsize after her dad was killed, because he hadn't had life assurance, or because they'd had no pay out for him dying on active duty. I had no idea if that would happen, I just thought it should; but what did I know? Yet her clothes, while too fucking big and baggy, were expensive looking and her backpack was a leather Michael Kors, which according to my mum was pretty good stuff. So, I was surprised that Sarah and her Mum lived in the small bungalow tucked beside three large detached houses.

"Nice house," I said as I stretched across her to look out through the window.

She shifted back a little into the seat, edging away from my body. "Yeah, it's nice, big enough for me and Mum."

I nodded and moved back, as I did, I got a whiff of her perfume and almost kissed her again. Her lips were soft and swollen and her hair was tousled like she'd just had wild sex. Swallowing back that thought I gripped the steering wheel and started up the engine.

"So, I'll see you at school tomorrow," I said, flashing a quick smile.

She nodded and picked her backpack up from the floor. "Yeah, see you tomorrow."

With her hand on the door, she hesitated, and she took a breath like she was going to say something, but when I cleared my throat she just got out of the car and practically sprinted up her driveway to the navy-blue front door. Once she was inside, I blew out a sigh of relief and stared straight ahead to the line of streetlamps edging the road. A kid walked down his path bouncing a football and then crossed over the road to bang on a door of a house where the security light had sparked on. I watched while the boy, of about ten or eleven, waited and kept on bouncing until the door was open and a lady with blond hair ushered him in. It made me wonder if Mum had never met Eric, would my life have been like that kid's; looking happy while I bounced my ball and went to visit a friend. If Eric had never beaten me until I had bruises mottling my back, just because I had knocked a glass off the table, or because I'd had the last of the milk for breakfast, would I have been different? Maybe if Mum had actually stopped it and not acted like she didn't know what was going on, I'd have been that kid going over to Ellis's house to shoot penalties, instead of sitting in my room plotting how to ruin the lives of anyone I ever met. No kid of nine years of age should feel that angry.

"Fuck," I growled to myself, looked over at Sarah's house, and then drove away.

When I got home my mum was surprised to see me. She knew how long the cheer and team meetings could go on, so she, Roger and Lori had eaten dinner and were watching a film together. She'd told me there was a plate of food in the microwave for me, but I couldn't bring myself to eat. The only thing on my mind was Sarah and her damn welcoming pussy, certainly not chicken pie and chips.

I gave some crap excuse about having a headache and escaped to my room. It wasn't like they would miss me watching TV with them, no matter how much Lori begged me to stay. Mum had been off with me for a couple of days since I'd lost my sister, but was acting now like it had never happened, like she'd never asked me if I could do anything right. Well, she might have been ready to forget but I wasn't.

As soon as I had changed into sweatpants and a clean t-shirt, I opened up my drawer and pulled out Sarah's notebook and flopped onto my bed with it. It was full of words; poems, one liner's, single words that were underlined or circled and I didn't think I'd ever read anything so raw or real.

I flicked to a poem that I'd read hundreds of times in the few days since I'd had the notebook, and despite the fact that I could recite it word for word, my eyes flashed over the page.

Fear is just an emotion that I know I cannot shake
And with the fear comes pain, pain that will not break
The black echoes of memories torture me and twist my soul
I cry and scream in the darkness of night and know I'm all alone

. . .

Every time I'd read it, a chill shivered through me as I thought about what pain Sarah must have suffered to write such words, but now I knew. It was about the death of her dad who had been killed in the most fucking horrible of ways. No wonder she had moved halfway across the country part way through a term; everywhere they went must have reminded her and her Mum of what they'd lost.

I flipped to another page that had the words '*I will survive him*' etched across the whole width of the page and underlined three times. Maybe it was about the man who had killed her dad, but when on the next page I read, '*He has taken what was mine to give but I will not give him anything more*', I wasn't totally sure. As I pushed it to the back of my desk drawer, I realised she was hurting from her past just as much as I was.

The next morning when I arrived at school, Ellis and Kirk were waiting in the car park for me, but there was no sign of Tyler. It wasn't unusual, he was often late and arrived just as the bell went.

Ellis was leaning against some kid's car with his arms folded over his chest. I smirked knowing no way would he lean up against his own car, a sweet ten-year-old, electric blue Audi TT that his dad had fixed up for him.

"What's up?" I asked as I fist bumped them both.

Kirk grinned and Ellis winked. "Nothing for you to worry about. Let's just say we took care of business and did something you're going to be pleased about."

"What?" I narrowed my eyes on the both of them and felt uneasy.

"I found something out about the new girl," Kirk replied as he reached out to wrap an arm around my shoulder. "I did a little digging in her old town."

My blood went cold and my heart tried to hammer its way out of my chest as Kirk's words filtered through to my brain. "What did you do?"

"Let's just say," Ellis said with a cocky smirk. "The whole school will soon know why she's here. Plus, we kind of twisted the truth a little."

Bile rose in my throat as I looked up the pathway towards the main entrance where hundreds of kids were filing into school; hundreds of kids including Sarah. Beautiful Sarah who despite everything I didn't want had totally messed with my head and rocked my world the night before.

Without a word, I pulled away from Kirk and sprinted up the path, pushing everyone aside without an apology. I skidded into the main reception and turned right for the sixth form corridor screaming at people to get out of my way. As I ran my eyes flickered around trying to see what the lads had done, but there was nothing, no one was interested in anything in particular, there were no groups of gossiping girls or lads laughing.

When I finally reached the bank of lockers where Sarah's was, I was breathing hard with the effort I'd made and the adrenalin rushing through my veins. As soon as I saw her, I slid to a stop. She was talking to Alannah who was smiling and waving her arms around. Whatever the lads had done hadn't come into play yet, which meant I might have time to stop it. I turned to go back and find Ellis and Kirk when I smacked straight into Tyler.

"Hey," I gasped. "You seen the others?"

"Not since Ellis picked me up this morning at the arse crack of dawn." He yawned and then grinned. "Hey, we have a surprise for you."

My heart sank. Tyler hadn't been late; he'd been the dick who put whatever shit they had planned in place.

"What did you do, Tyler?"

He smiled and nodded towards Sarah who was about to open her locker. When she did, she hesitated to put her stuff inside and turned to Alannah and said something. Alannah looked shocked and leaned over Sarah's shoulder as they both stared at something. Sarah crumpled to the ground with a pained scream, Alannah immediately following and cradling her in her arms.

I felt sick and I felt jealous. Sick at what they'd done to make her so anguished and jealous because it was Alannah comforting her and not me. Emotions I'd barely ever felt about anyone threatened to bring me to my own knees. Whether I liked it or not, I knew I cared about what happened to the tiny girl with golden hair.

People started to crowd around her and Alannah while others bypassed them and went to their own lockers. One by one I saw them pull out a piece of paper, read it and then all turn to stare at Sarah.

"What the fuck did you do?" I spat out at Tyler who was staring at the group with Sarah concealed in the middle. He had a smile of his face and his hands were stuffed into his jean pockets. *"Tyler."*

He turned to me and reached into his back pocket and then handed me a piece of paper. I unfolded it and read it, dread, pity and guilt all wrapping themselves around me.

Did you know Sarah Danes Dad was killed in a shootout with police?
No!
Shit, well, you should know the police shot the daddy of our new girl when he tried to hold up a jewellery shop, all because he didn't have enough money to buy our fellow pupil the diamond earrings that she demanded he get for her.

Underneath was a news picture of, who I guessed was, her dad being wheeled out of a jewellery shop on a gurney in a body bag, with the words; '*Michael Danes, 46, dies in jewellery shop robbery wanting earrings for his 17-year-old daughter*'.

I could tell straight away it had been doctored, probably by Kirk and his fucking freaky IT skills and I wanted to puke. There was no mention of her dad being a copper or that he'd tried to arrest the bastard; it was all twisted and the only truth was that he'd died at the scene.

"This isn't fucking true," I said. The piece of paper shook in my hands.

"Yeah we know," Tyler laughed. "But who the fuck is going to make the effort to check. Did we do good Cap or what?"

I turned to face him. In that moment, I wanted to punch the fucking life out of his eyes and wipe the stupid grin from his face. In that moment I hated myself for giving him, Kirk and Ellis the ammunition to fire at people without caring.

I looked back in the direction of Sarah. The group around her had dispersed and she was getting to her feet with the help of Alannah. As she straightened up, she lifted her head and found me watching, the stupid bit of paper in my hand. Her hand flew to her mouth and her legs almost gave way again. Even from the distance of the corridor I knew that there was hatred in her eyes.

18

SARAH

"How the hell have you allowed this to happen?" Mum paced up and down Miss Daniels' office, dragging a hand through her hair. "My daughter has been through enough. To have lies like this, especially about my husband, spread around the school is unacceptable."

Mum's voice cracked at the mention of Dad and she slapped the paper down on Miss Daniels' desk. Sinking down into the chair next to mine, she grabbed my hand.

"You okay, sweetheart?" she asked with tears welling at her lashes.

I nodded and gave her a smile. I couldn't fault her for how she'd been over the filthy shitty lies that had been spread about Dad. As soon as I'd called her, she'd dropped everything and rushed back from her job at the printing company she worked for. Even though Mr Henry her new boss seemed nice, she hadn't even hesitated. Her words had been 'I'm on my way'.

"I can only apologise, Mrs Danes." Miss Daniels sighed. "We are doing whatever we can to find the culprit."

I moved my hands to underneath my thighs so neither women

would see them shaking. I knew who'd been responsible because he was the only person I'd told about my dad and what had happened. I could see it on his face when he was watching me in the corridor earlier. He was like his beloved Bonaparte overseeing his victory.

"Well you make sure you do and I want everyone to know the facts. I will not have my husband's name tarnished in this way," Mum replied her tone harsh and low. "I'm taking Sarah home for the rest of the day."

"No, Mum." I grabbed at her forearm. "I'm not letting whoever did this win. I won't be shamed into going home. I already had to leave one school." I felt the colour rise in my face and glanced over at Miss Daniels. "I won't be pushed out of another."

"Are you sure?" Mum looked over at Miss Daniels, defiance in her eyes. "Because if you want to go home for the rest of the day, it won't be a problem."

"Honestly, Mum. I want to stay."

And I did. I would not let Adam Hudson and his gang of *boys* shame me into hiding away at home in my room.

Mum gave my hand another squeeze and then looked back to Miss Daniels. "Anything else happens here to upset my daughter and I will go to the education authority about it. Do I make myself clear?"

Well go Mum.

I had never heard her so angry before. When everything happened with Dad and then Mr Mills, she collapsed under the weight of it all. It wasn't until we'd got the court date for my rape trial that she'd finally came out of the fog that she'd been in and started to act like a mum again.

"Would you like me to call Alannah and get her to come and collect you?" Miss Daniels asked.

"No thank you, Miss Daniels. I'll be fine."

I wasn't. My hands were shaking. I had a pain in my chest, and my stomach was churning, but I had to appear unafraid, just like Dad told me.

"You can do this sweetheart. Just don't ever show your fear, because as soon as you do, they'll see your weakness and try and dominate you."

Mum gave me a hug and asked me again if I was sure, but I waved her away and left her with Miss Daniels, no doubt giving her more shit about what had happened.

The corridors were empty now, but it didn't make walking along them any less intimidating, knowing that only a couple of hours earlier they'd been filled with pupils all whispering about me and gossiping about a bunch of lies.

I stepped tentatively as my Converse squeaked on the polished floor, wanting to get to my class unnoticed, knowing that if I could get through English and then lunch, the rest of the day would be easier.

As I turned the corner, I jumped and screamed when Adam stepped out in front of me. His face was a hard mask of anger, his fists clenched at his sides.

You are my sunshine, my only sunshine.
You make me-

"This wasn't me," he snapped, thrusting the paper at me. "I know you think it was, but it wasn't."

My limbs wouldn't move. I couldn't get my legs to work to walk away from him or shift my arms to push him away. I couldn't even catch the paper that drifted to the floor and crunched under Adam's foot as he took a step closer to me.

"I know how painful it was for you, so I wouldn't use it against you."

I didn't respond but stood statue still, counting up to ten in my head and hoping that he would give up and leave. After a period of silence, Adam scrubbed a hand down his face.

"Say something, Sarah."

"Like what?" I shrugged.

"Like, you believe me."

I had only seen a handful of expressions on Adam Hudson's face – superior, cocky and… I thought of his face the night before when he'd come all over my hand, his face then had been filled with pleasure which had only enhanced his beauty, but I'd never seen the expression he was wearing now. It could have been guilt, maybe sympathy or even sadness, but whatever it was it was new, and it surprised me.

"Why would I believe you, Adam? Isn't this what you do?" I hissed. "Use things against girls to embarrass them, to shame them, to turn the rest of the school against them."

Adam's nostrils flared and he exhaled sharply three times before pinning me with a stare.

"It wasn't fucking me." His answer ground out through gritted teeth."

"It doesn't matter whether you printed the pages out and posted them in everyone's locker yourself. You told my greatest pain to whoever it was that did do it, and I'm guessing that person was one of the idiots that hangs on your every word."

My throat prickled and my nose twitched as I tried so hard to hold back the tears. They were tears of anguish, of fear and of disappointment. I had so wanted Adam to be the boy I'd seen a glimpse of the night before. The one who made me forget. I had known deep down, even in the throes of my orgasm, that this would happen, but I had desperately wanted to be wrong.

As Adam stared me down, I could feel the constriction in my lungs growing as the pain started to increase and threatened to drown me. My wrist tingled and I shoved my hand up the arm of my shirt and started to rub at the raised skin.

"Sarah, stop." Adam grabbed a hold of my hand that was on my wrist. "I've seen you. I know when you do that. You've got nothing to be scared of me for."

He was wrong. I wasn't scared. It was too late for that because he'd already done his worst, and I hadn't been as strong as I thought. When he put his fingers inside of me, I'd silently dared him to do something to bring me down and he had. He'd done something that stabbed like a knife into my heart with far more hurt than anything Joshua Mills had done to me, but I couldn't let him win. *I would not let him.*

I inhaled and took a deep calming breath.

"Just leave me alone, Adam." I whispered. "You've done what you had to do, now go and pick on someone else."

I pushed past him, my shoulder barging into his hard, muscular arm and with shaking legs walked away from the boy who I'd hoped might be my saviour.

My mum had messaged me to say she was going to pick me up at the end of school and we were going for a pizza for dinner. My feelings towards her were thawing somewhat and I tried to push aside the thoughts that it was a little too late; she was trying which was good.

The last time I'd seen Alannah had been first period after lunch, so I had quickly sent her a text to say that I didn't need a lift home. She'd messaged back to say she'd see me in the morning same time as usual, but about ten minutes later I got another message to ask if I could stop in at the sports hall first as she was struggling with one of the moves for the new routine – it appeared that after an hour of debating the night before, the team, as expected, had said yes to the choreography.

I'd texted Mum to say I'd be about ten minutes late and made my way to the sports hall. When I got there it was deserted, there was no sign of Alannah anywhere, not even her bag was in its usual place next to the big speaker she used. I groaned. I really didn't have time to wait for her but didn't want to let her down because I believed I owed her. I guessed that she had some feelings for Adam despite what he'd done to her, I'd warned her to stay away from him and then ignored my own advice. The guilt I felt was immense. I knew I'd have to tell her eventually, I just hoped that she still wanted to be my friend when I did. It may have only been a couple of weeks, but I liked being around her, and in that time she'd been more supportive than any of my old friends had ever been. They'd all turned on me pretty quickly when I'd reported Mr Mills, despite us knowing each other since nursery school.

I waited around for a couple more minutes and then sent Alannah a message to say I couldn't wait but we could catch up later if she wanted to. When I watched for the dancing dots nothing happened. I figured she must have been busy and got delayed, so decided to go and meet Mum. I was just about to leave when I heard a noise coming from the changing rooms. I wondered whether it was Alannah, so decided to go and find out.

As soon as I pushed open the door to the girl's changing room, I was faced with Adam Hudson for the second time that day. This time though he wasn't standing in front of me asking me to believe he wasn't responsible for trying to crush me. This time he was leaning back against the wall, his jeans pushed down and his hands on the shoulder of the dark-haired girl kneeling in front of him and blowing him like a pro. Her hand was between her legs and she was making noises worthy of a porno.

I gasped and as I did, Adam lifted his head and glared at me.

"Fuck off," he snapped.

The girl didn't even stop and her head continued bobbing up and down.

I didn't move but held my breath and looked into Adam's eyes. They were devoid of any emotion whatsoever. They were empty and vacant, and his features were like a solid mask.

"Seen enough?"

The girl hesitated, evidently realising they weren't alone, but Adam pushed a hand onto her head and encouraged her to carry on. When she did, I couldn't help but gasp, almost in awe at the power he had over girls. One touch from him and this girl was happy to degrade herself in the changing room. The thought caused me to give an ironic smile. I'd been this girl the night before, allowing him to have his fingers inside of me in a place where we could have easily been seen.

"Yeah." I exhaled on the word. "I've seen plenty."

Adam let out a short laugh and I knew then that he was not the boy I needed him to be. I turned around to leave, with my heart thudding in my throat, and ran across the sports hall to the doors. As I pushed them open, Alannah appeared in the corridor, walking in my direction.

"Hey," she said, flashing me a huge smile. "I thought you were meeting your mum."

"You asked me to meet you here." I choked over my words as air caught in my throat.

Alannah frowned and shook her head. "No, I didn't. I've been helping Marnie to get the choreography down. Tessa's grandpa died and her family are going to Wales for a week, so Marnie has to step in."

I sighed, not really wanting to get into an argument with her, but I hated it when I was right and was challenged. I pulled out my phone and showed her the text.

"I didn't send that," she said, peering closely at the screen. "It definitely came from me?"

I showed her and she gasped. "What the hell is he playing at?"

"Who?" I put my phone back.

"It has to be Adam. He borrowed my phone in maths because he said his phone had died. He must have sent it."

It all made sense, me turning up and there being no sign of Alannah and then finding Adam and that girl in the changing room. He'd wanted me to see them. It had all been part of his twisted game for me to see him being blown by a girl less than twenty-four hours after I'd wanked him off.

"I told you, Sarah," Alannah whispered as she put a hand on my shoulder. "He has you in his sights and you need to be careful."

She looked genuinely worried for me and it made my guilt ramp up another level.

"Alannah, it's fine. He's not interested in me."

"This morning, that had to be him, and now this. I'm scared for you, Sarah. You have no idea how manipulative he can be."

I chewed on my lip as I wondered whether this was the time that I should tell her, but as I opened my mouth, Marnie, a small bouncy girl with deep auburn hair, came running down the corridor.

"Sorry, sorry, sorry," she called as she skidded to a halt next to us. "Miss George kept me behind in French, apparently my accent is more comedy character than native French person." Marnie laughed and nudged Alannah with her shoulder. "So, shall we start now?"

I glanced over my shoulder at the sports hall and wondered whether I should warn them at what they might find, but at that moment the door opened, and Adam and the dark-haired girl walked out. Like some shit porno film, she was wiping the corners of her mouth while Adam adjusted himself in his jeans.

"Ladies," he said with his usual smirk.

We all ignored him and as they passed us, the girl looked over her shoulder and gave a sly smile.

"Who's that he's with?" I asked as I tried to ignore the clenching feeling in my stomach.

"Mackenna White," Alannah hissed. "She's his latest plaything."

"I heard she's on borrowed time," Marnie added as she turned back from watching them disappear down the corridor. "Jessica heard Tyler say that Adam was getting bored with her and was ready for a new toy."

Alannah eyed me warily and grabbed my hand. "Okay, Marnie we should go, we have a lot for you to learn. I'll see you in the morning?"

I nodded. "Yes, thank you. Usual time."

"Night, Sarah." Marnie waved and skipped off to the sports hall.

"Please be careful," Alannah whispered with one eye on Marnie. "You don't need his shit, Sarah."

"I'll be fine, I promise."

I gave her a small smile and then instinctively gave her a hug and told myself that I'd tell her soon about what happened with Adam, once I was sure I wouldn't let it happen again.

19

ADAM

From the minute the crowds had gathered around the edges of the pitch, and the girls had done their new cheer before the game, the noise had been louder than I'd heard at any game before. It was a week after all the shit with Sarah had gone on, and we were playing, Sexton High, our closest rivals in both distance and ability and it was currently three two to us with only three minutes of added time to go. We were definitely playing better than them; winning fifty-fifty tackles, being first to any loose balls and jumping higher for headers.

The whole team had put a hundred percent in, and I'd had one of my best games of the season. I'd scored a goal, had one cleared off the line and had put in a cross from my position on the right wing that had landed perfectly at the feet of our striker, Dante Duncan. He'd been fucking awesome and was no doubt Man of the Match. He hadn't stopped running and tackling from the kick off and the second of his two goals, had pretty much silenced the Sexton High fans. It had been a screamer from about twenty yards out. Maddison High supporters were going crazy, our subs and Mr Jameson were already celebrating, led by Kirk chanting 'Maddison... Eagles... Maddison... Eagles' and the cheerleaders were shouting just as loudly. This was going to be one our best wins of the season and I was pretty sure the party that our central defender, Brady O'Connor, was holding later would be carnage.

I wasn't in the mood for any party though and already had half my concentration on how I was going to get out of it. All I wanted to do was get the game won, get showered and go home. Getting my head back into what was happening on the pitch, I saw that Ellis had the ball in his hands and knew if he could kick it to me I was onside and in a shit load of space. There was only about half a minute of added time left, and Mr Jameson would probably scream at me to head for the corner flag, but fuck it, their keeper was off his line and I knew I could chip him. I pulled away from their left-back and screamed for the ball. Ellis saw me and kicked the ball from his hands, whipping it over the top of Sexton's midfield and with a shimmy around their central midfielder, I let the ball bounce and then hit a sweet half volley over their keeper and into the back of the goal. I'd known it was going in as soon as the leather left my foot and sailed through the air with a satisfying swoosh. When the net bulged it was only seconds before the rest of my teammates were jumping on top of me, thumping me on the back and kissing me like a bunch of girls with a puppy.

"Come on you lot," the ref shouted. "Back to kick off or I'll book the lot of you."

With high fives all round, we lined back up in our positions and waited for the whistle. Sexton High kicked off, with their striker passing to their left-winger and just as he was sizing up a pass to the overlapping striker, the final whistle blew.

Euphoria rushing through my veins, I let my head fall back, looked up at the sky and slapped a hand against my chest, where my

Maddison Eagles tattoo which I'd lied about my age to get, lay underneath my maroon and gold shirt. Everyone went crazy. At four two we had beaten our biggest rivals.

The bench and Mr Jameson wasted no time in storming onto the pitch to back slap us and haul Dante onto their shoulders for his performance. I didn't think I'd ever seen everyone so fucking happy about winning a match before. It felt good to beat Sexton High, and it felt even better to watch them slope off the pitch towards the changing rooms, not looking as damn cocky as they had when they'd arrived on their minibus earlier. We hadn't beaten them, home or away, in two seasons, mainly because they had a striker and a goal scoring midfielder who were scouted by more than one professional club. This season they'd both gone to the same EFL League one club, and Sexton were back to being average.

A hand slapped my back and I looked around to see it was Roger. I'd known he was there because I'd searched every face in the crowd, plus he was at every game to support me, usually without my mum, just like tonight.

"Great game, Adam," he said and gave me a quick smile. "That last goal was amazing."

"Yeah, thanks," I replied feeling unusually magnanimous towards him. "I saw an opening and took it, although Mr Jameson was probably shitting a brick that I wasn't keeping possession."

"Well, it was great." He shifted his feet and looked over his shoulder. "I'll get going and tell your Mum and Lori the good news. I take it you're going to the party."

I frowned wondering how he knew. We always told our parents we were headed to TJ's after a game.

"I was on the team when I went to this school, Adam. I do know what happens after a win, especially against your biggest rivals."

Someone jostled him, pushing into me, and he had to hold onto my elbow to steady himself. I wanted to snap at him to get his hands off me, but I really was feeling like a pussy.

"You okay?"

He nodded and took a step back. "Yeah, sorry about that. Anyway, don't be too late, you still have school tomorrow."

The pussy in me slinked off and left shitty Adam behind. "Yeah I do know, and for your information I'm not even going to the party."

"How come?" he asked, ignoring my attitude.

I shrugged. "Just not."

Roger evidently sensed our short truce was over and took a step away. "Okay, well see you at home."

I didn't respond, but watched him leave, wondering as I always did, why my mum hadn't come with him. She couldn't blame it on Lori because Mrs Jackson next door would sit with her. I could only assume that she just didn't give a shit about anything I did – story of my fucking life.

"Hey," Kirk yelled down my ear. "You ready to paartay?"

"Yeah I'll catch you up," I lied. "My mum needs to me to call home first."

Kirk raised his eyebrow. He knew I rarely did anything my mum asked, but there was no way I was going to tell him I was missing out on booze and girls just because there had been a face missing from the crowd tonight, and it hadn't been that of my mother.

Before the game started, during half time, even at points during the game, I'd searched the crowd and looked at every face, but none of them had been Sarah's. A mixture of anger and disappointment had surged through me; the anger being levelled at myself for caring. Why the fuck would she be there after the stunt I pulled with Mackenna? If I hadn't been such an angry, stupid dick, I was pretty sure I could have got her to believe me. Now, she wouldn't even look at me, never mind attend one of my matches.

Practically the whole of the fucking school had been there, but not her. Sarah had stayed away, and regret lay sour in my gut, giving me no inclination to party. For one thing, Mackenna would be there and I had pretty much cut her out since that day when I'd engineered for Sarah to find us. I hadn't even thought about doing anything to shame her into staying away from me. I told her it was over and that was it. Makenna White however was not one to give up easily and had bombarded me with messages and voicemails – she knew not to approach me in school, she was too fucking scared of what I might do or say if she did. She didn't need to know I didn't give a shit, but who knew, tomorrow was another fucking day so I could well change my mind. All I knew at the moment, was that my head was full of Sarah Danes and how fucking beautiful she'd looked when she came all over my fingers.

I wasn't sure what God was looking down on me, but on Saturday morning when my mum asked me to pick Lori up from dance class because she and Roger were going sofa shopping, I nearly bust a fucking bollock with happiness. Lori hadn't shut up about the fact they were getting to do some street dance a week earlier than expected and that Sarah would be running the class. It'd be the ideal opportunity for me to talk to her and persuade her that the thing about her dad was nothing to do with me. I wouldn't throw the lads under the bus, but I'd make sure she believed me. Why I was so fixed on it I didn't know, it wasn't like me to care about anyone's opinion of me, but Sarah had messed with my head to the point I couldn't even think about what cereal I wanted for my breakfast.

Mum had given me clear instruction not to let Lori out of my sight after the incident at the shopping centre, but Roger had told her to let it go and had dropped me twenty quid to take Lori to TJ's afterwards. It hadn't escaped my notice though that Roger had been the one to take Lori back to the shops for another of those fucking ugly swans for Mum's birthday a few days ago. So, for all he tried to get under my skin, get me to like him, I wasn't stupid, and I wouldn't be fooled by another of my mum's men. I still had a lump on the back of my head from Eric to remind me. I was grateful though because if I was taking Lori to TJ's maybe I could persuade her to get Sarah to come along too. I didn't know how I'd do that, but I'd manage it somehow.

Most of the mum's and dad's, or whoever had come to pick the kids up, were waiting in the reception of the building on chairs that lined around the edge, but apart from the fact there were no seats left and it smelled of stale coffee and fucking misery, I wanted to watch Sarah do her thing. I walked down the short corridor to where there was a double door into the studio and a one-way viewing window with another line of chairs against the wall opposite to it. There was one man in there, he was playing on his phone, while the two women also in there chatted about some shit to do with the dustbin collection times.

I grabbed one of the chairs, flopped down into it, and rested my arms on the window ledge, hunkering down so my chin was on top of my hands. Immediately my eyes found Lori right at the front, putting everything into the moves she was doing. I wasn't sure she was doing it completely right. She was going up and down, bent at the knees in a jerky motion and her arms, bent at the elbow, did the same. It was only when I looked at the kid next to Lori, a kid who seemed to have a better talent for it, I realised it was the robot they were doing. I broke out a huge grin as I watched the look of concentration on my little sister's face. She fucking loved it even if she wasn't that good; according to Mum, she wasn't going to be a ballet dancer either, too heavy footed apparently.

I couldn't hear what was said in the studio, but the kids all started to clap, and Sarah appeared in my view, as she walked towards the front of the class. Then she was in front of me, facing the kids and I had the best view of her perfectly rounded arse in tight, black leggings. I groaned quietly, remembering I wasn't alone, and leaned closer to the glass, desperate for a better look. Fuck, it was perfect. She still wore a baggy t-shirt, but it was short and gave me a glimpse of her pale skin and I knew I had to have her again. When she bent over at the waist and I could see the faint outline of a thong, there was no doubt I would do whatever I needed to do to make sure I had her again.

My jeans felt a little tight as I watched her walk forward a couple of paces with her arse swaying sexily and then clap all the kids. With her arms raised more skin was on show and I thought I was going to bust my zip.

"They finished?" the guy on his phone asked.

"Yes," one of the women replied and came to stand next to my chair. "Jasmine has been so excited about this class. She's not stopped talking about the new teacher and how pretty she is."

"I can see the attraction," the guy murmured under his breath, but I heard it and swung around in my seat to face him.

He took a step back at my sudden movement and when I pinned him with a narrow-eyed stare, he at least had the good sense to look sorry.

"Your kid in there?" I asked him pointedly.

He didn't look much older than twenty-four or five, but he was wearing a wedding ring, so should have known better.

"Yeah, the smallest one with the black hair in pigtails." He offered me a small smile, but I'd already got him marked as a creep.

"Yeah my sister too and the new dance teacher is my girlfriend."

The words were out of my mouth before I even considered how fucking stupid they were. Sarah Danes and I weren't even friends, let alone anything more. Maybe having had my fingers inside her I subconsciously thought I had some claim on her, but that was far from the truth. I wasn't even close to her forgiving me enough to talk to me, let alone anything else.

The guy looked down at the floor like a loser as a loud blast of chatter and laughter sounded, and I realised the kids were coming out of the studio. I glanced through the window to see Lori was trying to pull the zip up on her pink jacket but as usual was struggling. With a quick decision that the knob who'd come to pick up his kid wasn't worth the effort, I made my way to the door so I could go into the studio and help my little sister. As I did something in there caught my eye and it sent my heart clattering hard against my rib cage.

Sarah was on her knees in front of Lori and helping her with her coat. Lori chatted away and Sarah nodded or shook her head in response to whatever shit my little sister had blabbing out of her mouth. Once the coat was zipped up, Lori reached forward and wrapped her arms around Sarah's neck and hugged her tight. Sarah hesitated to hug her back at first, but when Lori didn't appear to want to let go, her arms came up and wrapped around Lori's pink clad body and squeezed tight.

Determination to make Sarah believe me flared to life, and I knew my sister was definitely my secret weapon.

As I stepped into the corridor, Lori came bounding through the door with a huge smile on her face.

"Adam," she cried. "You're here

"Hey, Munchkin."

"Where's Daddy?"

She looked behind me as if Roger might also be there, but she should have known better than that. It also didn't escape my notice that it wasn't Mum she was expecting; the woman really had given up parenting us both.

"They've gone shopping for a new sofa, so I'm taking you to TJ's."

Her eyes grew wide. "Really? Do I get to have a milkshake and a cheeseburger and chips?"

I ruffled her hair. "You get to have whatever you want." I peered through the glass in the door into the studio. "What about Sarah? Do you think she'd like to come as a thank you for helping you at the shopping centre that day?"

Thank God my sister was only eight and didn't understand bull-shit, because that had not sounded casual at all.

"Shall I ask her, or will you?" Lori jumped up and down on the spot her cheeks bulging with her smile.

"Maybe you ask, say you want her to come to say thank you. Maybe not mention it was my idea."

She didn't even question it. "Okay, wait one minute." She held a finger in the air and disappeared.

I thrust my hands into my jacket pockets as I waited for what seemed like hours. I didn't even look through the glass in the door in case Sarah saw me and immediately said no. I had my secret weapon though and if anyone could persuade her, Lori could.

After bloody ages, Sarah pushed through the door with my sister pouting behind her. This did not look like I was taking two girls for burgers.

"Hey, Lori," Sarah said as Lori came up beside her. "Can you take this to Clarice for me? She's in the office." She pointed with a key to a door a couple of feet away.

Lori rolled her eyes. "You can talk in front of me," she sighed. "I'm eight, not stupid."

I wanted to laugh but managed to stop myself. "We know, Munchkin, Sarah needs to talk to me about boring school stuff, so go take the key to Clarice."

"Okay." She sighed again. "Oh, and she said no to burgers by the way, so next time you want to take my dance teacher on a date, ask her yourself."

She took the key from Sarah and threw me a glare that said I was buying her ice cream as well and then ran off to the office.

"I don't know what you're trying to do," Sarah hissed when the door closed behind Lori. "But haven't you hurt me enough?"

"I told you that wasn't me. I've put the word around school that it was bullshit and no one is to mention it again."

"Well you needn't bother, Miss Daniels is going to make sure everyone knows the truth."

"*And* they'll still be warned not to mention it."

When a little breath escaped her lips, my eyes were immediately drawn to them; they were full and pink. I remembered the taste of them and how swollen they'd got after I'd kissed her.

"Stop staring at me." She narrowed her eyes on me. "Your little game isn't going to work, Adam. I know you got one of your friends to post those flyers around and I also know you used Alannah's phone to get me to the sports hall that afternoon. From what I hear it's just typical of the sort of trick you would pull to crush some poor girl who was stupid enough to fall for your charm."

Pure hatred addled her tone, and her arms were wrapped protectively around her body, like she was desperately trying to stop me from getting in. She forgot though, I had seen her without her barriers already. I'd felt her come apart without any fear, and she had loved it. This girl wanted me as much as I wanted her, whether she realised it or not.

"I admit the thing with Mackenna was a shit thing to do, but I was so fucking angry with you."

Sarah looked surprised and reared back. "*You* were angry with *me*? You are joking, right?"

"You wouldn't listen to me. I told you it wasn't me, I hadn't and still haven't told anyone about what happened to your dad, I swear. I saw your face when you told me. Even I wouldn't twist and use the

HATE STRUCK

pain that you feel against you. I'm not a good person, Sarah, but I'm not evil either."

I spoke low and slow, hoping that it would enforce the truth to Sarah, because whether I liked it or not, thoughts of her were constantly invading my head space. If I didn't get to taste or feel her again, I knew it would only get worse. I was scared that I'd become addicted without any hope of another fix.

Sarah looked at me speculatively and inhaled before letting it out slowly. "How did they find out then?"

I faltered, having no clue what to say because I could well drop Tyler, Ellis and Kirk from a great height if I said the wrong thing. It would only take Sarah one visit to Miss Daniels for the Head to investigate further and who knew, she could easily uncover the shit Kirk got up to with the school computer and CCTV. That would send the whole house of cards tumbling down, especially for Ellis, for a whole host of other reasons. I just hoped there wasn't some sort of camera on the photocopier in Mrs Stubbs' office or we really were done for, especially if she matched my face with the photocopied arse pics that had been posted all over her office.

"You may as well tell me, Adam," she sighed. "I'm not going to tell any of the teachers or anyone else, I swear. I just want to know why."

"Because I made you a target," I answered honestly. "And I'm sorry."

"But why. Why are you sorry?" she cried as she flattened her palms over her face. "This is how you treat girls. You manipulate them and then make *them* feel bad about it."

She dropped her hands and looked up at me and for a second she looked like she might cry, but she didn't. Her shoulders went back, and she straightened her spine to face me again.

"I was stupid to do what I did with you." She leaned closer to me. "It was a stupid lapse in judgement, but it won't be happening

165

again. I won't be another one of your victims, Adam," she said slowly but surely. "You've had your shot at me, now leave me alone because I will not be joining your little group of *cock suckers.*"

She pulled a duffle bag onto her shoulder and pushed past me with her head held high. I watched her go and realised my addiction had just got worse, because fucking hell if Sarah Danes saying cock suckers wasn't the sexiest thing ever.

20

SARAH

I parked Mum's car in front of the Tesco Express, and reached across for my purse. It was almost nine at night, but she wasn't feeling too good, she had a sore throat and could barely speak, so I'd offered to come and get some things that might make her feel better and the ingredients to make her some chicken soup. It was my nana's recipe, another member of my family who I missed like hell. She was the only grandparent that I'd known and was my dad's mum. Thankfully for her, she'd passed away almost two years before Dad, because having to experience her only son dying in that way would have broken her heart. Now Mum was all I had, so despite how I felt she'd let me down, I was determined to look after her.

As I wheeled my trolley into the fresh food aisle, I looked down at my list to double check what I needed and headed for the vegetables. Carrots were first on the list, so I reached for them, only for a large hand to land on top of mine. I startled and pulled my hand back. With a sick feeling in my stomach, I turned to look at whoever had thought it was okay to touch me.

"You've got to be kidding me," I groaned. "Are you following me."

Adam held his hands up in a surrender gesture and then nodded towards his own trolley. "My mum sent me. Apparently, it's not enough that I took care of Lori most of the day, I have to do this too, because she doesn't have the energy to buy food after shopping for living room furniture."

I ignored the bitterness in his tone and looked at his trolley. It had milk, bread and cheese in it and he also had a list threaded through the front, so I knew he was telling the truth.

"And you happened to wait until nine at night to do it?" I questioned.

"I put it off as long as I could, in the end she had to send Roger upstairs to force me to come. He did offer to do it instead, but well, you kind of know how I feel about him. I figured it'd kill an hour on a Saturday night."

"No party to go to?" I asked, lacing my words heavily with sarcasm.

Adam shrugged. "Not that I know of. Why do you know of one we could go to?" He wiggled his eyebrows. "We could go together."

"No," I quickly responded. "I don't like parties and I certainly wouldn't want to go with you anyway. Now if you don't mind, I have stuff to buy."

Adam stood to one side and waved his arm. "Off you go then."

I pushed my trolley past him and noticed that he took a step closer as I did. It meant that my arm brushed against his chest and I couldn't help but smell his aftershave.

Who the hell wore aftershave to go food shopping anyway?

After escaping Adam, I moved quickly around the aisles throwing the things I needed into the trolley, hoping that I didn't bump into him again. I didn't want to see him or be around him, he unsettled me. He made my head buzz with possibilities; if only he was a better person. I was already beginning to believe he was being honest about having nothing to do with the shit that had been written about my dad and that thought made me feel stupid and naïve. I knew what sort of a person he was, and it was exactly what I'd been led to believe he would do; the problem was he sounded pretty genuine when I'd seen him at the dance studio earlier.

I decided not to waste anymore thoughts on him and went to the magazine racks thinking that Mum might like a couple to read while she was laid up in bed. When I rounded the corner I groaned, Adam was already there leafing through what looked like a football magazine. I tried to manoeuvre my trolley back the way I'd come, but I was too late and Adam looked up and saw me.

"Now who's being a stalker?"

His grin and the word stalker sent a combined shiver down my spine. I physically shook myself to fling it from my body.

"I need some for my mum." I reached for the two closest to me.

Adam laughed. "Your Mum into cars and..." he stooped to take a look at the cover. "Fishing?"

I looked up at him to see a huge smile on his face. A smile that crinkled his eyes. He looked happy and carefree with the arms of his soft wool jumper over a white t-shirt pushed up to display his strong, veined forearms.

"She might do." I bit on my lip to stop my own smile. "You should see her cast a line."

Adam laughed loudly and dropped the football magazine back on the rack and reached for another.

"Here, try this one," he said and handed it to me.

"Adam! Really you think my mum would want this?"

We both started to laugh, and it felt good not to be in a standoff with him or trading insults. To feel like a normal teenager who could flirt with a hot boy in the Tesco Express.

Still giggling I stared at *Pole Dancing for Beginners*, wondering whether to take it for her as a joke, when the sound of gunshot rang out and a man's voice close to us yelled out.

"Get that fucking door locked now."

Without any hesitancy, Adam moved to me and grabbed my hand, pushing both our trolleys to one side.

"Come on," he whispered and pulled at my arm.

I couldn't move. Fear and panic were setting in as I started to shake. The sound of the gun ricocheted around my head, pulling back memories that I didn't want there.

"Sarah, please, we need to hide."

I just stood there, staring at him, as those unwanted recollections and reminders of the worst night of my life continued to punch through my brain.

Adam looked up towards the ceiling before his gaze landed back on me. "It's okay, Sarah," he said softly. "I can see in the security mirror, there's just one man and he's over by the tills." He moved closer to me and placed both his hands on my shoulders and looked me directly in the eyes. "The manager and assistant are up there, but I don't think he knows we're here, so we can hide. There's an office just down the end of this aisle. Do you think you can come with me? If it's unlocked, we can hide in there."

I looked over his shoulder to where he wanted us to go and sucked in a breath. It was only a small store, but we were in the last aisle, so could possibly get there without being spotted.

"I'm scared, Adam," I whimpered.

"I know. And I know this must be the worst thing to happen to you, but we will be okay. I promise, I'll take care of you." His voice was soft and cajoling and when his hand cupped my cheek, I couldn't help but lean into his touch. "Okay take it really slow and be as quiet as you can." He looked down at my feet and smiled. "Thank fuck you're a girl who likes trainers and not those fucking high hooker shoes."

I couldn't even smile at his attempt at a joke, I was so petrified. Adam gave me a nod of encouragement and then took my hand in his and started to lead me down the aisle towards the door where he said the office was. We were almost there when the man shouted again, and another gun shot went off. I shuddered to a halt and screamed, howling as if I'd been the one shot.

Adam slapped a hand over my mouth and wrapped an arm around me as my body began to convulse with sobs. He pulled me close and I sagged against his broad chest, grateful for the small sense of comfort it brought me, despite the fear still clawing at me.

With my whole body shaking and my chest heaving, there was no way I was going to be able to walk. Adam must have realised it too because he hauled me into his arms and we started to move again.

"Fucking stop where you are." A voice boomed behind us.

The air left my lungs as Adam's arms tightened around me, his big hand shielding my head.

"I'll take care of you," he whispered against my ear. "We'll be okay."

"Get up here now."

"Okay, okay," Adam ground out. "We're coming."

He started to move slowly, his arms still cocooning me in the safety of his body.

"Move it and put her down. She needs to walk up here."

"She's scared man," Adam's deep voice rumbled. "Can't you see that?"

"I don't fucking care. Put her down."

Adam stopped walking and whispered into my ear. "I'll be with you, I'll hold your hand, but you have to walk, Sarah, okay?"

"Don't let me go, please." I moved my face away from his chest to look up at him. His eyes were so soft and caring I inhaled sharply on a sob and my chest heaved.

"I'll hold your hand the whole time, I swear."

He slowly dropped me to my feet and placed a steadying hand on my waist as he raised his brows in a silent question. I nodded and felt his hand wrap around mine. When I turned to face the gunman, I was surprised to see how slight he was, but my eyes soon left his body and his masked face to focus on the gun in his hand.

"No," I cried, when I saw it pointing at me. "No don't shoot us, please." The noise started off small in the pit of my stomach, but as the gun wavered in front of me, it built and built until it became huge; ear piercing and earth shattering.

As I screamed out my fear and the culmination of the pain I'd experienced for the last year, I heard Adam shouting behind me. His voice was anxious and loud, and I felt myself being dragged behind him. Through my tears I saw his back and felt his arm wrapped around my waist and my body being pulled against his.

There was more shouting and then Adam turned, grabbed my shoulders and gave me a shake. "Sarah you have to stop," he yelled. "You have to be quiet."

"I don't want to die, Adam," I screamed. "I don't want to go the same way as my dad. My mum, what will my mum do?"

Adam closed his eyes and breathed in. Once again he pulled me against him and dropped a long kiss to my forehead.

"Please, Sarah," he whispered. "Please try and stop. I swear we will be home soon, but your crying is making him anxious. You have to be quiet."

"I mean it, man," the masked man bellowed. "Shut her the fuck up, or I will."

Adam turned sharply. "Okay, can't you see how fucking scared she is? I'm trying." He turned back to me and shook me as he stared right at me. "You have to stop, Sarah. I mean it, stop *now*, okay."

His voice wasn't harsh, but it was hard enough to make me realise that I needed to listen to him. Slowly my cries quieted to hiccups and once the noise had almost stopped, Adam stooped down and cupped my face.

"I've seen you counting your breathing, so do it with me now, okay?" He nodded and started to count in time with each bob of his head.

"Nine. Ten. That's it," he said with pride as though I'd just taken my first steps. "Keep going, slow and deep that's it."

"Get over here," the gunman shouted. "Now."

Adam let out a deep breath and his nostrils flared. He was holding on by an edge to his patience, any other situation I'm pretty sure he'd have lost it. Just like he had in the sports hall with Davies the boy who'd been rude about the keepers' sister.

"Now, I said."

"We're coming, okay. Let's go," he said to me and grabbed my hand tightly in his own, giving it a reassuring squeeze.

As we walked towards the man in the mask, my feet started to drag, but Adam was there encouraging me to take each step. When we finally reached the front of the store, the man pushed us forward to where an elderly couple, the manager and an assistant were sitting on the floor, their backs against a wall.

"Get down there with them." He gestured with his gun.

The assistant flinched and let out a squeal, but the manager placed a comforting chubby hand on her shoulder. She looked at him and reached up to link her fingers with his. I was glad he was able to comfort her. My dad had been alone when he lost his life and that was one of the things that haunted me the most. He'd died without anyone to hold him while the life drained from his body. If I was going to die in a Tesco Express, at least I'd have Adam with me.

As he led me to sit on the other side of the elderly couple, I looked up at him and smiled. "Thank you," I whispered.

He gave me a soft smile back, which made his eyes sparkle, and gave his response by squeezing my hand again. When we dropped onto the floor, he turned to the old couple who both looked pale and gaunt.

"You okay?" he asked.

"I'm so scared," the lady said. "He doesn't seem stable."

"Joyce, we'll be fine. Just stay quiet and do what he says, love and it'll all be over soon." Her husband took her hand in his.

My throat constricted with the feeling that I was going to puke. I knew it would only cause the man to get angrier, so I took a few deep breaths to try and abate it. I placed my hands flat on the floor to steady myself and immediately Adam's little finger linked with mine. It was his way of telling me he was there without saying the words.

"Where's the money kept?" the man growled at the manager.

"There's only what's in the till," he replied. "I go to the night safe at eight every night."

"It's true," the assistant said with a small nod. "Every night."

"You're fucking lying," he snapped.

"I swear, I'm not. You can check the office."

The man looked down the shop towards the office where Adam and I had been going to hide. Then he looked back at us and then finally at the locked door. He seemed to be thinking about his best plan of action and I hoped that didn't include killing us.

"You," he said, and pointed the gun at the assistant. "Get the money from the till."

"I'll do it," the manager said, moving to get to his feet.

"No, she does it." He pointed the gun at her again. "Now."

The assistant who was wearing a badge which said 'Rita' on it, struggled to her feet and moved to the till. It struck me how slow and calm she was considering there was a gun pointing at her. I looked up at the gunman and saw him wipe a bead of sweat from the part of his forehead which wasn't covered by the mask which was actually just a wool scarf tied around his face.

As Rita opened up the till and pulled out all the money, throwing it into a plastic bag, a car horn sounded outside and we all jumped, the gunman more than the rest of us. He moved to the window and looked through, peering at the small car park outside.

Adam leaned closer to me. "He has no clue what he's doing," he whispered from the side of his mouth.

My mouth dropped open with shock. I knew instinctively what he was thinking.

"Adam no." I shook my head with wide begging eyes. "Please."

"I can take him, Sarah. I'm bigger than him, he's wired and he's fucking stupid."

"Shut the fuck up," the gunman bellowed. "I've told you, no talking." He turned to Rita. "What the fuck is taking you so long, hurry up."

"I'm coming," she said, her voice quaking. "Here you go."

She passed the money to the man who lowered his gun to his side while he peered inside the bag. Adam shifted beside me and I knew he was going to try and jump him, but I couldn't let him. How could I watch him get shot and die? I'd never get over someone else in my life being killed for the sake of a few hundred quid.

"Just go." My voice came out louder than I expected and gained his attention. "You have the money, so go."

As the man lifted his gun again and stared at me, I heard Adam groan beside me.

"You really think I'm just going to leave you all to call the coppers on me?" he replied. "Do you think I'm stupid?"

I shrank back against the wall and Adam's hand grabbed mine.

"I'm sorry," I said and clutched his bicep. "I couldn't let you try. I couldn't watch him shoot you."

He exhaled slowly and kissed my temple. "It's okay. I understand."

"I hope so, because you saved me tonight and I just wanted to save you."

The way his eyes shone as he looked at me made my insides warm with a depth of feeling that I could only assume came from the fear that was swamping me. I could only see good in him and all the things that I'd thought might be possible if he were a better person suddenly seemed more attainable.

I reached up and kissed his cheek. "Thank you for taking care of me."

"We're not going to die, Sarah," he said with a small laugh. "We're going home soon."

"I said no fucking talking." The gunman stalked toward us with the bag in one hand and the gun pointing at Adam in his other. "You need to be quiet unless you want me to take you out first."

"No," I cried holding my hands up to him, palms forward. "Please no. We'll be quiet."

The man pulled back the trigger and pointed it, his shaking hand making it wobble between the two of us. There was defiance in his bloodshot stare, and I knew he'd already made his mind up.

I closed my eyes, held my breath, and waited to join my dad.

Whereas not so long ago I'd wanted to be there with him, I'd wanted to die, now I was getting better each day. I wanted to live, and to grow and to continue losing the pain around my heart. My eyes were tightly closed but I could feel it in my bones that the cold steel of the gun was pointed at me. I knew without any doubt that the bullet would leave the barrel and go straight to my heart. I was the one he would choose to kill first.

I held my breath and imagined my dad's face as I readied myself for oblivion, but the pain and blackness never came, instead Adam's arm was wrenched away from my hold. My eyes flashed open and I screamed as he hurled himself at the legs of the man holding the damn gun with the barrel cocked.

When the gunshot sounded, I was sure Adam must have been shot. My heart stalled and everything around me sounded elongated and distorted; like the world slowed down as they both flew through the air toward me. Then without warning, my pulse thudded back into action and the screaming and shouting became crystal clear as a pair of dead eyes stared up at me. Rita and Joyce were both screaming, the store Manager shouted "Fuck" over and over, while all I could do was silently scream and grip my hair as I looked down at the two bodies that had landed next to me.

After an eternity of time that hung in the air, Adam finally rolled over and onto his back, breathing heavily as he let his arms flop to the floor at the side of his body. My chest heaved as I stared at him, desperately waiting for him to speak, or move again, to show me that he wasn't hurt.

When he did an ab roll to sit up, I finally extinguished the anguish from my lungs.

"Adam." I scrambled over to him and literally threw myself on top of him. "You stupid idiot, why did you do that? Oh my God."

I clung to him and let out a sob, tightening my arms around his neck as he shifted forward.

"I'm okay," he said against my hair. "Except I can't breathe."

I loosened my grip. "I'm sorry, but I was so scared. I thought..." I turned to look at the prone body of the gunman.

"No, don't look." He immediately pulled me to his chest, shielding my view. "I don't want you to look. Keep your face close to me." He manoeuvred us both to our feet, with his hands strong and tight on me all the time.

"I think we should get everyone to the back of the store," I heard the Manager say.

"Yeah," Adam replied and with my face still cradled against him, he slowly walked us down the aisle in the direction of our abandoned trolleys.

Once we were all gathered together, Joyce started to cry.

"I thought he was going to kill us all," she sobbed as her husband pulled her into his arms.

"Thank you, son," the elderly man said to Adam. "But it was a bloody stupid thing to do."

"I couldn't risk not doing it." Adam looked down at me and swallowed. "He was getting too desperate."

"The police should be here soon," Rita offered slumping to sit down on the floor. "I pressed the panic alarm when I went to get the money."

The Manager rubbed a hand over his face. "Shit, Rita, if he'd seen you."

"Well he didn't, so you can let me have tomorrow off as thanks." She grinned at him, but I noticed the wobble in her chin.

"It's the least I can do."

Only seconds later we heard sirens and saw the flash of blue illuminating the walls and ceiling; the police had arrived.

I was still in Adam's arms when we finally walked outside into the car park that was a buzz of activity of police and paramedics. As soon as I felt the cool night air on my skin, he gently pushed me away and looked down at me.

"Are you okay?" he asked, his hands running over my hair, my shoulders and my arms.

With tears rolling down my cheeks, I nodded. "I'm fine, you made sure I was okay. You made sure we were all okay. Thank you."

He pulled me closer again and wrapped me into a hug. I shivered at the press of his lips against my forehead.

"Hey, you two kids need to come and get checked out," a police officer said. "Just go to the paramedics, but then we'll need to ask you some questions, is that okay?"

"Yeah sure," Adam replied and when I shivered again, he hugged me tighter. "Do you have something to warm my friend up, she's had a big shock, her dad died at the scene of a jewellery shop robbery."

"Oh, sweetheart, I'm so sorry." The police officer ran a hand over my back and the weird thing I noticed was that I didn't shrink from his touch.

"Come on," he continued, "let's get you both warmed up, take your statements and then you can go home."

Adam took my hand in his, and just as he'd done for the last hour or so, didn't leave my side until we were finally allowed to go home with our parents three hours later.

21

ADAM

I sat upright in bed. My skin slipped with sweat and my breath came as harsh gasps. I'd had a nightmare and was back in the shop, only this time I didn't tackle him and bring him down, and it was Sarah who was shot in the chest. Her lifeless body was propped up against mine with her hand still on my bicep, but no matter how much I shook her or shouted in her face, she wouldn't wake up. It had been terrifying and felt so fucking real, I'd even called out her name when I'd woken, thrashing the bedcovers as I fought for her to wake.

I scrubbed an open hand down my face and flopped back against my pillows as I tried to banish the images from my head. I'd been able to hold it together at the station when we were giving our statements, but the minute I'd got into the house after Mum and Roger brought me home, I'd run up to my room and locked the door. Roger had knocked quietly a few minutes later, but I ignored him and pretended to be sleeping. I knew he only wanted to check on me, but I preferred to deal with everything that had happened alone.

It wasn't long after that I heard Mum crying and telling Roger that she shouldn't have sent me for the shopping, that it could easily have waited until the morning. I was glad I'd been there though. If I hadn't been, I wasn't sure Sarah would have held it together and the bloke robbing the place was so erratic I knew in my heart that he'd have shot her – just like in my dream.

As I lay in my bed, the house felt too quiet. I knew it was early, but I couldn't hear anything, no creaks or groans, not even the sound of Lori's soft snoring drifted as far as my room. I felt agitated by it and couldn't wait for the sun to come up and for the usual breakfast noises to sound out. I snatched my phone from the chest of drawers next to my bed and looked at the time; 4 am. I wondered whether Sarah would be awake, whether images of last night were disrupting her sleep too. I had her number; I'd sent it to my phone when I'd used Alannah's, acting like mine was dead. At the time I wasn't sure whether I'd ever use it, but I'd never even considered that if I did, it would be to check she was okay after almost being shot dead.

Near the end, when he'd pointed that gun at us, I'd kept my stare on him the whole time. If he was going to shoot me, he was going to look me in the eyes while he did it, but there was no doubt where his gun was pointed, and it wasn't on me. He was going to kill Sarah and make me watch, just to prove a point in some sort of fucking pissing contest. I just couldn't sit there and watch that, so I'd lunged for him. Thank fuck he was wacked out on something because for all he was erratic, his reflexes were slow, and he hadn't seen me coming when I'd headbutted him right in the dick and sent him flying. It hadn't taken much to wrestle his aim from Sarah's chest to his own and with all the jostling he'd squeezed the trigger and – bang he was dead.

"Fuck," I muttered into the darkness as everything began to play over in my head again.

I couldn't handle it, I needed to get out of the house, or at least check on Sarah. I dialled her number and was surprised when she answered on the third ring.

"Hello," she whispered. "Adam is that you?"

I let out a relieved breath and moved to a sitting position. "How did you know?"

"Not sure who else would be calling me at four a.m. I guess you got my number from Alannah's phone?"

I smiled. "Yeah. Too obvious?"

"A little." She paused for a few seconds, but I could still hear her breathing. "You can't sleep either?" she finally asked.

"I did, but had a nightmare, but I guess being held up in a Tesco Express when getting milk will do that to you."

"I suppose. Did the officer taking your statement at the station tell you the man was a drug addict?"

"Yeah," I sighed. "Said he was homeless too. All the best people come to Maddison Edge."

Sarah giggled softly on the other end of the line and it was a great sound, mainly for the fact that she was actually still here to make it.

"There'll be no come back on you will there?" she asked.

"No, apparently the CCTV recorded it all. It was clear I was trying to..." I paused, thinking carefully about my words, not wanting to say I was trying to save her life. I didn't want her thinking any more about what might have happened. "I was trying to resolve the situation."

"That's good," she said quietly. "It wouldn't be fair. You saved us."

"Yeah, main thing is we're safe," I replied. "Anyway, how's your mum? This had to have been doubly hard on her."

"She's okay. She cried a lot and I had to stop her from sleeping in the chair next to my bed, but mostly she's angry. Apart from me being in danger, it's resurrected a lot of hatred for the man who shot my dad too. It brought it all back and dredged up some shitty memories and feelings for her."

I shifted again and changed the position of my pillows, I wanted to be comfy while I talked to Sarah because I didn't want anything to distract me from having a long conversation with her. On the way home, Roger had begged me to talk to him and Mum about it, but I'd clammed up, the only person that I'd wanted to discuss it with was now on the other end of the line.

"I totally get that," I replied. "It's a wonder she hasn't decided to lock you in the house for the rest of your life."

Sarah made a soft whimpering noise and I thought maybe she was going to cry, but she carried on talking, her voice full of resignation.

"He was going to shoot me."

Her statement surprised me. I'd thought I'd have to always keep that fact from her, but someone must have told her.

"Did someone say something?" I asked.

"No," she sighed out. "I just felt it. When he was waving the gun between us and I closed my eyes, I knew it would be me." She blew out a breath and I got a sense that she was trying to gather her thoughts, so I stayed silent and waited until she was ready. "I want you to know something, something important."

"Okay," I replied tentatively. "But you don't have to tell me, we're not even friends remember."

Sarah huffed out a laugh. "I think you can safely say after tonight and how you helped me, we *are* friends. I'm pretty sure I'd be dead now if it wasn't for you."

I didn't want to lie to her and deny it. I had no problem lying to most people but somehow it didn't seem right to do it to her. Whether she meant to or not, in a matter of weeks Sarah Danes had started to change me and I wasn't sure I was ready for it. I also wasn't sure whether I could change totally or whether it was just for Sarah, the girl with the golden hair who tried to act brave every single day.

"Aren't you afraid I'll tell everyone?" I asked, closing my eyes and hoping that she saw some light in me. "You know I'm not a good person, Sarah."

I wanted to be able to tell her that I would take her secret to the grave, but what if the black hatred inside of me meant I used it against her? I didn't want to do that to her, but what if I had no choice?

"I happen to think you're a better person than you think you are." Her voice pitched low. "And, I'm not scared if you do. I've realised after tonight that life is too short to have secrets, particularly those that hold you down, the ones that make you drown in misery. All you do is spend your time hiding from life and trying to make sure no one finds out the real you. It's time consuming and tiring."

She had a point. I'd spent the last nine years keeping a secret that I thought would make people, my friends, think less of me. Yet to keep that secret I'd become the sort of person no one liked or gave a shit about anyway.

"If you tell me, I'll give you a secret of mine, in return," I offered as I pulled up the duvet against the cool chill in my room.

"You don't have to," Sarah responded. "But if you want to then I'll be happy to make a pact with you."

"Oh yeah," I laughed. "What's that?"

"You tell anyone my secret and I'll tell yours."

My first instinct was to tell her to fuck off, I couldn't be black-mailed, but then sense kicked in. This was Sarah, she wasn't like that, she was trying to make light of the fact that we were both about to tell the other something that could potentially break us.

"That's a deal. So, you want me to go first." I was more than willing to do that to prove to her that I could be trusted.

"No," she breathed out. "I need to say it now before I lose my nerve."

"Okay, so tell me."

Sarah cleared her throat. "I-I, shit I thought this would be easier."

"You don't have to tell me." My heart twisted for her; it was obvious that whatever it was caused her a lot of pain. Pain that she had to endure on top of that she felt for the loss of her dad.

"I do, I want to," she continued, and I heard her take a deep breath. "I tried to kill myself three months ago."

Her words hit me like a head on collision with a juggernaut. She'd wanted to die.

"Sarah," I whispered her name into the darkness. My throat felt thick with worry and regret at every fucking awful thing I'd said to her; the fucking shit stunt the lads had played on her. "Why?"

I felt the bile rise in my throat at the thought that it might have been someone like me who'd pressed her into making such a heart-breaking decision; a decision that would probably kill her mum in turn.

"Sarah, what happened? Why? Was it losing your dad?"

"Not as such, but," she sighed, "that's another secret, but I guess I can't give one without the other."

Something slammed inside my brain. Whatever it was had to be too big to tell a stupid fucking dick who relished in bullying girls and making them feel like shit. "No, Sarah, you don't have to tell me. I don't want you to tell me."

I closed my eyes against the words that I knew were coming. She'd gone this far and if I'd learned anything about Sarah in the last few weeks, it was that she was brave, and she would see not telling me as being cowardly.

"I was raped," she said softly. "There was a teacher at my last school and when my dad was killed, he saw that I was lonely."

I heard her draw in a breath and I could imagine her rubbing her wrist or wrapping an arm around her waist. The tells were all there now I knew. She was battling to overcome the most hideous of things that could ever happen to a woman, all the time she was grieving too. This girl, this tiny girl with the golden hair, was braver than I'd given her fucking credit for.

"He preyed on me, Adam. He saw that my mum wasn't coping and had mentally left me, and he made me think he was looking out for me, but he wasn't. He exploited my unhappiness and raped me. And then," she said with a light laugh, "he tried to tell me that I loved him, that we loved each other and that I was just scared at the depth of my emotions."

"The fucking bastard." I drew my knees to my stomach as a sharp pain hit me. "Tell me he's fucking dead, Sarah, or at the very least in prison."

I started to breath heavily as I waited for her to tell me what I needed to hear, because although I barely knew her, I had a bone crushing need to protect her. From the minute I'd seen her she'd fascinated me to the point of wanting her more than any girl before. I'd treated her like a piece of shit because I couldn't express my own feelings without hurting those around me. I was a maelstrom of anger and pain. Everyone got caught in the tornado of my life and was thrashed around to the point of pain because of me. Sarah had been one of those people and yet she'd tried so hard to stand up to me, to keep away from the vortex, while all the time dealing with something so monstrous it had driven her to attempt to take her own life.

"I- I don't understand," I stuttered. "How did you survive it all? How do you get through each day?"

"I just do, I have to. I know we barely know each other, but I just wanted to share my secret, finally."

"How fucking ironic you wanted to share it with me, the arsehole who has been making your life shit since you got here."

There was silence on the line, and I wondered whether Sarah

had realised that she'd made a bad choice in telling me, but then I heard something on the other end of the line.

"Sarah, you still there?"

"Yes, sorry, I heard my mum going to the bathroom, I thought she might come in and check on me."

I looked up at the ceiling not able to see anything in the darkness except flickering pictures of Sarah in pain from grief, from fear and from desperation.

"What happened to that bastard, Sarah?" I whispered.

"The jury didn't believe me," she replied, and my insides began to burn with anger. "It was my mum in the end who found out what was going on and called the police. He was arrested and I had to testify." Her words were rushed but clear like she needed to get them out before they poisoned her. "It was an anonymous testimony I was Miss A. and he told everyone that we were lovers and I'd got angry when he'd ended our affair. The jury believed him, they believed it when he said I'd kept the underwear that he'd torn from my body as a memento of our first time and they believed him that I was just a vindictive little bitch."

Sarah sounded defeated and I wished I'd gone with my gut and actually gone around there to talk. How could I hold her and comfort her from two damn miles away?

"Shit I'm sorry, Sarah."

"It gets worse," she said on a shaky breath.

"Worse?" I asked incredulously. "How much worse can it get?"

"For me it did. He lost his job, so he left town and I went back to school."

"That's good though, isn't it?"

"Not when almost every single person in the school hated me and made sure I knew it. He was a really popular teacher; one of those cool, easy going ones, you know the sort."

"Yeah, but even so, he fucking raped you," I hissed.

"According to them I'd ruined his life, so they were determined to ruin mine."

"What did the teachers do about it?"

"Not much," Sarah said her voice flat and deflated. "The head just told my mum it'd die down eventually. Some of the parents of the GCSE kids even complained about me, saying that if their kids didn't pass their art exam without him, it would be my fault."

"Fucking cunts."

Sarah laughed. "Yeah well, that's one word for them."

"Do you know where he went?"

"No idea, but I know he's back in town."

"Where you used to live?"

My heart thudded in my throat because my first thought was that she meant Maddison Edge.

I heard her breathing heavily and not for the first time wished I'd just fucking gone around there to see her.

"Yeah, where I used to live. The town I had to leave."

"Bastard."

Silence fell between us. I wanted to fill it but wasn't sure what to say. What words were there for something so awful. It wasn't like we were really close and I knew how to support her, apart from which I was a fucking seventeen year old who had no idea how to treat people, never mind beautiful, tortured girls.

Finally, Sarah started to speak. "I hate him, Adam. I hate that he gets to carry on with his life, more or less, and I had to move away. I had to watch my mum break down all over again and I hate that I'll live with those fucking shit memories for the rest of my life."

"I can't believe he's allowed to go back there."

"As far as the law is concerned, he did nothing wrong, except, according to him, have a sexual relationship with a pupil."

"I'd fucking kill him for you if I could." Shit, I'd never heard anything so gut wrenching in all my life. She'd been through enough and the sick bastard had preyed on that. "I'm so fucking glad you didn't succeed in killing yourself though, because that would have meant he'd won."

"Yeah well," she replied. "I'm trying to be stronger to prove he didn't. It was a moment of weakness and I'll regret it for the rest of my life."

"When?" I asked screwing up my eyes and wincing. "When did you try, you know, to kill yourself?"

"After the trial..." She cleared her throat. "When my friends and most of the school, turned against me. When they all accused me of lying and believed his version of events. It was supposed to be a secret, it wasn't reported on or added to my records, so I don't know how, but someone at school found out and thought it their duty to tell everyone."

How she'd broken down in the corridors last week came back to me. Tyler, Kirk and Ellis had forced a replay of all the shit she'd gone through at her other school. I wasn't innocent in that. I'd been the one to bring her to their attention. I'd been the one who'd put a target on her back, and I'd been the one who'd singled her out from the minute she set foot in school.

"I'm so fucking sorry, Sarah," I groaned. "More than you will ever know."

"It happened I-."

"No," I butted in. "I mean for everything I've put you through. You should really fucking hate me and I would understand if you did."

"I told you, I think you're a better person than you actually know, Adam, and you kind of saved my life, so I think I owe you."

"I just did what I thought was best."

"Yes and that was to save me and everyone else in that shop."

We stayed silent for a while, neither of us spoke but we didn't hang up either. I think we were both just happy to have someone else on the end of the line. Someone in the room to share our inner thoughts with.

"I guess it's my turn now," I eventually said.

"Only if you want to," Sarah replied. "But I've got to say Adam, I doubt you'll beat that one."

The sound of her amusement lightened my darkness a little and within seconds I joined her in laughter and then began to tell her *my* secret

22

SARAH

"You're right," Adam said. "It's nowhere near as big as yours."

"If you don't want people to know, there's a reason for that, a reason that's just as important to you as mine was to me."

Adam laughed on the end of the line. "You're fucking amazing you know that?"

"I don't know about that. I just know my dad would have wanted me to fight and it took doing what I did to realise that. You know I believe he was looking down on me all that time, especially that night I tried to end it all." I smiled as I thought of how protective my dad had always been and possibly still was being.

"How come?" Adam asked.

"I cut one wrist and then passed out when I saw the blood."

"I-I, oh shit Sarah," Adam said with soft laughter. "I hate to say this but that's...."

"Ironic?" I giggled despite grimacing. "Yep, I know which is why I like to think it was Dad helping me out. So, go on tell me your secret. What has you lying awake at night?"

I wasn't sure how much more I could take because telling Adam everything had wrung me out like a dishcloth. I felt raw and weary, but I knew it was important to him to tell me.

"I'm not even sure why I never told anyone, well I do, but it seems pretty trivial now."

"Nothing is trivial if it upsets you," I whispered, snuggling further down under my covers.

"Well, my dad left when I was five. Mum threw him out to be more exact and I have no clue where he went. I got a kiss on the head, he told me he loved me, and then he left. That was the last I saw of him."

"That must have been awful. God, Adam you were just five years old?"

"Yeah, it was bad, and I remember crying for a whole week, but Mum just kept saying we were better off without him. I didn't believe her though. The man taught me how to play football and to ride a bike, he loved me, and I loved him. Believe it or not, that's not what has me so fucked in the head." He sighed and then continued, "When he went Mum started to go out with all these different men, the first long term one was a bloke called Dean, he was pretty cool and took me fishing or to cricket matches even though both bored me. He lasted around six months until he couldn't handle my mum's moods any longer. Jimmy was next and he lasted a lot longer. He stuck around for three years and he's Lori's dad. I didn't like him as much, but he was okay and he didn't shout or hit me; he didn't actually communicate with me in any way to be honest. Then Mum found out she was pregnant, and Jimmy just left. He took a load of our stuff with him, including my Xbox, some of Mum's jewellery and our TV, but he did leave us something; a whole load of debt, oh and Lori of course."

"So that means Roger isn't Lori's dad?" I was surprised. She had the same colouring as him and they seemed close.

"Nope, Jimmy is but he's never seen her and never wants to. He texted Mum to tell her that just after she was born."

"Oh my God, no," I whispered as I felt an ache in my chest at the thought of someone not wanting sweet little Lori.

"Yeah a real charmer. So, that was 'dad' number three gone. Or I like to think of him Stepdick Number 2." Adam gave an empty laugh. "That pissed me off as well, that Mum got me to call them dad. I fucking hated it."

"Especially if you still missed your real dad," I offered. "I can't imagine calling anyone else Dad, ever."

"Yeah, well, she didn't get it and thought I was just being a dick about it."

Adam let out a long sigh and I had a feeling his secret was about to be revealed. I also had a feeling that it was something he shouldn't be ashamed of.

"So Mum decided we needed a fresh start and a friend of hers told her about this little town just outside of Manchester called Maddison Edge where a friend of his had a house to rent and he also knew there was a job going at the local library for an administrator and his friend had offered to get Mum an interview."

"Wow," I replied. "That was lucky, my mum had to go out to Bidston Green an hour away to get her job. And your Mum was pregnant too, good job they were willing to take her on."

"Yeah," Adam groaned. "I'm pretty sure the *friend* of Mum's was a married man who just wanted her out of town, so he got his friend involved who pulled some strings. Anyway, I was nine and Mum was pregnant with Lori."

"And that's where Roger comes in?"

"Nope, he's dad number five. Stepdick Number 4 would you believe. He came into our lives about a year and a half ago and he moved us in almost straight away. Him and Mum married a year ago.

Good old Roge who wants to be my dad but will never be. None of them are good enough to fill his shoes."

"But he still left you," I whispered.

"I know, and that's all down to my mum. She burned his pictures, Sarah. She made it really clear he couldn't see me again, she didn't care how her being a bitch to him affected me."

"I'm so sorry, Adam."

"It's fine," he replied. "I got used to him not being around, it was all the other knobheads who she tried to replace him with that I hated, especially Eric. It was when she started work at the library that she met him."

Adam fell silent and I heard him moving around and I wondered if he had changed his mind about telling me.

"Adam, you don't have to do this you know."

"No, I want to. You told me something far worse and I should just stop being a fucking pussy about it. So, we moved here, she met Eric and within a month he'd moved in and yet again I was encouraged to call him Dad; but by then I'd pretty much lost any respect I had for my mum and wasn't going to do it and I told Eric that the night he moved in. And that night..." he paused and coughed, and I held my breath hoping his story wasn't anything like mine. "Well that night when Mum went to bed early because she was six months pregnant by then, he took me into the kitchen washed my mouth out with soap and then punched me."

I gasped and held a hand to my chest as I imagined a nine-year-old Adam being beaten by a man who'd been brought into the house to be a father figure to him.

"Did you tell your Mum?" I asked pushing a hand against my quivering chest.

"Yeah," Adam replied in a quiet voice. "Told her the next day and she took my football off me for a week for lying."

"Oh my God, Adam."

I had an understanding now of why he was so hostile to Roger. He probably didn't trust him not to leave like the other four men who were supposed to have been his father.

"She never believed me the second, third or fourth time, so I gave up telling her after that," Adam continued. "Although I sometimes think she knew really. Eric brought good money into the house though, he said he loved her and when Lori was born, admittedly he didn't have much interest in her, but he didn't hate her being around. Why would Mum risk that for a mouthy nine-year-old kid? He hit me pretty much two or three times a week, sometimes worse than others but never where it would be seen. The only time he seemed worried was when he hit me around the back of the head with his belt and the buckle cut my head open. It was a big ugly square thing with his initial in the middle."

I felt sick at the thought of what he'd gone through. I'd lost my dad in the worst possible way, but at least he'd loved and cherished me for the seventeen years I'd had him. What was worse, Adam seemed so matter of fact about it all.

"Did the hospital report him when he took you to be stitched up?" I asked.

"He didn't take me; he was a porter at casualty, so we always had shit he'd taken from there lying around the house. He patched me up with some butterfly stitches and told me to tell my mum I'd fallen in the garden."

"And no one ever suspected? None of your teachers or friends?"

"No, I made sure I always wore a vest or t-shirt under my school shirt."

My stomach rolled as the line went quiet. He must have been so scared and on edge all the time, always wondering when the next beating was going to come.

"Your Mum never ever said *anything*?"

"No, she said she never knew because Eric always did it when she wasn't around. She had to wonder why I'd suddenly become introverted and moody though. Even Ellis' Mum noticed the change in me, and we'd only been friends for a few months. Like I said though, maybe the fear of losing Eric was worse than the thought of her kid being beaten up."

That was just a horrific scenario, but hadn't my mum missed the signs too.

"So, what happened in the end. How did it stop?"

"The day I turned fourteen. By then I was almost six feet tall, so when he came at me, I punched him first," Adam replied his tone low and hard.

And there it was, 'I punched him first'. That's what he'd been doing all his life since then.

"Not long after that," Adam continued, "he met a woman on a boy's trip to Benidorm and never came back. Left Mum high and dry; but at least I wasn't getting beaten on any longer and Lori didn't seem to miss him, but he didn't do much with her anyway. Once he was gone, that was when Mum suddenly started to ask questions and decided to believe me."

"Five years, Adam," I cried, my voice breaking on his name. "He beat you for five years and your Mum said she had no idea. No one else noticed or stopped it?" The phone quivered next to my ear as my hand started to shake as thoughts of how lost and lonely he must have felt raced through my mind. He was just nine years of age and must have been so bloody scared every single day.

"Yeah, five years, Sarah. Five years I acted like a pussy. I let that man put his hands on me and hid it because I was scared that if I said anything he'd leave Mum, and then Lori wouldn't have a dad, or worse we'd be taken into care and me and Lori would be separated. I wouldn't have been able to stand that, and I didn't want to have to move again; I loved it here. It was the first place that'd felt like home since my dad had left. I had friends, kids liked me and..." He sighed. "Kids were scared of me. You know what they say, the bullied becomes the bully, well that was true for me. I was knocked around at home, but at school, even then I damn well ruled the corridors. Once I got to high school, I got worse because I hung around with sixth formers who thought their shit didn't stink, I guess their attitude rubbed off."

Everything about Adam clicked into place. All the reasons that he treated girls like they were nothing. Why he always took the first strike. Why he demeaned girls when he was finished with them. It was all he'd known for a big part of his life. It was how his own mother had been treated by every man she'd been with, apart from Roger, and as for him, Adam simply didn't trust he wouldn't be like all the others and leave them eventually.

"Why keep it a secret now though?" I asked.

"Because if I don't everyone will judge her," he replied on a shaky breath. "They'll all say she's a bad mother and she should have done something to protect me, and—"

"And she should," I blurted out. "She's your mum it's her job, Adam."

"Yeah I know," he snapped. "But she's *my* mum and only I get to say that about her. Can't you say that about your mum too? Didn't you say your Mum checked out on you?"

I sighed because he was right. "Yeah, you're right, but *five years?*"

I found it so hard to believe his mum didn't know. How could she not have known what was happening to her son under her very nose. My abuse happened away from home, so Mum had no real way of knowing exactly what was wrong with me, but I was sure she'd have noticed bruising on me.

"Plus, you know if people at school find out I was beaten until my back and stomach were black and blue, don't you think someone will try their luck with me and think it's okay to take me down? My credibility would be shit."

"And, so what?" I cried. "Being known as a bully isn't credible. That's not who you want to be remembered as. If you just let yourself be you, you'd be surprised at how many people would actually want to be your friend because they like you, Adam, not because they're scared of you."

"And what about my friends," he growled. "People are scared of them, because of me. They have every girl in school after them, because of me."

I sat up and swung my legs out of bed. "Then let them do it on their own, but you can't carry on being the bully. You have to stop and just be you. Just be Adam Hudson the brilliant football player and lover of Napoleon Bonaparte. Be the boy who actually has a big heart if he'd just let it out once in a while."

He snorted an empty laugh and the heaved out a breath. "How can I be anyone different when my whole life is mapped out for me?"

"It doesn't have to be," I replied as I stood up and walked to my bedroom window to pull back the curtains to the quiet darkness outside. "You're not Eric and you're not his son. You don't have his bad blood inside of you."

"I mean that I'm being forced to get a job, when I actually want to go to UCL and study history," he groaned. "Mum says they can't afford to send me, and she didn't even bother filling in my student loan forms. So, I have to get a job when I really want to learn about the world and what it was like and what it might become. I want to travel and discover things other than complex set plays that might get us a goal in a match. I need to keep learning, Sarah. I need to see things that changed the world, I need to go to uni to give me that chance, but I have no bloody choice. How the hell do I change who I am if I can't do what I want or need?"

I stopped with my hand on the curtains enthralled by Adam's passion for the things he didn't think he had any chance of having.

"Everything that has happened in your life has moulded you into the person you've become and most of that wasn't your fault; but if you don't make a stand then how can anyone have any sympathy for your situation?"

"I don't want fucking sympathy," he ground out. "I just want to live my life how I want to, but if I can't I don't see how I'll ever change."

"You'll change because you'll make a stand, Adam. You tell your Mum that you're going to UCL. You tell the people who've already had their youth what *you* want to do with *yours* and you stick by it. If you don't, you'll become a product of circumstance and that will lead you down a very wrong path."

I heaved out a breath, not only because I'd felt nervous to say those words to the boy who'd bullied my friends and made it clear he didn't like me either, but because I needed to listen to them too. They were my mantra as well and I needed to tell my mum that I was not going to do languages at Lancaster after having a year out. I would take that year and spend it preparing for Kingston University and getting on to their degree course in teaching dance and choreography.

"Wow, nice speech." I breathed a sigh of relief at his light tone.

"Yeah," I replied as I bounced back on my bed. "It's kind of what I needed to tell myself too."

"How come?"

"Let's just say me and my mum have had a similar conversation about Kingston Uni. I want to study dance and choreography to teach or work in film and television; she wants me to study languages and then die of boredom as a bilingual secretary."

Adam laughed loudly and I was glad that he hadn't taken offence at my words, because I truly did think he was a better person than he gave himself credit for. It wasn't too late to let everyone else know that too.

"So, we could both end up in London," he said with a flirtatious tone.

I grinned and didn't want to think about what that statement might mean. Slow, baby steps were what was needed in this friendship.

"Yeah, and maybe I'll meet you for coffee sometime. Although I'm taking a year out, so you might be waiting a while."

"You are?"

"Yeah," I replied heavily. "After the year I've had, Mum and I both agreed I wasn't quite ready for University."

"And what will you do in that year?"

I shrugged even though Adam couldn't see me. "Not sure. I don't know if I'm ready to travel especially as I'd have to do it alone, so maybe I'll help Clarice out full time; or get a job of some kind. I hadn't really thought about it, you know with everything that's happened."

"I do," Adam said, in a soft gentle voice. "I totally do."

"Well it's still dark, but I'm wide awake, so I think I'll go and start on the bacon and eggs for breakfast. What about you?"

"Hmm, not sure, maybe I'll start on that new leaf and do the same. I could make breakfast for everyone. Or maybe I'll still act like a dick for the rest of the day and then land it on Mum and Roger that I'm going to try clearance for a late entry to UCL once I have my results."

"You think they'll take it okay?"

"No idea. I just know Mum thinks I'm shit at school and only capable of working some crap job for the next fifty fucking years."

"Well tell them otherwise. Let them know you're a history and maths genius. Think of it as your Battle of Austerlitz and show them how strong your right and left flanks are."

I grinned as I heard Adam's laughter on the other end of the line. What had been a hideous night the night before had resulted in something positive at least – Adam and I had some semblance of a friendship, and he might finally have the nerve to change his future.

"Okay," he said and yawned. "You may well be wide awake, but I think I have the ability to sleep for another couple of hours yet, so I'll let you go."

"Okay and thanks for checking on me."

He sighed. "No problem, that's what friends are for."

We said goodbye and then the line went dead and suddenly I didn't feel so wide awake. The moon was still casting silver patterns through the window, so maybe a couple more hours of dreamless sleep wasn't too bad an idea. I slid back into bed and snuggled down, falling asleep for another three hours, until I was woken by breakfast in bed from my mum who I gave the biggest, brightest smile to.

23

SARAH

Walking into school on Monday morning, it was pretty clear that everyone had heard what had happened to Adam and I. Groups of kids were huddled together whispering and breaking off their conversations as I approached, some even took pictures of me on their phones.

"At least this means they've forgotten the crap about my dad," I muttered to Alannah as we walked into our French class. "Or maybe the bitter irony of it will fire up the gossip even more."

"I can't believe how calm you are." She looked at me warily as we dropped our books on the desk. "I thought you'd be freaking out and maybe not even come to school today."

I'd called Alannah to tell her what had happened, and she'd been the one to freak out. When I mentioned that it had been Adam who held me together, I thought she may have passed out, she went so quiet. Finally, she had cleared her throat and said, 'Just don't expect him to continue being a decent person, Sarah, just because he was when faced with death'. I didn't tell her about our phone conversation in the early hours of the morning. I didn't want a lecture from her, but I also didn't want to have to tell her what we talked about.

Adam and I had agreed they'd be our secrets, but I couldn't say I wasn't worried that Alannah was right, and he'd go back to being Mr Shithead and tell everyone everything I'd told him in confidence. I was second guessing my decision and just hoped I wasn't wrong about him.

"I'm fine," I told Alannah.

I didn't tell her that Mum had called Eleanor, my therapist, and insisted on an immediate session via Skype, or that the night in the store hadn't been as bad as being raped by one of my teachers because I'd had Adam with me.

"Are you sure?" she asked, her tone soft and caring. "It must have brought back so many memories."

"It was hard," I admitted. "And I was so scared at the time, but I don't know, Alannah, I kind of feel…" I paused as I tried to find the words to convey how I felt. "At peace I guess."

"At peace?" She pushed her glasses up and wrinkled her nose. "How?"

I shrugged. "I don't know. It kind of feels like it helped to close a chapter in my life. Like it was the end of the bad stuff."

Alannah sat down in her chair and looked down at the desk. She didn't understand me, I knew that, but I couldn't tell her that part of my cleansing had come from talking of my rape and suicide attempt to Adam. It felt like ten weights had been lifted from my shoulders, not just one.

"Not going to lie, Sarah," Alannah said eventually. "I don't get how you're not screaming in a corner and refusing to come out of your room, *ever*, but if you feel okay then I'm glad. You'd tell me, right, if you ever feel the need to scream in that corner?"

"Yes, Alannah, I promise."

I gave her a smile and felt glad that she'd been the one asked to take care of me, because she was becoming a really good friend.

———

I'd been looking out for Adam all morning but hadn't seen either him or his mates. When I sat down for lunch with Alannah and Amber and my heart missed at least three beats as he walked into the dining room it shocked me. I hadn't realised how much of an affect he was starting to have one me. The fact that he looked hot didn't help. He sauntered in wearing his usual jeans and t-shirt, but today he was wearing a pair of Adidas Gazelle's and a baseball cap which he had pulled down low over his brows.

"Does he think he's a damn celebrity or something?" Amber asked with a snort of laughter. "Hiding his face from the paparazzi."

If I had to bet on it, I'd say he'd worn it to make himself look even sexier because of all the attention he'd be bound to get today; but I chose to keep quiet. If Alannah didn't understand how much Adam had helped me that night, Amber certainly wouldn't.

As the four of them approached our table, I felt my legs begin to shake and reached under my jumper for my wrist. I was nervous about how Adam would be with me, whether he'd give me that cocky smirk of his and then announce to everyone that he wanted to tell them my darkest secrets.

You are my sunshine, my only sunshine
  You make-

Adam looked up at me and when his eyes caught mine, he pushed up the peak of his cap and gave me the softest smile. It was filled with light and energy and made me feel hopeful that maybe our friendship would help us both in some way.

When he paused at our table, I held my breath and waited to have my hopes decimated by him.

"Hey, Sarah, how you feeling?" he asked, concern reflected from his eyes.

I gasped, ever hopeful and always scared.

"I'm fine, you?"

He shrugged, pulled his cap off, ruffled his hair and then pushed it back on again. "Okay."

His gaze stayed pinned to mine and I knew he was trying to tell me so much without having to say the words. He was there for me, he'd had another nightmare, he wasn't going to let the man who'd almost killed us win, and more importantly my secrets were safe with him.

"Are we getting lunch or not?" Ellis groaned. "I'm fucking starving."

Adam rolled his eyes and turned to him. "Yeah, just give me a second."

"Oh shit. Do we have to play nice with her now you've bonded over a gun pointed at your heads," Kirk said with a loud laugh.

Adam rounded on him. "Shut the fuck up, you insensitive dick. Do you have any idea what we went through?"

The whole of the dining room went silent as Adam grabbed hold of Kirk's shirt.

"I wonder why I'm friends with you sometimes." Adam got right in Kirk's face. "You're nothing but a prick."

"It was just a fucking joke." Kirk reared back from Adam. "Since when can't you take a joke?"

"Come on lads," Tyler said as he pulled them apart. "Both of you stop acting like idiots and let's get some lunch."

Adam let go of Kirk's t-shirt and took a step back. "I'll come in a minute, and I'm sitting here."

Without looking at either me, Alannah or Amber he pulled a stool from under the table and sat down.

"Looks like we have a new table, lads." Ellis slapped Kirk's back. "So, let's grab food before I eat your fucking big fat head."

"You girls don't mind if we sit here, do you?" Adam looked around at the silent, staring faces in the dining room and then raised a questioning brow at a boy and a girl on the next table. When they went back to their food and everyone else around us started up talking again, he turned back to us and flashed me a smile.

"So, you've really been okay?" he asked.

I nodded and swallowed the huge lump in my throat. "Yeah, fine. What about you?"

"Good, good. Roger organized some therapy sessions for me, but I'm not sure I need them."

I placed my hand over his and our eyes met as something unspoken passed between us. The air was highly charged, and I had a desire to sit there all day just feeling the warmth of his skin.

"I think you should," I said on a swallow. "Go to the therapy session. You have no idea how something like that can affect you. I should know."

He leaned closer to me and whispered in my ear. "I meant what I said, Sarah, I won't tell anyone anything at all about what we talked about."

He pulled his cap off again and put it on the table. His hair hung in his eyes, which made him look boyish and cute and my heart flipped over.

Licking his lips, he gave me a shy smile and just as I began to feel excitement about what he was going to say, two trays landed on the table.

"Got you something for lunch," Kirk said sullenly. "Peace offering."

Adam looked up at him and then at the tray with a chicken salad and an apple on it. "Thanks, but you need to apologise to Sarah too."

"Oh my God," Alannah whispered. "What the hell have you done with the real Adam Hudson?"

I gave her wide eyes and turned to Kirk. "It's okay. You don't need to."

He shook his head and pushed a bowl toward me. "Yeah, I do, so I got you a pudding."

"What is it?" I wasn't a lover of desserts and this looked just like a stodgy brown blob in the middle of custard.

"Jam roly poly, apparently," Kirk replied with a grimace. "Not for me, but I figured you might like it."

I actually didn't like the look of it, but he'd been good enough to apologise, so I picked it up from the tray and placed in front of me.

"Seriously," Alannah said with a frown. "Am I in a coma and dreaming all of this?"

"No," Amber replied. "It's all weirdly real."

"You can go and sit somewhere else," Adam offered as he picked up his knife and fork.

"We were here first." Alannah sounded tentative, but she looked him directly in the eye.

"And why would that stop me from making you move?" he threw back.

I inhaled sharply and looked at Adam who had turned to cutting up his chicken. The disappointment I felt at him being his usual self, after everything we'd said to each other, felt like a lead weight had been dropped into the pit of my stomach. He would never change, and I was stupid to even think he could.

I turned to Alannah to suggest we did in fact separate ourselves from them, when Adam stopped me in my tracks.

"I'm messing with you, Alannah. I just decided to stop being a dick around you girls. Almost getting shot kind of a changes a person."

He'd said everything he'd wanted to and was ever going to say in one sentence and his ego insisted that should be enough of an explanation. Apparently, he was right, it was perfectly sufficient, because Alannah silently picked up her spoon and began to eat her fruit salad.

Not for Amber it seemed.

"Seriously," Amber hissed. "That's all we get as explanation for you turning from a dick to a normal human being?"

Adam shrugged. "Not sure what else I can say."

"Well what about an apology for one." Amber's brown eyes were sparkling with anger as she leaned across the table closer to Adam. "You made my life a misery, and then just because you almost got a bullet to the head, we're supposed to forgive you? Oh, and FYI the fact you didn't get shot dead is *most* unfortunate."

"*Amber.*" Alannah gasped at the same time as she gripped my forearm. "You can't say things like that."

I was so shocked at Amber's comment I couldn't speak. I sat watching her with my mouth open. It hadn't even registered with me about my dad until Alannah had almost cut the blood supply off in my arm—I'd just been shocked because it was such a vile thing to say to anybody.

Adam looked over at me with his hand gripped tightly onto his fork and eyed me warily. I gave him an imperceptible nod and let out a long breath and turned to Alannah.

"It's okay," I whispered to her. "She didn't know."

"Of course, she knew," Kirk said with a smirk. "She got the same memo as everyone else."

"Kirk," Adam growled. "Why don't you keep your fucking mouth shut."

"What? I haven't said anything." He said the words but the way he narrowed his eyes on Adam told me he knew exactly what he'd said and the fury burning in Adam's eyes told me he knew too.

"Move over," Ellis said as he and Tyler arrived at the table with their lunches.

Kirk moved on to the next stool along, so he was opposite to Adam.

"I'm sorry, okay."

Adam didn't respond but the situation thankfully seemed to be diffused as he went back to his lunch and Amber pulled out her Kindle and with a sigh began reading it.

Alannah leaned closer to whisper into my ear. "This is so weird you have to admit."

I looked around the collection of people at the table and nodded. "Yeah, you're right."

Not sure what else to do, I reached for my pudding and stuck a spoon in, scooping up some of the stodgy blob along with some custard.

When I put it into my mouth at first it didn't taste too bad, but as I started to chew it just tasted like fatty dough. I looked over at Kirk who was watching me with a smile, and I didn't want to appear rude after he'd got it for me, so nodded and smiled.

"Hmm, lovely."

Kirk continued staring as I ate two more spoonful's and it struck me as odd that he was so interested in what I thought of his peace offering, but when I felt the itch begin at the back of my throat, I knew exactly what he'd done.

I threw the spoon down and clutched at my throat. "What is it Kirk?" I croaked already knowing the answer.

Adam looked up and dropped his cutlery, reaching across the table for me. "Sarah." His voice rose. "What's wrong? You don't look right."

I pointed at the dessert. "I-I... banana... allergic."

Second by second my throat closed a little more and I struggled to drag out a breath. I frantically felt around for my backpack, but everything got fuzzy too quick and started swimming in front of my eyes.

"Kirk, what the fuck is it?" Adam yelled as he knocked his stool over and scrambled over the table, pushing trays of food out of the way.

"What the-." Tyler was just about to spear a tomato with his fork when it disappeared.

"P-p-p." I clutched at my throat.

"Oh my God," Alannah screamed. "What's wrong with her?"

Everything pitched black; voices became distant echoes as it got harder and harder to breath.

I was about to die.

24

ADAM

"Kirk you fucking idiot, what did you do?" I screamed at my friend whose face had morphed from smirking to panic.

"I didn't know," he cried. "I just thought her throat got itchy."

"Alannah, where does she keep her pen thing?" My eyes darted between her and Sarah as I pushed out ragged breaths.

Alannah's hands were gripping her hair. "I don't know what you mean."

"She's allergic. Tell me now, what the fuck it is?" I pointed at the pudding while looking around for Sarah's backpack. Kirk had said her record stated she carried it everywhere.

"Sarah, where is it? Can you tell me?" I gripped her face in my hands and begged her to help me save her.

"It's banana custard." Kirk sounded scared and so he fucking should, because this was the most fucking stupid thing he'd ever done.

"What are you staring at?" Ellis yelled at the groups of students who had stopped eating and were gathered around watching. "Someone ring 9-9-9, or at least get a teacher for fuck's sake."

"EpiPen," Amber cried. "She needs an EpiPen, my brother has one for his nut allergy."

"Fuck." I picked up Sarah's backpack, unzipped it and emptied everything onto the table. Pens, notebooks, rulers, even tampons rolled out. "Amber what the fuck am I looking for?"

My eyes went back to Sarah whose face was going a shade of deep red, her lips were swelling, and her eyes were closing as she swayed in her seat.

"It looks like a huge needle." Amber quickly sifted through Sarah's things. "It'll have a big yellow sticker on it. Like a warning sign."

"Where the fuck is it." I snatched up the backpack and looked inside. There was a zip pocket, but it wasn't in there. I felt all over the bag with my fingers, hoping desperately that I'd find the fucking pen. Then, thank fuck, I felt it in a side pocket.

"Amber what do I do?" I asked frantically.

"Give it to me, I'll do it."

She held her hand out for the pen, but I shook my head. "Just tell me what to do." I wanted to be the one who helped her, I didn't trust anyone else. It had to be me because if I didn't have the pen in my hand, I'd smash Kirk's face in for doing this.

"Snap the cap off, hold her leg still, make a fist around the pen and then stab her outer thigh and count to ten." Amber barked the instructions at me as one of the lunchtime staff came running over with Mr Raymond.

"Adam what's happened?" Mr Raymond rushed to my side. "You know what you're doing?"

I blew out a breath, nodded and then stabbed Sarah in the leg and counted to ten.

"Did it click?" Amber cried.

I nodded and pulled the pen out and held it in front of me like it was some sort of lethal weapon. "What do I do with it?"

Amber handed me the storage case. "Put it back in, it'll need to go to hospital with her."

"Well done." Mr Raymond sighed and squeezed my shoulder. "Ambulance should be here soon."

All our eyes went to Sarah who was already breathing much easier, her face losing the beetroot red colour too.

"You okay?" I ran a hand down her hair.

She nodded and her eyes went to the pudding and then to Kirk before she fell against my chest.

"Sarah." Mr Raymond knelt down next to her chair and placed a hand on her shoulder. He didn't notice her flinch, but I felt it and held her closer to me.

"I'm going to get Miss George to come in the ambulance with you, okay?"

Sarah nodded and glanced up at Miss George with relief in her eyes. I could have kissed Mr Raymond for suggesting it.

As I sat with Sarah in my arms, I saw Kirk move in my periphery. He was going to bolt because he knew what he'd done, but before I could say anything, Ellis shoved him back into his seat and then gave me a nod. My best friend knew exactly what I would need when this was over.

A couple of minutes later and Miss George appeared with two paramedics. They dropped their bags at my feet and one of them gave me a smile while the other gently pulled Sarah away from me.

"Well done," the older of the medics said to me. "You probably saved her life."

I let out a huge breath of air and felt my scalp prickle as I thought about how twice in a matter of days, I'd nearly lost her. I knew she wasn't mine to lose, not yet, but I felt like she could be one day.

"We're going to take her to the hospital now," the paramedic said, after he'd finished checking her out. "Who's coming with her?"

Miss George stepped forward. "That would be me."

"Valentina, I'll call her mother," Mr Raymond said and then turned around to face the rest of the dining room. "Okay people let's all get back to class, lunch break is over."

As Mr Raymond herded everyone out of the dining room, Sarah was put onto a gurney and covered with a blanket and when the paramedics started to wheel her out, she reached out a hand for me.

"Thank you, again," she said with a small, tearful smile.

"My pleasure, but let's not go for strike three, hey?"

Her chin trembled but she still managed another upturn of her lips. When she was wheeled away, it took everything in me not to run after her and insist they let me travel in the ambulance. The thought of letting her out of my sight was crippling. It was like the night in the Tesco Express and then the sharing of secrets had created a bond between us and no one else was supposed to step inside the circle that held us together.

I kept my eyes on Sarah until I didn't have any sight of her anymore and then with a sigh turned to look at Amber and Alannah, who were putting everything back into her backpack.

"What you going to do with it?" I asked.

Alannah's eyes slid to mine. "I'll take it to her house later."

I nodded and then turned to Kirk who was whispering heated words with Ellis and Tyler.

"You're a fucking idiot." I shoved the pudding across the table and he just managed to catch it before it toppled off the edge of the table and onto his jeans. "You knew she was allergic to banana."

"How the hell did you know?" Alannah asked. "She hadn't even told me."

I breathed out heavily and kept my eyes on Kirk. "It doesn't matter. He just did, we both did."

"You're a fucking prick," Amber snarled and I wasn't sure

whether it was directed at me or Kirk; probably both. "Alannah, let's go."

Alannah picked up Sarah's bag and gave me a warning look. "Don't do anything stupid, Adam. He's a dick and he will have to live with that knowledge for the rest of his life. That's his punishment."

Tyler and Ellis both burst out laughing, but Kirk shook his head.

"You have no fucking sense of humour any of you." He smirked. "She was fine and if she'd just fucking told someone where her damn pen thing was, 9-9-9 wouldn't have been needed."

"Do you have any idea what an allergic reaction can do to someone," Amber cried. "She couldn't breathe, you loser."

"Chill, Amber, you're just mad that Adam seems to want Sarah to suck his dick these days instead of you."

The red mist dropped like a curtain in front of my eyes and I couldn't stop myself. Alannah made a grab for me and Amber screamed as I launched myself over the table and sent our lunch leftovers flying. Stools skidded across the room, and the table upturned as I grabbed hold of Kirk's shirt at the neck and pulled my fist back.

"Adam, no," Ellis yelled. "Think about this."

I paused but Kirk made my mind up for me.

"You're going to hit me, one of your best friends, just because of a pair of tits and a welcoming pussy."

"Too right," I hissed and then punched him.

The red mist turned black and with screaming and shouting whirling around me, I punched him again, and again and again. I would have done it again too had Mr Raymond not grabbed hold of my arm and Miss Daniels not yelled at me to stop.

25

SARAH

I felt nervous as I walked up the driveway to Adam's house and I wasn't sure why. All I was here for was to thank him for saving my life – again, well to thank him and to ask his parents not to be too hard on him.

Alannah had called at my house with my stuff and told me that Adam had been suspended for the rest of the week for punching Kirk. Apparently, Miss Daniels had wanted to make it two full weeks, but Mr Jameson had begged her not to as the Eagles had a match on Tuesday night after school. Kirk, who had a black eye and a thick lip had also pleaded on Adam's behalf, but Alannah had a suspicion that was more to do with Ellis and Tyler than Kirk feeling bad about what had happened.

As for me, well I was feeling okay. After a quick check at the hospital, my mum had insisted I take the rest of the week off school. With the robbery and then the pudding incident, she'd pretty much put me under house arrest, which was why I hadn't seen Alannah until the night before when Mum had finally let her visit.

Adam and I had exchanged a few texts over the last couple of days, but he'd never once mentioned his suspension. The only thing he's said was that Kirk was a dick, otherwise all conversations had been about our history project, his upcoming match and the fact that Murray, the man who managed the Tesco Express, had offered us and the elderly couple free shopping for a month. Mum had rolled her eyes at that one, but I was pretty sure it wouldn't be long before she went down there to take advantage of Murray's kind offer.

I straightened down the blue check flannel shirt I wore with denim shorts, thick black tights and boots and knocked on the black front door.

After I knocked a second time, I saw movement through the frosted glass. I couldn't see exactly who it was, but with the height and swagger, I guessed it was Adam. When the door swung open, I was proved right and even though I was expecting him, I stood like an idiot with my mouth hanging open.

I was a teenage girl, and with a hot boy looking like a snack wearing grey sweats, a white slim fitting vest and mussed hair in front of me, it was no wonder I'd become catatonic with want.

"Hey," he said, his face breaking into a warm smile. "What are you doing here?"

I looked him up and down and drank him in. I didn't think I'd ever seen him look so damn sexy. There was no doubt he was handsome, but there was something different about him. Today he had that added extra layer of something special. His eyes were brighter, his smile bigger and his skin appeared to have some sort of lustrous glow to it.

"Have you been to a health spa?" I slapped a hand to my mouth. "Oh shit, I didn't mean to say that out loud."

Adam grinned and ran a hand through his already messy hair, allowing a view of a bulging bicep. No wonder girls were hypnotized by him, he was beautiful when he turned on his charm. Yet today there was no brash smirk or ego on display, just Adam.

He cocked his head to one side and drew his brows together as he looked at me with a grin. "Nope, but if you want to come in, we can paint each other's nails."

"Oh God, I'm sorry." I dropped my head to my hand and groaned.

Adam laughed. "Don't worry. I get it, I'm hot."

My head shot up expecting to see the sneer I'd become used to, but he was smiling and most definitely not trying to be a prick.

"You want to come in?" He stepped to one side.

"Is that okay? I'm not interrupting anything am I?"

"Nope, not at all. You couldn't have come at a better time, I'm bored, and pizza is on its way."

I moved inside and instantly felt the warmth of the heating as opposed to the chill from the January wind outside. I'd borrowed my mum's car so hadn't worn a jacket, but even a few minutes on the doorstep had been enough to chill me.

"You mind taking your boots off," Adam said with a sigh. "Mum doesn't like outside shoes indoors."

"Oh God, my mum is the same." I bent to untie the laces of my Dr Martens. "She freaks if I even step one toe on her clean tiles."

When I stood, Adam was watching me with his hands linked behind his head, giving me a glimpse of a trail of dark blond hair leading down into his sweatpants. It was so bloody sexy. I groaned inwardly; it was hair for goodness' sake. I had no idea what was wrong with me other than the shot of epinephrine I'd had from the EpiPen must have done something to my hormones.

"Is your mum home?" I asked as he continued to watch me.

Adam frowned and then grinned. "Why Sarah Danes, don't tell me you want me alone so we can make out."

I felt my skin heat as memories of Adam's fingers inside of me flitted through my head. This boy had the ability to turn me into a quivering wreck if I let him. He was self-assured and experienced, everything I wasn't, and he knew that; but I also had a sense that he liked it when I acted tough with him.

"I think we've already been there, don't you," I replied trying to sound nonchalant. "No, I wanted to speak to her actually."

"My mum." He raised his brows. "What the hell do you want to speak to my mum for?" He turned and started to walk across the entrance hall towards an open door which I could see led into a large lounge area. It was cosy and comfy with a grey and ochre coloured rug covering a hardwood floor, a large grey L-shaped sofa with ochre coloured cushions and all the walls were the same grey as the sofa. There were family photographs along the mantel over the fireplace which had a log burner in it and at the windows were white wooden blinds.

"This is a lovely room," I said.

"Thanks, I'm sure my mum will be happy you said that. She likes to decorate now she has Roger's money." He rolled his eyes and walked over to a low coffee table to pick up the TV remote and turn off the television.

"You don't need to do that. If you were watching something."

"It was just some reality TV crap. I told you I was bored. So, why do you want to speak to her? Is it about Lori and her non-existent dance skills?"

I knew I shouldn't, but I couldn't help but laugh. "She tries really hard."

Adam's brows quirked high and he gave a pained expression. "That's one way of putting it. My little sister has all the elegance of an elephant on roller skates."

"Ah poor Lori, she so wants to be a dancer."

"She does, but we know it isn't happening. So, come on, tell me what you want to speak to Mum about."

I chewed on my lip not sure whether I should say. It felt stupid now.

"Go on," Adam said and pointed to the sofa. "Sit down though, and then once you've told me, I'll get you a drink."

"But your pizza will be here soon." I glanced over my shoulder towards the door, as if the pizza boy would suddenly appear.

"Yeah and you're staying, right? I ordered enough for two, I must have had a premonition you were coming over."

He gave me one of his sexy grins and I warmed from the inside out.

"So, sit."

I did as I was told and perched on the edge, while he dropped on to the chaise section and kicked his legs out in front of him.

"Well," I said, as he looked at me expectantly. "I kind of wanted to plead your case."

"*My* case?" He poked a finger at his chest.

"Yeah, I heard you got suspended."

Adam sighed and let his head drop back against the sofa. "Alannah?"

"Yep, but why didn't you want me to know?"

"It wasn't that I didn't want you to know," he replied. "I didn't specifically say 'don't tell Sarah', but I didn't tell you because I thought you'd had enough to deal with over the last few weeks, year even..." he paused and eyed me warily. "Not that it matters to you what happens to me."

Oh my God, Alannah was right, this was not the real Adam Hudson. This one seemed unsure and caring, where the one I'd had dealings with over the last month had been harsh and coarse. That night at the Tesco Express was bound to have changed us, no one had a gun pointed at their head and stayed the same, but Adam had done a total three-sixty.

"It does matter, Adam," I replied. "You saved my life twice, so I'd be a pretty shitty friend if I ignored the fact that you'd been suspended because of me."

"No, Sarah," he growled. "I got suspended because of Kirk and the fact that he's a dick."

His lip curled in disdain as he exhaled heavily. This was the Adam Hudson expression that I was used to, but now I'd seen the other side of him I liked this one even less, so decided to move the conversation on.

"Actually, something Alannah said kind of got me thinking."

"Yeah, what's that?"

He still looked angry, but when he moved the pillow at his back and got himself into a more upright position, he lifted his chin into a defiant tilt. He knew exactly what I was going to say, but he really didn't need to put his walls up because life was most definitely too short. So, as long as he was being honest about changing then I could let go of the past.

"How did you and Kirk know I was allergic to banana?"

He puffed out his chest and looked me square in the eye. "I think you know the answer, but I suppose I should tell you anyway." I nodded and waited until Adam finally let out a long exhale. "You know Kirk's pretty good on computers, right?"

"I heard something like that, yeah."

"Well he hacks the school computer all the time."

I should have been angry, shocked even, but with the level of manipulation and bullying that Adam and his mates did, there had to be something that he was using to help him to do the things he did.

"It's on my records," I said with resignation.

"Yeah." Adam dropped his gaze from mine for a few seconds and then pushed his legs off the sofa and leaned forward. "One thing though, he never mentioned what happened at your old school and I know you said it wasn't on your records and was private. I'm worried though, that he's found out and is going to use it against you. In fact, I don't even think he got the information about your dad from there. He just did some digging where you used to live. Which is another reason why I'm worried he knows but is keeping it to himself."

"Wow," I said raising my brows. "You really are changing. Worried that Kirk may use something that could bring me down, isn't what I'd expect from you."

"*Expected*, past tense." He narrowed his eyes. "I told you Sarah, I'm changing."

He was either the best actor around or he was actually being honest with me. His eyes were dark and there was a set to his jaw that said I shouldn't question him, so I didn't. There was still a tiny part of me that worried he might suddenly shed the new improved image he was trying for though and use everything I'd done or said against me.

"You're right, none of its on my record," I replied. "And as far as I know Miss Daniels is the only one who knows about Mr Mills, although she might have told the rest of the staff." I shrugged. "I have no idea, but unless Kirk's gone back to my old school and talked to my old friends, he won't find out. You can stop worrying about it, Adam."

"You sure?" he asked. "Because I've got to be honest with you, if he does something to hurt you, I'm not sure I'd stop at three punches."

I reared back. "Woah".

"Don't tell me you're surprised," he said as he looked up at me through long lashes that most girls would die for.

"Well, yeah," I replied. "He's your best friend."

I couldn't believe he was sticking up for me, over Kirk.

"Ellis is my best friend," he stated.

"Okay, but he's been your friend for a long time. You've known me a month and yet you're saying you'd be on my side if Kirk tried to use my past against me."

Adam's forearms rested on his knees as he contemplated me. "Yeah, I think I would."

Silence fell between us and I could practically feel the static building in the room. The energy floating around made it hard to breathe, and when Adam's lips parted and he sucked in his bottom lip, I knew that from the way he was looking at me that something was going to happen. Determination glinted in his eyes as he told me without words what he wanted.

My body hummed with the possibility of being held in his strong arms while his long fingers revisited the places they'd already been. I wanted his powerful body to shroud mine as we brought each other pleasure, I needed his beautiful blue eyes to look into mine and give me a host of promises when words would never be enough. I was desperate to feel the hardness of his smooth length inside of me, empowering me to be free with every delicious thrust of his hips.

"I can't understand why I feel the way I do," Adam said, his voice a hushed whisper alongside the tick tock of a clock on the mantle and the gentle moan of the heating. "I mean there's no denying you're beautiful, Sarah, but this isn't just about you making me feel hard and horny. This is about you making me crave to change. At night I lie awake thinking about you, desperate for the daylight not just so I can see you, but so I can start to make changes in my life and in me. I have to be worthy of you before I can even touch you."

As Adam leaned forward, with an intensity in his gaze that I'd never seen before, I couldn't stop the flutter of air from leaving my lips. It was a soft sigh of appreciation and when I saw Adam's chest hitch, I knew he'd heard it.

"You've already touched me," I replied, my eyes never wavering from his face.

"I shouldn't have." He shook his head and breathed deeply. "I wasn't the person you needed that night, you needed someone who would have cherished you, someone who would know you were worth so much more than a quick finger fuck against a wall."

His words were hard and coarse, but they were said with truth and gentleness.

"I wanted it too."

Adam's lips upturned into a slight smile, but I could see in his eyes that he was remembering how hot and sexy that quick ten-minute fumble had been.

"I know, but it still doesn't mean you didn't deserve better."

I conceded to what he was saying and stayed silent as I continued to bask under his intense stare.

"I'm not going to lie, Sarah, and say I'll suddenly be this fucking awesome lad who you deserve. I'm seventeen-years-old, I'm a dick and an idiot at best. I've done things that I'm not sure even my mum would forgive me for, so why the fuck I'd expect you to I don't know. Shit, I have no damn idea why I want you to forgive me or why you make me want to change, it's fried my fucking brain thinking about it, but I do."

His words felt like a salve to both our souls. He knew he wasn't perfect, had never been and never would be. He knew I was damaged and had issues that would always weigh me down. Yet he felt I deserved something good and he wanted to be that good in my life. Instinctively, I dropped from the sofa and crawled over to him and pushed up on my knees. We were eye to eye as I reached up and cupped his face in my hands, my palms cool against his warm skin.

"You've been like a hurricane in my life," I whispered. "I didn't want you, or welcome you, and when I got caught up in you, I thought I'd be destroyed, but somehow I've come out the other side and I feel stronger for surviving you."

Adam put his hand on top of mine, and he started to rub the inside of my wrist with his thumb. His hard skin soothed the scar which was so often my comfort.

"I was sure I was going to crush you," he whispered. "I was desperate to. From the moment I set eyes on you, I fucking craved you and I knew I couldn't let you in. I didn't want to let you in, so it was easier to make you hate me."

"Typical Adam Hudson," I said around a soft laugh. "Getting the first strike in before someone hurts you."

He arched a brow. "You see how well you know me, after just a few weeks. My own mum doesn't get that. She just sees me as her troublesome brat who might steer her nice little boat of domesticity toward the rocks."

Sadness filled his eyes and I knew so many of his troubles and the way he was with people were as a result of his mum's behaviour, with both men and her son.

"She loves you," I stated not entirely sure I was stating the truth, but unable to watch the desolation on his face any longer.

"Yeah, maybe, but she loves herself more."

His words sounded final and resolute, so I chose not to continue any further conversation about his mum. I didn't know her, and it wasn't my place to state what I'd gotten from that one meeting at the shopping centre, which was that Adam was right.

"How the hell have you done this to me?" Adam asked, his thumb still caressing my wrist. "How have you made me want to change? I was happy being a dick."

We both laughed and the air around us lightened.

"I haven't," I said, scooting a little closer so that our lips were inches apart. "The good person was always in there it simply took almost getting killed to make you realise that it wasn't a secret that you had to keep any longer. I didn't change you Adam, *you* did."

If I'd been expecting some announcement from Adam that he was going to kiss me, I would have been disappointed, but only for a second, because as soon as his lips hit mine, I was rocketed to the heights of delight.

Adam's fingers on one hand raked through my hair, while the other cupped my cheek as our breaths became more ragged with each sweep of his tongue against mine. As his teeth nipped at my bottom lip, I let out a needy moan and pushed myself forward, forcing his legs wider apart. When my chest touched Adam's, he fell backward onto the sofa and pulled me up with him, our mouths remaining locked together the whole time.

"You were wrong you know," Adam groaned as his lips moved to my neck. "You make me a good mad."

His hand reached down to cup my bum and when he pressed me into him, I could feel how hard and swollen he was beneath his sweatpants. Greedily I found his mouth with mine and gripped at his vest, urging him to kiss me some more. When his other hand landed on my bum to join the first, the need to thrust my hips was too great, and with a soft undulating wave, I rocked against Adam's erection.

"I-I-I have too many layers," I panted as Adam's hips pushed up to meet mine creating the most delicious friction between my legs.

Without warning his strong arms lifted me up and flipped me over so that my back was on the sofa and he was above me. His forearms were either side of my head as he lifted his hands to gently brush the hair away from my face, and as he looked down on me, I didn't think I'd ever seen a more beautiful sight. Eyes full of warmth and the colour of the clearest lagoon, contemplated me with intensity.

"You have to be sure, Sarah," he whispered. "Because I'll stop at any point if you need me to, but it'll fucking kill me. I'd rather wait until you're totally ready than start and then not have the opportunity to worship every fucking inch of your skin."

I was desperate for his worship, twice over if necessary, but he was right, it was something I had to be sure of. It wouldn't be fair to either of us to have to stop. I knew that the thought of having Adam inside of me didn't fill me with fear or dread. I'd had his fingers and now they didn't feel nearly enough. I was desperate to change my memories of what sex was like, what feelings it evoked. I didn't want it to feel dirty or degrading, I wanted to relish the release it brought and enjoy the ultimate high. I wanted to have sex with Adam Hudson.

"I'm ready," I whispered. "For everything."

ADAM

"I'm ready for everything," Sarah said, her lips red and puffy from my kisses. If I hadn't had the biggest craving of my life to be inside her, I may well have blown at that moment.

She looked beyond beautiful with her sunshine blonde hair fanned out around her and her mouth parted in readiness for my tongue to enter her mouth and sweep against hers.

My cock was painfully hard and pushing against my sweatpants. I knew there was probably already pre cum on the end of it to show how much I needed her. When Sarah's hand snaked up the back of my top and she scraped her fingernails over the curve of my muscles, I lost every bit of restraint I had left in me. With a level of desperation that I didn't know existed, I reached for the button of her shorts and practically ripped it open before tugging at her zip. As I pulled her shorts down her legs, Sarah lifted up, dragging her shirt over her head without undoing any of the buttons and threw it to one side.

After the pain and humiliation that she must have gone through with the fucking animal who raped her, I would have expected her to be shy and conscious of being half naked beneath me, but she surprised me. With the confidence of a girl who knew what she wanted, and a determination to get it, Sarah lay back and stretched her arms over her head. She wasn't wearing a bra and though her tits were small, they were pert with the prettiest pink nipples I had ever seen. She wasn't nearly as tiny as her baggy clothes made her seem and finally getting a look of her slim waist that curved gently at her hips reinforced that she really did need to stop hiding herself.

As Sarah looked up at me with anticipation, I forced myself not to take her nipple into my mouth until I had her completely naked. She needed to be savoured, not rushed as if I couldn't wait to move on, because that would be a lie. The hope she'd forced into my soul made me wonder whether I would ever want to move on from her. I hooked my fingers into the waistband on her tights and slowly peeled them from her skin and off the ends of her legs and when I threw them to join her shirt, I couldn't help the groan that escaped from my mouth. She was wearing a pair of white cotton knickers, so plain and simple yet as sexy as fucking hell against her creamy skin.

"You're so beautiful," I whispered as I lowered myself down and locked my eyes with hers. "More than you know."

With my gaze still on her, I dropped an open-mouthed kiss on her breastbone and her eyelashes fluttered as she let out a little sigh. How the hell I didn't rip off my clothes and her knickers and then thrust inside of her I didn't know, but somehow, somewhere I found the control I needed. Not only did I want to take my time with her, but she needed me to go slow, even if she didn't realise it. I would be her first since him and I had to erase her memories of him.

Still watching her, I kissed down her stomach until my mouth was at the edge of her knickers and when I smelled her fucking juices, I felt ten feet tall. I had done that to her before I'd even put a finger on her. My lips and tongue had barely touched her, but she was wet and ready to let me enter her willingly.

I kissed down to the apex of her smooth, toned thigh and when my finger whispered over the white cotton, I heard a soft, mewling sound.

"You like that?" I asked as I drummed a soft beat against her sex with two fingers.

"Hmm hmm."

Unable to speak, Sarah's head went back, her rock-hard nipples pointed skyward and her hips thrust upward as her back arched. She was more responsive than I'd expected, and I couldn't help but feel a level of pride that I'd never felt before, not even when I'd won player of the season for the whole of the county the year before.

For all I wanted to prolong Sarah's pleasure, I was also aware that I was in danger of embarrassing myself. She was so fucking hot, I was pretty sure I might blow like a geyser at any contact, even if it was an accidental touch from her knee or elbow, so I eagerly dragged her knickers down her legs and threw them to join the rest of her clothes. I'd been right, they were soaked, and her neat triangle of blonde pubic hair glistened with her juices at the opening to her pussy.

With my dick straining to be set free, I scooted down the sofa and lifted Sarah's legs to lie over my shoulders. She was too far gone down the rabbit hole of pleasure to question me or to care what I was about to do, but I felt I needed it as much as she did. I hadn't gone down on many girls, not that I was a chauvinist or anything like that, but weirdly most seventeen-year-old girls were a little shy about letting a lad give her head. We fucking loved it, but according to Kirk's older brother, girls learned to love it more as they got older. Sarah on the other hand didn't appear to have any problem with it, because as soon as my tongue licked her like she was the sweetest lolly I'd ever tasted, she gasped and dragged her fingers through my hair, pushing my face closer to her.

Fuck, she didn't taste *like* the sweetest lolly ever, she *was* the sweetest. She tasted hot, sweet and delicious and as my tongue moved up and down in long strokes, I knew I'd found heaven.

After a few more licks, I took Sarah's clit into my mouth and sucked on it, causing her to squirm beneath me. She was so fucking wet, it was unbelievable, her juices were dripping down to her arse crack and I didn't think I'd ever seen such a perfectly pink pussy.

The soft, quiet sounds that Sarah made as I licked and sucked only spurred me on more until I couldn't stand it any longer and had to clutch my cock to ease the pain of its throbbing. My balls felt heavy and ready to explode and if Sarah dragged her nails across my scalp one more time, I knew I would.

"Adam," she gasped. "I need you."

I wanted to get on my knees and give a prayer of thanks, because for all my best intentions, I was as horny as hell and I needed to fuck her.

I pulled back and when Sarah's eyes opened to watch me, I couldn't help but grin.

"What?" she asked breathily, her complexion flushed.

"You," I replied. "You look thoroughly fucked and I haven't even started properly with you yet."

She smiled shyly, but dropped her legs further apart, exposing more of her pussy to me, a silent invitation, a wordless command that I wouldn't disobey.

"You need to be naked first," she said with a smile, looking so damn cute and sexy.

I reached behind and pulled my vest up and over my head. "Whatever you say," I replied.

Sarah moved her hand and I knew when her lips parted that she liked my Eagles tattoo. It was on my left pec and if I flexed it the wing actually looked like it was moving.

"Wow," she whispered. "I had no idea."

"Let's such say it got me grounded for a few weeks, seeing as I used fake ID to get it." I grinned at her and reached over to the side table for my wallet and pulled out a condom and then pushed down my sweatpants and boxers, all in one go. My cock, hard and eager, bobbed against my abs and as soon as she saw it, Sarah's eyes widened. It wasn't huge, but it was big enough and even if I said it myself, it was a fucking pretty cock compared to most I'd seen. I liked to keep things neat and clean down there and I could see that Sarah was impressed now that she was actually getting to see it and not just feel it in the dark recesses of an alleyway.

As I stepped out of my clothes, I kept my eyes on her, and she only had eyes for my cock. When her hand instinctively went to her nipple and she began to roll it between her fingertips, I groaned. Fuck she had no idea how sexy she was, or how tied up she had me and that was before I'd been inside of her.

"Sarah," I whispered. "Look at me."

When her eyes met mine, the blush on her cheeks became that of embarrassment, so I took hold of her hand and kissed her knuckles.

"Don't ever by embarrassed for wanting sex," I said softly. "It's sexiest thing in the world. I only want you to look at me because I need to be sure that this is definitely what you want."

"I do," she cried.

"I know you say the words, Sarah, but I need to see it in your eyes too. When I put this condom on, I want to still see that desire and when I lay on top of you about to enter you, I have to see you want the same thing."

She didn't answer but pulled me down to her and when our faces were close, she raked her fingers through my hair and kissed me with an eagerness that answered every question I'd had about what we were about to do.

"You taste of me," she said against my mouth.

"Yeah and it's fucking delicious." I pulled back and with a grin passed her the foil wrapper. "You do it."

She looked a little unsure and her eyes flittered from me to the condom in her hand. "I've never done it before."

"I'll show you, just take it out."

As Sarah ripped open the foil, I palmed my cock which was aching more than I ever thought possible, so much so I wanted to take the condom from her and put it on to save time, but I knew I had to let her have some control. After what felt like an eternity, but was only seconds, Sarah pulled herself up so that her face was level with my cock. She looked at it eagerly and then dropped a kiss on the end of it. It wasn't the full-on blowjob I'd have welcomed, but it made my heart thud louder in my chest. This girl would most definitely be the one person who fucked me up the most, I could feel it in my bones.

Tentatively she took hold of me and then placed the rubber on the end of my cock.

"Pinch the end," I said. With her concentration still on her task, I ran a hand down her hair and around to her cheek. Once she'd done as I asked, she looked up at me, her eyes full of questions. "That's it, now roll it slowly down."

As her tiny fingers worked the latex down my length, I blew out a breath. Her touch was featherlight and gentle and it sent more waves of need swirling around my body, until I thought I might self-combust. Finally, when she was done, she looked up at me and gave me the biggest smile, proud at what she'd achieved. For some girls wrapping up a lad's cock was nothing, but to Sarah it was everything.

"I need you pretty soon," I gasped as Sarah's smile brightened a little more.

"I want you too," she replied and floored me once more when she lay back on the sofa and opened up her legs for me again.

"Ah fuck," I muttered and dropped down and braced myself above her.

I hooked a hand under her leg, just at the crease of her knee and lifted it. Instinct told Sarah I wanted it on my shoulder and with her pretty pink painted toes pointing, she placed it just where I wanted it. Her other foot went to the floor, which only opened her wider and the sight was spectacular. With a lingering kiss to her inner thigh, I couldn't wait any longer and settled between her hips to push inside of her.

As soon as I gave my first thrust, I knew that this would be the best feeling I'd ever experience. Whatever happened, Sarah would always be the best sex I'd ever have because of what it meant to both of us; it was the beginning of the end of our pain.

With every thrust I made, Sarah drew me in and tightened around me, enticing me to go harder and deeper. Nothing had ever felt so good, I had never felt so addicted and each time I pulled out I couldn't wait to push back inside of her. Our pace was steady, but not slow. I had to force myself not to go faster, not to scare her, to still allow Sarah that control; but when I hitched her leg higher and her fingers tightened in my hair, I couldn't help myself.

Faster, harder I went as Sarah began to buck beneath me. Her hips moved wildly and with abandon and I felt her walls squeeze me.

"Adam," she gasped. "Don't... don't stop."

I couldn't if I tried. I couldn't even speak so my lips found her collar bone and sucked hard. As Sarah gasped and pulled harder at my hair, I knew I was about to come, but she had to get there first, I had to give her that, so I lifted my chest away from hers and dropped my mouth to her nipple and sucked and licked it, nipped at it with my teeth and gave it the attention that I knew Sarah wanted it to have.

"Adam," she groaned and shuddered beneath me. Her body

tensed, her head went back and a cry for God came screaming from her mouth.

As her heated form continued to pulse around me, I used the power in my thighs to piston my hips faster and harder, until my balls start to throb from within and tighten up. With every stroke the sensation rose, and the anticipation built and as my heart pounded and my body tensed, I let out a loud groan, and exploded into a world of ecstasy.

We were both breathing hard and a fine sweat had formed on our bodies. I realised I'd never before put that much effort in sex. I'd done what I'd needed to do to get us both off, but with Sarah that hadn't been enough. I'd needed her to understand how I was ready to change for her, and for her to know that this was different for both of us. It wasn't cheap, meaningless or unwanted, it was sex between two people who cared, who wanted what the other had to give. It was the sort of sex that marked the start of something.

"Are you okay?" I asked and dropped a kiss to her neck.

She nodded but didn't speak; she was breathless and boneless as her arms dropped to her sides.

"I'll take that as a fucking hell yes." I laughed and lifted myself on to my forearms, not wanting to crush her yet wanting to keep her beneath me for as long as possible.

She giggled and looked up at me. "That wasn't what I expected."

"Good," I replied and slowly pulled out of her, taking a hold of my dick and the condom as I did so. "That means it was like nothing before, which also means in time we'll wipe away those memories."

She stilled and I wondered if I'd said the wrong thing by mentioning what she'd been through.

"Hey, I'm sorry," I said. "I didn't mean to upset you."

Sarah frowned and shook her head. "You didn't, it's just that you said in time."

I sat back on my haunches and looked down at her, startled when my heart flipped over. She looked beautiful and she'd been fucking amazing, but the feelings that were wrapping around me were weird. I had a strong desire to cuddle and kiss her all night and I knew this was so much more than my usual hook ups. I felt like I needed to put a label on us, and it needed to be written in indelible ink.

"Yeah, in time we will."

"So, you want to do this again?" she asked.

"Yeah, don't you?"

"Of course, but it depends."

"On what?" I asked shrugging one of my shoulders.

I knew I was being a dick about it and should just go right out and say it – 'yeah and I think you should be my girlfriend' – but changing your personality from prick to reasonable human being doesn't happen overnight.

Sarah eyed me warily and then with a little huff, leaned up on her elbows and gave me a spectacular view of her tits.

"You really are an idiot at times," she sighed.

"What?" I reared back and subconsciously thought about the condom still on my dick. "Any chance I can get rid of the wrapping before we have our first argument?"

Sarah sat up fully and crossed her arms over her chest, which pissed me off, because I no longer had my spectacular view. "No, you can't. Just be honest with me, Adam. Do you want me as a fuck buddy or something more?"

"Will *my* answer make a difference to *your* answer?" I asked and tried hard not to smirk. Like I said, there was still an element of dick-head in me.

"Yes," she snapped. "You know it will. You know that no matter how amazing sex is with you I can't just be a fuck buddy. I told you before I will not be a member of your cock sucker gang."

241

I just didn't know when to quit. "Officially you'd be part of my sex gang. Oh, and noted that the sex was amazing."

"Oh my God, you fucking loser." Sarah threw a cushion at me and it hit me right in the face. It was a bloody good throw too because it knocked me onto my back. "Well that was the first and last time, so suck that you knobhead."

Sarah scrambled off the sofa and reached for her clothes. Before she'd got very far, I snagged her around the waist, pulling her back until she was flush against me.

"Shit, Adam, your dick is still wet and its touching my bum," she cried.

I couldn't help the laughter that rumbled from deep within my stomach, and when Sarah jumped up and started wiping at her backside with one of my mum's cushions it just got louder.

"Stop laughing," she said and threw me a glare.

"I can't help it, but make sure you don't leave too much jizz on my mum's soft furnishings."

She stopped and looked down, horrified. "Oh no, your Mum is going to kill me," she squealed and dropped the cushion like it was a hot potato. "We need to wash it before she gets home." She paused and looked at the clock on the mantlepiece. "What time is she due home? I need to get dressed and go. Oh my God, she'll think I'm one of your cock sucker gang and that I'm the easy new girl that drops her knickers just to make friends. She'll—"

I was up and in front of her, taking her mouth with mine, before she had chance to get herself more anxious. The kiss was everything I never thought a kiss could be; it was sweet, warm and welcoming.

"I still think you're a prick." Sarah pouted, breathless as she circled her arms around my neck.

"I know and I'm sorry." I did something I'd never done before and rubbed my nose with hers. I thought I'd feel stupid doing something like that, but it felt good and intimate. "You're just too easy to wind up."

She blinked quickly three times and I figured I was about to get blasted again, so jumped in quickly with another apology.

"Again, I'm sorry, and to show you how much I mean it I'll tell you exactly what I want for us."

Sarah swallowed hard and I saw the worry pass over her face. I hated that I had been such a bastard in the past that she would think I'd do something shitty after the amazing sex we'd just had. I forged on, desperate to put her mind at rest.

"I want us to do this again and again, but not as fuck buddies or a weekly hook up. I want us to go out, be together, mutually exclusive. Girlfriend and boyfriend." The words out of my mouth surprised me, and I had to admit to feeling a little unsure. I'd never wanted to date anyone, let alone be exclusive. It wasn't me, but Sarah made me want it, but only with her.

I expected her to smile or at least say okay, but she just stood there and stared at me. Her fingers knotted together, but I felt a huge sense of relief that she wasn't rubbing at her wrist; the scar of her pain.

"Sarah, say something."

It was my turn to feel anxious and I was shocked at how much I wanted what I'd offered to her. If she said no, I wasn't sure how I'd react—probably like a dick, because I was after all a work in progress.

"You do?" she asked, her voice soft and low.

"Yeah, I do."

The moment that she smiled was the moment that I knew I really was gone for her. The relief was almost on a par with that I felt the day Eric walked out of our lives; that was how important I knew Sarah was going to be to me.

She threw herself into my arms and hugged me tightly before smacking a hard kiss to my lips. When her hands crept toward my hair, I groaned and gently pushed her away as I'd already figured out that this was her tell when she was horny.

"Sarah, we have to stop."

"Why?" she asked and looked at the clock again. "Oh, shit will your parents be home soon?"

"Nope, but my cock is wading in a balloon full of jizz and I think the pizza is here."

As she pulled away from me someone banged on the door and we both turned towards it and burst out laughing.

I grabbed my sweatpants and threw Sarah her shirt. "Kitchen is through there, plates are in the first cupboard on the left, and there'll be some cans of Diet Coke in the fridge. I'll go and pay, while still wearing the fucking condom I should add."

She smirked and saluted me, and I watched her walk into the kitchen, pulling her shirt over her head, as she gave me a glorious view of her arse.

27

SARAH

I couldn't help smiling as I watched Adam eat his pizza, he was a typical boy and had the all the finesse of a Gorilla at feeding time. Almost a whole piece was stuffed into his mouth quickly followed by a mouthful of coke.

"Ugh," I groaned. "That's gross."

"What is?" he said around a mouthful of pepperoni.

"Drinking while you have food in your mouth. My dad used to eat chocolate and drink coffee at the same time. He said it helped to melt the chocolate and mixed them together."

Adam smiled and reached up to tuck a strand of hair behind my ear.

"You don't really talk about him much."

I smiled as I thought about my dad, the twinge still there in my heart.

"It hurts you know. Plus, it's not really like we've been best friends since I got here."

Adam took another swig of his drink and his eyes considered me like he was studying one of those picture puzzles where there's a hundred cats and you have to find the one rabbit.

"What?" I asked and wiped at my mouth with my serviette. "Do I have food on my face or something?"

Adam shook his head. "I'm just trying to figure out why I even thought I could break you. You're so fucking strong and brave, anyone can see that."

He pushed the pizza box away from us and reached out to pull me onto his lap. His strength meant he lifted me like I was a toddler and when he placed me down to straddle him, I felt my stomach swarm with the recently hatched butterflies of a new relationship.

We'd had an amazing afternoon, once Adam had told me his family had gone away for the weekend and had left him behind, and that I didn't haven't to worry about his Mum finding us. There'd been two rounds of sex, which meant we had to reheat the pizza, but mostly I'd enjoyed just talking and getting to know each other better.

"I'm glad you think I'm brave, because I've got to be honest, I don't feel it most of the time."

"I know," Adam replied as he linked his arms around my waist and gave me a quick squeeze with his forearms. "But the fact that you tried to hide it proves you actually are. You've had so much shit thrown at you this last year and yet you tried to battle with me every step of the way."

I let out a long sigh and snuggled closer to his warm body. "I couldn't let myself be dragged under again. I had to take control of my life and not let another man manipulate me."

Adam startled and pulled back from me. "I'm nothing like him, he's a fucking rapist."

His voice was low and hard and his eyes dark with anger and disappointment as he spat out the words. His face was curled into a sneer of displeasure and I wondered if the fine gossamer thread that tethered his goodness to him might have been snapped, allowing the blackness back inside. Concerned that I'd ruined things between us, I gave Adam a soft smile and placed a hand against his cheek, and when he visibly relaxed, I felt relief and empowerment in equal measures. This boy said I had him tied up in knots, but I was beginning to think we were tied together from some other past life. Everything had happened so quick between us. Maybe it was too much and we should have stayed friends for a while longer, but I couldn't see how anything could be better than the now.

"That wasn't what I meant," I said with my eyes still intently on Adam's face. "And you know it, and if you don't, then maybe all this was too soon."

"No," he replied quickly. "It's not too soon and I do know, it was just with you talking about us both in the same sentence, it shocked me." He paused to take in a deep breath. "Do you think that's how people see me, as some sort of monster?"

His eyes were shadowed with guilt where usually there was confidence and defiance and I knew that the manipulative bully had all been a pretence to hide the Adam I was seeing today. As I'd pretended to be brave, Adam had pretended to be someone no one would dare challenge. There was that link again; two sides of the same coin.

"I think people will see what you want them to see," I replied and kissed him gently on his lips. "You want me to see the real you so that's what you give to me, I just hope more people get to see that too."

"One thing's for certain," Adam sighed. "We'll certainly shock them at school on Monday."

"About that," I said tentatively, wanting to voice a thought that I'd been mulling over. "The fact that until a week ago we were pretty much sworn enemies, do you think people will think I'm easy for having sex with you? Do you think I'm easy? Oh my God, do you think they'll think I've joined the *cock sucker* group?"

Adam rolled his eyes but said nothing as he watched me trace my finger around his eagle tattoo. I was fascinated by the delicate intricacies of the bird's feathers. Its talons, so life like, looked as if they really were clutching a football.

"Don't overthink it," he said and lifted my chin with his finger and gave me a gentle smile that only a few weeks ago, I'd have never thought him capable of. It warmed me and eased my worries and insecurities. "And, no, I don't think you're easy. I know how hard that must have been for you."

"But that's just it, Adam, it wasn't," I replied. "Having sex with you felt so natural and easy. At no point then or in the alleyway did I get a flashback or a memory to make me want to stop. I know it's been nine months and I've been having therapy, but was it wrong for me to want you like that? You're my first sexual experience since then and it felt right, should it have?"

I had no idea, so I wasn't sure how Adam would know, but I was being truthful when I'd said nothing had worried me or made me want to stop. In fact, my thoughts of Joshua Mills had been far more infrequent the last couple of weeks. I hadn't even thought about the fact that he was living in the town I'd practically been hounded from. I didn't feel scared anymore, because I was confident my mum would keep me safe, I was confident I would keep myself safe. More than that, I was confident Adam would keep me safe.

"Why would you think it was wrong, hmm?" He kissed my forehead and then wrapped his arms tighter around me, encasing me in security right at that very moment.

"Because..." I struggled to say the words, not because I couldn't find them, but because I was worried that he might believe them to be true. "Because if I was happy to have sex with you, wanted to have sex with you, does that mean that I enjoyed what he did to me too? Was it not so bad if I could do again just months later?"

Adam's arms around my body got firmer. We were so close I

could practically hear his heartbeat. I could definitely feel it under my fingertips at his chest. The steady, strong beat was the matching rhythm to my own heart and I marvelled once more how we could we be so in tune with each other. We were carefree together, which was a miracle after what had passed between us, and what we'd both had to endure?

"The difference this time," Adam replied as he toyed with a strand of my hair. "Was that it was consensual, and you had some control in the situation. We went at your pace and if you'd said stop, I told you I would have, right away."

I looked up at him and grinned. "You're actually quite a nice person. You should let more people know."

Adam's eyes narrowed. "Not a fucking chance. This is reserved for you, babe and no one else."

***

As Adam's family were away for the weekend, I went home to sleep on the Friday night, but only because my mum would never have let me stay over. She thought I'd been at the library catching up on schoolwork, it didn't occur to her that I had all the textbooks I needed in my backpack and a Mac and the internet at home if I'd really wanted to study. Adam had joked that I should tell her I'd been studying biology because that way it wouldn't be a lie. He'd suggested that one just before I went home, while he was doing things to me that I'm sure would have horrified my mum.

Saturday morning came around and I was up earlier than was acceptable for a weekend, but I was standing in for Clarice and doing a Street Dance class for her while she took a break to visit her parents in Birmingham.

Mum was still sleeping, which wasn't a surprise as it was only six-thirty, so I crept around the house after I'd showered and dressed, gathering my things together including a change of clothes as I was going over to Adam's afterwards. I'd actually told Mum the truth about that, to a point anyway; she thought a few of us were going over to do a history project. Again, it wasn't a total lie, Adam and I *might* discuss the map we had to create of Napoleon's most famous battles, but it was unlikely. I was excited to think that there might be more biology lessons on the agenda for the day.

We were in the first couple of days of February with cool early mornings, so when I stepped outside and zipped up my jacket, I was surprised to see Adam's car parked at the end of our driveway. He was leaning against the bonnet and looking down at his phone. His hair was blowing in the breeze, but he looked warm with his Eagles hoodie on underneath his trucker jacket and I would have done anything to go to his house and snuggle up with him on the huge sofa in his living room.

"Hey, you," I said as I approached the car.

"Oh shit, I didn't hear you. Sorry, I was texting Ellis."

I frowned. "At quarter to seven on a Saturday morning?"

"Yeah, he wanted to go into Manchester and get a jacket he'd seen in a magazine. We were going to leave at eight-thirty to get there early so he could get back to help his dad with something."

"Oh okay, that's fine," I replied, a little disappointed but trying to hide it. "You didn't have to come to the house to tell me not to come over later, you could have texted me."

He smiled and shook his head. "I was texting him to say I'm not going. I'm going to spend the day with you instead."

I took a half-step back not sure I'd heard him properly. "Say again."

Adam grinned and pulled me to him by the ends of my scarf, until I was between his legs.

"I'm spending the day with you. I told you I would, so that's what I'm going to do."

"Didn't you promise Ellis first though?"

He shrugged. "It was kind of a loose arrangement. Kirk's going too and I don't want to be in his company."

My heart sank because I might have Adam in my corner now, but I really didn't want to make an enemy of Kirk or be the reason he and Adam stopped being friends.

"Hey," Adam said stooping down to look me in the eye. "It was dangerous what he did, and then to mouth off about it afterwards, well that was just a dick's trick. But stop worrying, we'll be fine in time. Now come on let's go, you've got a dance class to give."

"Oh God, Adam," I gasped as he pumped into me, his fingertips digging into my bum. "Don't stop."

I was naked from the waist down and being fucked hard on Adam's Mum's kitchen counter and it was everything I had never known sex to be before I'd met him.

My top half was covered in one of his football shirts emblazoned with his number seven and name, and it was so big that the neck dipped low enough that you could practically see my nipples. To me that seemed to make it pretty pointless wearing it, but Adam apparently liked it. We'd had sex earlier after we got back from my dance class, and I'd thrown it on to go to bathroom and he hadn't let me take it off since.

As the sensation of my impending orgasm continued to grow and sweep through my body, my heels dug into Adam's tight bum. I didn't want to think about how he'd gotten so skilful at sex, but all the same I couldn't help but be thankful. My body felt as though it had been worshiped over the last two days, worshiped and cherished almost to the point of exhaustion. I was addicted to Adam and how he made me feel during sex. Every part of my skin tingled, my nipples were sensitive and there was the most bloody wonderful ache between my legs. Adam Hudson may have only been a boy in age, but he treated me like a woman and hadn't once made me feel scared or unsure; he was more of a man than Joshua Mills would ever be.

"Shit, Sarah," he said through gritted teeth as his hand appeared between us. "I need you to come, I'm going to fucking blow any second."

His long fingers reached for my clit which was so swollen and sensitive that two strokes were all it took to set the firecrackers off inside of me. Wave after wave of sensations that were pleasurable and painful all at the same time rushed through me like a tidal wave.

"Adam!"

"Fuck," he cried and picked up his pace.

He pistoned his hips and clung to me until finally he groaned out and shuddered against me. Our chests heaved in unison and when Adam's smile crinkled his eyes and lit up his face, I knew that whether or not I'd rushed into things with Adam, I wouldn't have done anything differently. I knew from experience that your life could be snuffed out when doing something as simple as doing your job, or you could suffer a trauma so great that you didn't even want to live any longer. I wouldn't allow myself to regret being a teenager and having sex with a boy I liked.

"I've never had so much sex in one forty-eight-hour period." Adam said against the heated skin of my shoulder before dropping an open-mouthed kiss upon it. "My cock might drop off."

I slapped his arm and rolled my eyes. "Nice image."

"Yeah and what the fuck would you do if it did?" he asked with a wry smile. "I'd have to start using my magic fingers."

"I could always get a boy who still has his dick," I replied with a nonchalant sigh.

Adam laughed and pulled out of me. "Sarah, we both know one

of my fingers will perform better than any other lad's cock, so no, babe, you won't."

He smacked a kiss to my lips and then moved away and discarded the condom in the kitchen rubbish bin.

"Adam," I hissed, jumping down from the counter. "You need to wrap it in tissue, what if your Mum finds it?"

He winked and gave me one of the cocky smirks I was used to. "They shouldn't have left me here as punishment then should they."

"So, you wanted to go and visit Roger's parents with your Mum, your eight-year-old sister and your stepdad who seems to irritate you just by breathing?"

He thought about it for a second and then shook his head. "Nope, because then I wouldn't have had the most sex that I've ever had in forty-eight hours."

With a grin he bent to pick up his jeans and stepped into them along with the boxer briefs still inside. "Maybe I should thank Kirk after all."

I lifted up onto my tiptoes to kiss him and patted his cheek. "Good to know that knobhead is still in there somewhere."

Adam laughed loudly and I soon joined in, surprised at how quickly we'd fallen into an easy, carefree relationship. No one would recognize us as the two kids from school who hated each other.

As I started to walk away, determined I was finally going to get changed into clothes, there was a knock at the door.

"Have you ordered more pizza?" I asked.

"Nope. Although it's not a bad idea."

"I told you I'd cook. We can go and get some of that free food from Murray."

Adam walked out into the hall with me and as I moved to the stairway slapped my ass.

"Don't even think about taking that shirt off," he hollered over his shoulder as he opened the door. "I haven't finished with you yet."

"Oh my God, so it's true."

The voice made me stop with one foot on the bottom step and my heart sank.

"Alannah," I whispered to myself, closing my eyes and hoping that it might be just a dream.

It wasn't.

"I don't believe this," she cried. "How the fuck could you?"

2 8

ADAM

When I'd told Sarah I'd never had as much sex in a weekend as I'd had with her, I'd left out a major piece of information – it was *the* best fucking sex I'd ever had. I didn't know why I hadn't told her, maybe because I was still a prick at heart, or maybe I was ashamed that the experiences I had to compare it with were nothing more than meaningless hook ups.

There weren't that many if I was being truthful, not full sex anyway. Yes, there'd been lots of blow jobs and finger fucks, but sex, well I'd only had four partners before Sarah, not as many as she would think. Admittedly Mackenna and I usually had sex when I was hooking up with her, but two other girls, Tamsin and Meghan, had been one-offs. Tamsin had been my first and it had been unspectacular at a party for Ellis' fifteenth birthday, she was seventeen and even less experienced than I was. At least I'd been blown off and wanked off a few times by Pippa Jennings our neighbour. The summer was boring when you were fourteen and your friends all had parents who actually took them on holiday. As for Meghan well she was the girl I'd been caught fucking in Mum and Roger's bed earlier in the year, pretty shit sex where I hadn't even orgasmed. Then there'd been the one-off threesome with Amber and Ellis, which I couldn't say I'd enjoyed too much either; I couldn't concentrate on Amber riding me while I could see Ellis from the corner of my eye getting his dick sucked.

The point was, that was why I hadn't told Sarah that sex with her was the best, because anything before her didn't count anyway. I was well and truly hooked and it was a good job I wasn't really talking to Kirk because he'd take one look at my fucking stupid soppy grin and give me shit for it all pissing day.

On Monday, when I arrived at school and jumped out of my car, the first person I looked for was Sarah. Our run in on Saturday with Alannah had upset her, but on Sunday when we'd gone to Manchester to go to the ice-skating rink and the cinema, she'd seemed a little happier.

Alannah had yelled at both of us, but mostly Sarah, and I was so close to bringing mean Adam back out to warn Alannah off. The things she'd said hadn't been wrong; I was a dick, a mean bastard, a cunt – who knew Alannah would have such a wide vocabulary – and a bully. Whether I'd show those tendencies again, I had no idea, I just knew I couldn't stand the thought of ever hurting Sarah, not ever.

When she'd called Sarah a stupid prick tease, I totally lost it. That was when I threw her out and told her if she couldn't apologise to Sarah then she needed to piss off.

It had been a totally unfair thing for Alannah to say, especially as I knew what Sarah had gone through from that fucking teacher of hers. I was also fucking petrified that her comment would make Sarah feel as if she were to blame. I knew Alannah had no idea that Sarah had been raped and probably wouldn't have said it if she'd known, but she didn't, and she had. I'd kept a close eye on Sarah the rest of that evening and the following day at the ice-rink. I asked her every few minutes if she was okay and her answer had always been yes, but her eyes had been frosted over and her voice empty of sincerity.

I got to the sixth form corridor without bumping into Ellis, Tyler or Kirk and I was glad. There was only one person that I wanted to see, and she was beautiful and blonde and wore clothes that were far too big for her. As I rounded the corner, there she was. I felt a weight lift from shoulders. I moved forward with a huge smile on my face only to falter when Alannah stepped up to her.

"Fuck," I muttered when I saw Alannah's arms crossed over her chest and her tense stance. I ran toward them and skidded to a halt just as Sarah took a deep breath ready to talk.

"I'm sorry, Alannah, I really am. I know I should have told you, but it just happened. I didn't think for one minute that Adam and I-."

"Oh, and here he is," Alannah bit out. "Your *boyfriend.*"

"Listen, Alannah," I growled, standing close to Sarah. "Whatever issue you have with me, fine, but don't take this out on Sarah."

Alannah pushed her glasses up her nose and scowled. "She knew what you did to me."

"What Alannah?" I cried. "What the hell did I do to you that you didn't want to do? Tell me that."

Her nostrils flared as she considered my question. "You know *and* you made me stay at TJ's that night." She turned to Sarah. "He did things to make me stay. He. Made. Me. Stay. You can't think that's right?"

Sarah glanced at me warily and I knew then that I'd fucked up by not telling her every single thing I'd done. I should have come clean because she was bound to go back to hating me once Alannah told her all the sordid details.

"I'm probably not going to like it, Alannah," she replied. "But I am going to give him the opportunity to tell me."

I almost choked with the shock that she was going to give me a chance. She wasn't going to immediately believe Alannah and then throw me to one side. I drew in a breath and placed a hand on Sarah's shoulder, and she looked up at me.

"We do need to talk. I should have told you things over the weekend."

"If you weren't fucking like Duracell bunnies," Alannah replied, her tone dripping with sarcasm. "You could have."

"Alannah," Sarah groaned. "You're really not helping."

Alannah shook her head and looked at me with eyes that held a whole host of curses that she wanted to cast upon me.

"What about what him and his gang of idiots did to Amber? Did you know they told the whole school she had a threesome with him and Ellis and that she asked *him*?" She pointed an accusatory finger at me. "To pee on her. That's why she spends lunchtimes alone and has no friends hardly in this school."

Sarah's eyes went huge. "*Adam!*"

"What?" I shrugged. "We did it, she did it. If she was ashamed of it then she shouldn't have accepted."

Sarah took a step away from me. "But you didn't need to tell everyone. That's just nasty, Adam."

"And you still want to be with him?" Alannah's resting bitch face suddenly became animated. "Come on Sarah, let's just go."

My heart halted as Sarah moved beside me. I kept my eyes on Alannah, not able to watch Sarah leave, so when a small hand wrapped itself around mine, I held my breath.

"Alannah, I know exactly what sort of person Adam can be, was, but he's changing, and we want to see how this goes between us."

I finally let out the breath I'd been holding on an extra-long exhale, briefly closing my eyes.

"I don't know if it'll work," Sarah continued. "But if I don't give

Adam a chance, give us a chance, then how will I ever know. I want us to be friends, Alannah, but I want to be with Adam too."

Alannah's nostrils flared and her glasses slipped again. She didn't say another word, instead she swivelled on her heels and stormed away, her red tartan skirt flipping with each stomping step that she made.

"Why didn't you tell me about Amber?" a small voice asked.

I turned to Sarah who was watching Alannah disappear up the corridor.

"I didn't think it was important." I knew it was a shit response, but I had nothing else to offer.

"Bullshit." Sarah glared and tugged her hand from mine. "You didn't tell me because you knew I'd think you were a fucking shit for doing it."

"You knew what I was like when you decided to come to my house on Friday, Sarah, so don't give me that crap. I'd given you enough shit for you to be aware I wasn't the *nice boy* you wanted me to be."

She stared at me and shook her head. "You're a knob."

She then followed in the same direction as Alannah and I felt as though I'd had the air snatched from my lungs.

29

SARAH

Ugh, Adam Hudson was an absolute dickhead and I could easily have strangled him, if I could have reached. As I slammed into French class, I was met with the frosty glares of Alannah and Amber. Amber stepped forward and I held up my hand.

"No, I'm not interested, Amber. I get that you hate him and that you're going to warn me off, but sometimes people change."

"And sometimes they don't," she snapped. "Do you know how he humiliated me in front of the whole school?"

I nodded. "I heard, not the full story I suppose, but I know what he said about you."

"You do remember how I sit alone at lunch, because Adam fucking Hudson says so?"

I let out a sigh and knew everything she was saying was true. I really should hate him for what he'd done to them, and for how he'd treated me with the whole Mackenna thing, but I couldn't. I thought about him all the time, I wanted to be with him all the time; I craved his smile and was mad on him. I knew he'd orchestrated some pretty horrible things to happen to the girls in this school, but with me he was different. He treated me with care and respect. He was gentle and patient, but how did I explain that to the two girls in front of me without sounding like I was just like them and being controlled by him.

Although now I'd stormed away from him I no longer knew what we were.

"When I went to your house on Saturday and your Mum said you were at Adam's doing your history project, I almost laughed in her face." Alannah added taking a step closer to Amber and I. "I had no idea I'd find you there barely dressed and smelling of... sex."

I glanced warily around the classroom, worried that other people were listening in. No one seemed to be interested thankfully, but I was pretty sure word would soon get around.

"Can we talk about this at lunchtime," I sighed and pinched between my eyes.

Alannah looked at Amber and nodded and then they both stalked off to their seats.

When I walked into the dining room, I didn't get the feeling that everyone was talking about me, but that didn't mean they weren't. I looked around to see Adam, Ellis, Tyler and Kirk were at their usual table, but they didn't appear to be having their usual banter. Each one was silently eating, apart from Tyler who was spinning a football on his extended finger. I then saw Amber and Alannah were sitting together but they weren't talking either. With a sigh I walked over to them and flopped down onto a stool opposite them both.

Alannah looked up slowly and peered at me over the top of her glasses. "Adam dumped your ass already?" she asked with a smirk. "Did he tell you not to sit with him?"

I glanced over at Adam who had now spotted me and was watching carefully, having pushed his plate to one side.

"I want to sit with you." I hadn't bought any lunch, not that I had the stomach for it anyway as it kept knotting and unknotting itself, leaving no room for food.

"Have you seen sense?" Amber asked without looking up from her food.

I frowned kind of wishing that she'd go back to quiet, unassuming Amber.

"Listen," I said and leaned closer to them both. "I know exactly what I'm getting in to. If this all goes wrong, then there'll only be me hurt. I'm not asking you to become his best friends or to double-date, all that I'm asking is that you accept my decision. You can even say you told me so if it doesn't work, okay?"

Alannah let out a short breath and slammed her glass down on the table. When she looked at me though, I could see understanding in her eyes.

"Just be careful, Sarah. He may seem like Mr Nice Guy now, but once he's bored of you, he'll use whatever he can against you. If you've got more secrets than what happened to your dad I'd make sure Adam doesn't find out."

It was kind of pointless to tell her he already knew my darkest secret, and I knew his. I had a feeling that if anyone found out what we shared with each other, Adam would style that shit out far better than I would.

"You may be about to get yours sooner than you think," Amber snorted and nodded her head in the direction of Adam's table. "Someone looks salty."

I turned to find him stalking toward us with a look of grim determination on his face. He pulled up next to our table and looked down on me with his fisted hands on his hips.

"Is that it?" he asked. "We're done just like that?"

I frowned at him and not for the first time appreciated just how handsome he was. Childish anger seemed to suit him because his lips were pouty and his eyes as wide as a puppy dog's.

"What are you talking about?" I asked, pushing to my feet.

"She's realised that you're a dick, Adam, so just go and plot her demise why don't you?"

We both looked down at Amber who was starting to piss me off.

"Have you?" Adam asked, turning his attention back to me.

"No," I snapped. "We had an argument, Adam. If I wanted it to be over, I'd have told you. I'm not the sort of person to play games."

He flinched at my barb and brushed a hand over his hair. "So, what's happening, Sarah?" he asked, his voice quiet as he leaned closer to me. "Why are you sitting over here?"

"Because you're a bloody idiot," I groaned and dragged him to me by his t-shirt. "We need to have a serious talk, but we're not over."

I pulled his mouth to mine and to gasps and jeers, I kissed him with everything I had. I ran my fingers through his hair and nipped at his lips and made sure he realised we definitely were not finished business.

"Sarah," he groaned against my mouth.

I didn't answer him but simply relished his hands on my waist, his tongue duelling with mine and his hard dick pressing against my stomach. My nipples hardened and wetness flooded my knickers as my drug of choice continued to give me everything back, and more. I was addicted to this boy even though I knew he could break me, the fact that he'd saved me in his own way, and he'd helped to repair my broken soul, meant I didn't care.

When we were breathless and unable to keep it PG any longer, I pulled away and gave him my biggest smile.

"Does that answer your question?" I asked.

"Get a fucking room," Ellis shouted across the dining room.

Adam nodded and gave me one last nip at my lip. "Yeah it does. Now are you coming to sit and have lunch with me or not?"

I looked over my shoulder to Amber and Alannah who were in varying stages of pissed off.

"No, I'm staying here."

"Sarah," he growled.

I patted his chest. "Go back to your friends and get over it, Adam."

When he smiled, I knew we were back to being carefree and the sensation of freedom washed through me. We were too young to be weighed down with the issues we had. We were seventeen years old and on the cusp of the rest of our lives; however long this lasted I would strive to enjoy it.

With a sigh, Adam walked back to his table. I sat down at mine, feeling as though I could finally eat something.

"Don't get too comfy," Amber said with disdain in her eyes. "Because I promise you, he will make you suffer one way or another."

I smiled but somewhere in the recesses of my being felt the shiver of impending pain.

30

ADAM

It was match day and we were going to be playing The Saints, of St Jude's High School. Two places behind us in the Division 1 rankings for the North Western title, we weren't taking anything for granted, especially as a new striker had joined them at the beginning of the last term. He was fast on the pitch with the ball and had scored in every match he'd played. He'd pretty much turned their performances around, shooting them three places up the division to fourth.

Mr Jameson had made us learn some new set pieces and we'd had practice every day for the past week, he was so determined that they wouldn't win. According to Ellis' dad, Mr Jameson had bad blood with their coach, it was something to do with a dirty tackle from Mr Riley when they played at under 18 level; Mr Jameson at City and Mr Riley at United. The tackle was high and had resulted in Mr Jameson breaking his leg in two places which pretty much shit on his chance of a professional career.

"You set for tonight?" Sarah asked, as we walked hand in hand from the car park.

She and Alannah had made up, to a point. Alannah still hated me and warned Sarah about me every single day. Over the last week things had calmed down enough that she still gave Sarah a lift into school, but I always insisted on walking her to class.

"Yeah, as we'll ever be. I was up until late last night watching videos of their keeper on YouTube. I think I know what his weaknesses are." I tapped my temple and grinned.

"Of course, you do."

She rolled her eyes playfully and then reached into her jeans pocket when her phone buzzed with a text.

We stopped and let a few kids pass us by as Sarah read the message and groaned.

"What is it?" I asked and looked over her shoulder.

"It's my mum, I forgot I have a therapy appointment this afternoon. She's picking me up at lunch to go to it."

My heart sank with disappointment. "You're not going back to Kent for it are you? That means you'll miss the match."

Sarah swung around to face me with a smile. "It'd be a bloody long way to go. Don't worry, I'll be there. Eleanor has an office in Liverpool, so she's going to be here for a few days seeing some of her clients in this area, so I'll be back in plenty of time."

I nodded and let out a breath. "Good, I really want you to see me play tonight."

"Well, I will, but even if I don't make it, you have another match on Tuesday."

"Yeah, I know," I replied, a little distracted.

I didn't know what it was, but I felt as though she had to be there tonight, like she might well be my lucky charm. Which was kind of stupid as she'd never watched me before. In the week we'd been together we'd seen each other every day at school and most nights after school. Although, seeing as we had nowhere to go, it had all been pretty PG after our fuck fest of a weekend. I wasn't feeling the desire to let my mum know about Sarah just yet; I didn't feel as though she deserved to know anything about the good in my life, seeing as she'd not really cared about me for some time. I hadn't wanted to take Sarah to the old club house in the BMX park where I usually met girls, or even have sex with her in my car, because she deserved better than that. That meant we'd had to limit ourselves to some hot and heavy kissing and over the clothes groping in her bedroom, with the door left ajar, because her Mum had insisted upon it; apart from the one quickie while her mum was having a bath.

Sarah had decided to be upfront about our relationship to Mrs Danes because that was their deal, no more secrets, and to be honest she took it better than I'd expected. She'd invited me over for dinner, told me not to hurt her daughter and that any time I was over Sarah's bedroom door had to be left open. At least she hadn't made us sit in the living room and watch TV with her.

As Sarah put her phone back in her pocket, I spotted Kirk walking toward us.

"Fuck," I muttered. "He better not say anything he regrets."

Sarah looked over her shoulder and tugged on my hand. "Be nice, he's your friend."

We hadn't really spoken since the day he'd given Sarah the banana custard. I'd been suspended for the rest of that week and this last week we'd done what we could to avoid each other. Ellis and Tyler had tried to get us to shake hands and forget it, but he still sported a bruise around his eye, a scab on his lip and I could have lost the girl who was starting to mean everything to me. He was a prick as far as I was concerned, and it would take some serious grov- elling for me to forget what he'd done.

I knew I was a hypocritical shit because I'd done some fucking nasty things to girls at Maddison High School; but I'd never have gone that far. Kirk had no idea that she actually had the EpiPen on her, or that any of us would know how to administer it. He'd risked too much for me to forgive and forget so easily.

"Hey," Kirk said as he levelled with us. "Can we talk?"

He looked between me and Sarah, his eyes were hesitant as his hand rubbed at the back of his neck. We'd been friends for nine years yet at that moment our bond was gone and there was an invisible wall keeping us apart. The things that had happened over the last few weeks had made me reassess my life in lots of ways, not least of all my relationship with Ellis, Tyler and Kirk and my assessment hadn't been good. They acted like entitled pricks, and I was the head entitled prick who'd instigated most of the shit they'd pulled. It was no wonder they were starting to pull crap off their own backs; I'd made them believe it was okay to a be a cunt because of who we were. That certainly wasn't anything I was proud of and knew it was time I put things right. As far as Kirk was concerned, a wall had been built between us after what he'd done to Sarah, and I wasn't sure I ready to breach it.

"Of course," Sarah said brightly, bouncing on her toes and flashing me a smile.

I threw her a glare and not for the first time wondered how the fuck she could even consider forgiving him; she'd been on my back all week to talk to the fucker.

"I just want to say sorry, to you, Sarah. What I did was stupid and dangerous, and I shouldn't have done it."

Sarah turned her lips in between her teeth and nodded, but when Kirk turned to me, I crossed my arms over my chest and stared him down.

"I get why you did what you did," he said as he kicked at the path. "I'd have punched me too. Things could have ended a lot differently if you hadn't acted so quick."

"You think?" I asked leaning my top half closer to him. "It was a dick move."

Kirk took a breath and I had an idea he was going to say something that I wasn't going to like, because when I narrowed my eyes, he closed it again.

"Well thank you for apologizing, Kirk," Sarah said and nudged me.

"Yeah, appreciated," I ground out.

Kirk licked his lips and stuffed his hands into his jean pockets. "So, you two really are a thing then?"

I pulled Sarah to my side, every instinct I had wanted to protect her from one of my closest friends, although I wasn't so sure about the basis of our friendship anymore. As I looked at him it occurred to me that he had been useful to me but there wasn't much other reason why I'd kept him around. Ellis and I were really close, but Tyler and Kirk kind of got dragged into our plan to rule the school. Every leader had to have his fucking minions and I'd made them mine and now someone I cared about had been hurt. I couldn't help but feel guilty that I'd somehow been responsible. Like the dick I was though, it was much easier to blame Kirk; after all I hadn't given Sarah the pudding, he had.

"Yeah, we are," I replied. "I realised a lot of things while I sat in that Tesco Express with a crazy fucker holding a gun, and one of them was how I feel about Sarah."

She shifted at my side and without looking at her, I knew from the direction of Kirk's gaze that she was looking up at me. I had no fucking clue what I'd done to deserve her forgiveness, but she cared about me and for some reason thought I'd earned a chance to be allowed to change. The way Kirk's mouth thinned, I had the feeling he wasn't so sure about anything between Sarah and me.

Sarah cleared her throat. "So, I promised Alannah that I'd go over some English lit notes with her, I'm going to run and find her." She kissed my cheek forcing my eyes to hers. "I'll see you when I get back from my appointment, okay?"

I didn't want her to go, I wanted to spend the last few minutes before the bell went kissing her and holding her close, stamp my foot and demand she stay, but I wasn't going to act like a fucking tantrum throwing toddler, especially not in front of Kirk.

"Okay, see you when you get back. I won't be in science Mr Jameson has called a last-minute practice."

I leaned down and not giving a shit that Kirk was watching, took her mouth in mine and kissed her long and hard.

When I finally pulled away, he had turned and was looking around anywhere apart from at us.

"See you," I whispered and gave her hand a last squeeze before she ran off toward the main building.

"We okay then?" Kirk asked when I turned back to him.

I noticed that his tone was a little harder than it had been when Sarah had been there, but I gave him a single nod and with a little doubt held my hand to him.

"Yeah, we're good."

He gave it a shake, his hand firm around mine. "I better go, I need to shit before the bell goes."

"Yeah, I'll cover for you," I said, managing a small smile, but when Kirk walked away, I still felt the difference in our friendship.

The morning had gone pretty slowly, even our practice session dragged. I knew my set pieces and I knew how important the game was to Mr Jameson. Also, on the surface, things seemed back to normal between me and the lads. Kirk laughed and joked along with us, but I had to admit to struggling not to look at him in a different light.

"You really okay with him?" Ellis asked, as always seeing right through me.

I kept my eyes on Kirk who was talking to Mr Jameson and shrugged. "Not sure. I want to be but there's something that's stopping me."

"Don't fucking punch me when I say this." Ellis leaned in closer. "But you've been friends for a long time, you've known Sarah six weeks tops and for a month of that time you fucking hated her."

I rubbed the bridge of my nose and considered Ellis' words. "Not sure I did to be honest, man. I think I had a thing for her from the get-go, but just didn't want to admit it."

He leaned forward and his gaze followed mine. "He's a dick, we all know that, and I know you're not as tight with him and Tyler as you are with me, but don't push him out over some girl you're likely to get bored of in a few weeks."

I inhaled a deep breath through my nose and tried not to turn around and punch him as he'd predicted; I'd already alienated one friend and I certainly didn't want to do that with Ellis too. I figured it was best not to speak and to let him come to his own conclusions on what my silence meant.

"Looks like someone is here to see you." Ellis pointed toward the door of the sports hall and when I followed where he gestured, my heart jumped at the sight of Sarah.

I glanced up at the clock and realised she must have been about to leave for her therapy session.

"I'll be back," I whispered to Ellis. "Cover for me if Mr Jay asks."

Ellis nodded and kept his eyes on Sarah. I wasn't sure what he thought about her, or our relationship, I just knew he'd supported me. He hadn't even bitched when I'd blown him off to be with her over the last week, which had been a lot; she'd even gone to my first therapy session with me. He was a good friend and I made a vow to spend a little more time with him soon; if only I could stop my obsession with my new girlfriend.

Taking advantage of Mr Jameson being occupied with Kirk, I

skirted around the edge of the sports hall to where Sarah was waiting.

"You about to go?" I asked, ushering her into the corridor.

"Yeah, my mum's stuck in traffic, so I have a few minutes before she gets here." Sarah looked up at me and smiled. "I just wanted to wish you good luck."

"I thought you said you'd be back."

Disappointment hit me just as it had earlier when she'd told me about her session. I pouted like a sulky kid.

"I will be, but I may not get a chance to see you before it starts."

A sense of relief flooded me and took her hand in mine. "Well, that's good. Come on I'll walk you out to the car park and wait for your mum with you."

"No way, you have practice. Go back in and I'll see you later. I'll be here I swear." She reached up on tiptoes and kissed my cheek. "Go."

"Nuh uh. I need more than that." I leaned down and pushed with my tongue to open up her mouth, seeking something far more fulfilling.

As I grabbed her arse, Sarah groaned and pushed herself against my hard dick and gripped my hair, pulling it roughly.

"Fuck," I muttered, knowing what that meant. "Sarah, you have to go otherwise I'm going to have to take you into the changing room."

Her body tensed and she pulled away from me, dropping her hands to her sides. When she glanced toward the door, I wanted to punch myself in the nuts. It was where she'd seen me getting a blow job from Mackenna.

"Sarah," I groaned. "I'm sorry, I didn't think."

She shifted her expression into a weak smile and shook her head. "It's fine. It's me, I just..."

I noticed her hand go up the sleeve of her jumper and pulled her to me, kissing her again, stopping her mid-sentence and stopping her from rubbing the scar that reminded her of the hell she'd been through.

"No, don't be sorry," I whispered when I let her mouth free. "I'm the one who should be sorry."

She shook her head. "No, it was before we were together, and I need to get over it."

I brushed the hair from her eyes and held her face. "Things are so different now. We both have a lot to get used to. I'm probably still going to be a dick from time to time, but we will get there, Sarah, I swear."

Finally, she gave me a bright smile. "I know. I'd better go and let you get back to practice."

"You want me to wait with you?"

"No, she said she was about fifteen minutes away, so you should get back, but I'll see you later."

I hesitated and almost agreed with her, but with a quick glance at the sports hall, shook my head.

"I'm at least walking you out to the car park."

"I do know where it is." Sarah giggled and slapped playfully at my chest.

"Yeah I know, but I might want a taste of those fucking gorgeous lips of yours before you go."

Sighing softly Sarah held out her hand and I gladly took it in mine and led her down the corridor.

"You fancy doing something after the match?" I asked letting go of her hand and draping my arm over her shoulder instead.

She looked up at me with narrowed, considering eyes. "Isn't a party or TJ's the usual thing for you boys after a match?"

"Yeah, but I don't fancy it tonight. I prefer to spend it with you."

I pushed open the double doors into the sixth form corridor and stood to one side as some little kid, evidently in year seven if the size of his blazer was anything to go by, came rushing past us, with a hurried 'sorry'.

"Shit where's the fire?" I glanced over my shoulder to see him running at full pelt.

Sarah laughed and patted my chest. "You really are changing. A few weeks ago, you'd have had that little kid pinned up against the wall and warning him 'do you know who I am'."

I burst out laughing at the gruff tone she put on. "Was that supposed to be me?"

She grinned and nodded and looked so cute I couldn't help but lean down and kiss her.

"You're such a hilarious little fucker aren't you?"

"Yep." Sarah puffed out her chest with pride and shined her nails on her soft, pale grey jumper that dropped off one shoulder.

I rolled my eyes before pulling her to me and kissing the side of her head. "Go to therapy and I'll see you at the match later."

With a huge fucking grin on my face, I pushed open the main door and let Sarah go in front of me. I was so distracted by the swing of her arse in her tight, short red skirt that I didn't notice her pull up to a stop.

"Shit," I mumbled as I stumbled into her.

"*Adam.*"

My name was a horrified gasp, sounding so pained that my head shot up and my arm instinctively wrapped around her waist, pulling her back against my chest.

"Sarah, what's wrong?"

"No, he can't be here. God, no."

As I looked out toward the car park, her body began to shake in my arms as she began whimpering about Joshua Mills. My eyes focused on a man walking toward us; a figure I recognised. The closer he got the more Sarah's body shook and the faster my heart thudded against my breastbone. Eventually the man stopped in front of us and looked me straight in the eyes and when he smiled, I felt the bile rise.

"Hello, son, it's been a long time. Sarah, fancy seeing you here."

To be continued in Love Struck

mybook.to/LoveStruckMaddisonHigh

ACKNOWLEDGMENTS

There are so many people to thank for this book, and so little time, but here goes.

Firstly, to my wonderful group of BETA readers, who gave their feedback, warts and all on this book. I appreciate all of your honesty it was invaluable in the process of writing what I hope is a good story which people will want to read. So, thank you, Lynsey Goddard, Claire Cutler, Lesley Robson, Donna Wright, Cal Sleath and Kirsty Adams. It was an absolute pleasure.

To Anna Bloom you've been with me from the first word to the very last and I can't thank you enough. The editing process was easy and fun, and I especially loved your comments about Adam and the advice texts from your teenage neighbour!

On that note, also thank you to my niece Libby and nephew Harry, who steered me right on the teenage lingo, because even though I think I'm down with the kids I'm evidently not, as the words 'lingo' and 'down with the kids' prove.

Thank you, Lou Stock for making me the perfect cover for Hate Struck. I adore it. Also thank you for being a dream to work with, you never once grumbled about my last-minute changes which were completed before I'd barely had time to sit back and hope my request wasn't too late. You're a star and I can't wait to see what you come up with for Love Struck.

To all my Angels, you're a bunch of people who I'd gladly share my last supper of lamb roast with. Not only do you make me laugh, but you put up with my obsession, okay some people may say stalking, of Matthew Noszka, but when have you ever complained about the pictures hey? Yep, never!

Which leads nicely on to my gratitude to Matthew himself. *Thank you* for being my muse for Adam, well most of my more recent heroes to be honest. *Thank you* for everything you bring to my life. *Thank you* for your face. *Thank you* for your body. *Thank you* to your parents for having you. Simply *thank you* for being you.

Mr A and the lovely Mrs A senior, deserve a special thank you for this book as they waited on me hand and foot while I was writing it. Not only that, but they were subjected to spending the whole of the Christmas period sitting in the house, drinking alcohol and eating chocolates because I wouldn't move from my desk. It was tough for them let me tell you.

Finally, the biggest thank you of all goes to you for reading not only the book but these acknowledgments. I sincerely hope you enjoyed the first part of Sarah and Adam's story even though at times you may have wondered if this was the same Nikki Ashton who writes about fanny farts and penis' caught in zips. It is a big change for me, and it was hard trying to write something without any humour, but it was a story I really wanted to tell. My biggest hope is that you stick with me for part two; Love Struck. The pre order link is below, if you want to find out what happens next for two young people who deserve some good in their lives.

That's it for now and I'll see you soon for the continuing story of Sarah and Adam.

mybook.to/LoveStruckMaddisonHigh

NIKKI'S LINKS

If you'd like to know more about me or my books, then all my links
are listed below.

Website:
www.nikkiashtonbooks.co.uk

Instagram
www.instagram.com/nikkiashtonauthor

Facebook
www.facebook.com/nikki.ashton.982

Ashton's Amorous Angels Facebook Group
www.facebook.com/groups/1039480929500429

Amazon
viewAuthor.at/NAPage

BOOK LINKS

Guess Who I Pulled Last Night

mybook.to/NAGuessWhoIPulled

No Bra Required

myBook.to/NANoBra

Get Your Kit Off

mybook.to/GetYourKitOff

Rock Stars Don't Like Big Knickers

myBook.to/NARockStars1

Rock Stars Don't Like Ugly Bras

myBook.to/NARockStars2

Rock Stars Do Like Christmas

myBook.to/NARockStarsXmas

Cheese Tarts and Fluffy Socks
myBook.to/NACheeseTarts

Roman's having sex again
myBook.to/RomansHavingSex

I wanna get laid by Kade
myBook.to/NAVJKade

Box of Hearts (Connor Ranch #1)
myBook.to/BOH

Angels Kisses (Connor Ranch #2)
myBook.to/AngelsKisses

Secret Wishes (Connor Ranch #3)
myBook.to/SecretWishes

Do You Do Extras?
mybook.to/DoYouDoExtras

Pelvic Flaws
mybook.to/PelvicFlaws

Elijah (Cooper Brothers #1)
mybook.to/ElijahCooper

Samuel (Cooper Brothers #2)
mybook.to/SamuelCooper

The Big Ohhh

mybook.to/TheBigOhhh

Hate Struck

mybook.to/HateStruck

Audio Books

preview.tinyurl.com/NikkiAshtonAudio

Printed in Great Britain
by Amazon